DAYBREAK

OVER

APPALACHIA

The people and events of the past
that helped shape our present

Don R. Watts

DAYBREAK OVER APPALACHIA

The people and events of the past that helped shape our present

Through the tender mercy of our God; whereby the dayspring from on high hath visited us, To give light to them that sit in darkness and in the shadow of death, to guide our feet into the way of peace. Luke 1:78 & 79 KJV

DON R. WATTS

Copyright © 2012 by Don R. Watts

DAYBREAK OVER APPALACHIA
by Don R. Watts

Printed in the United States of America

ISBN 9781622305841

All rights reserved solely by the author. The author guarantees all contents are original and do not infringe upon the legal rights of any other person or work. No part of this book may be reproduced in any form without the permission of the author. The views expressed in this book are not necessarily those of the publisher.

All scripture quotations are taken from the King James Version of the Bible. Public domain.

www.xulonpress.com

Protection

All rights reserved. No part of this book may be reproduced or transmitted in any form or by any means without the publisher's prior written permission. It is set in the context of the Appalachians and a must read for the lover of Americana. Any similarity to actual persons and events is coincidental. Asterisks are used to connote name changes. The author will not be held responsible for any errors expressed or otherwise.

Dedication

Foremost, to the Chief Shepherd, my Senior Partner and Heavenly Father, who has kept me in line, and provided me with experiences I trust you will enjoy.

To my wife, Ruthie, for her encouragement, support and labor of patience towards the writing of this project.

To my sons, Casey and Jeremy, who have given to this endeavor.

To family and friends for their contributions and influence in this writing.

SOME THINGS ARE PERMANENT

A word spoken cannot be withdrawn;
A log split cannot be un-sawn.

A fire set cannot be unburned;
A bullet sent cannot be returned.

A line written cannot be blotted;
A bad act cannot go unspotted.

All evil deeds someday are caught;
Only God can truly say, I forgot.

A NOTE TO READERS

―⚭―

To think of Appalachia is to envision mountains and character. The name may be a weak expression of an Indian word meaning "eternity," while others insists it means "place of the footprint" in reference to tracks made in the mountain snows. To choose either of the definitions opens up endless possibilities to behold. Looking over one's shoulder at Appalachia reveals a great deal as to how she has molded the lives of her inhabitants. This book has set out to expose her character and the mark she has made upon so many - how she exposed the weak and strengthened the daring.

The author views Appalachia with respect for her beauty, her natural treasures and her people. She is admired for her vast coal supplies that lie deep beneath the earth. Heavy green forests line the landscape. Mountain peaks and valleys serve to guide creeks and rivers to distant destinations. These all make one hungry to see what is around the next bend and satisfy that inherent curiosity in man.

I have seen her bountiful river bottom growths, fresh bubbling mountain springs, and abundant wildlife. Among all these, mountain walls and vast underlying rocks have prevented a great abundance of tillable fields. The land declares an unwillingness to change, yet sets a captivating grip on her settlers. This beauty and abundance, particularly of wildlife, has been the nemesis of many men, making it difficult to leave. The insatiable desire to revel in her natural resources sometimes placed undue hardships on their families. In spite of all the challenges, families have adapted and found perhaps the most important things in life. They conquered the mountains to have something of their own, and independence grew as they escaped the entrapment of slavery known elsewhere.

The rugged mountain isolation affected every aspect of life, influencing mental and cultural ideas. Geographical isolation served to seclude the mountaineer from modern aggressive people, and disadvantaged him when doing business. The aggressive took advantage of the mountaineer when purchasing land and minerals from him. The mountaineer often did not see the monetary value of property and precious minerals, neither could he market products if he had. He also had the conviction that the land was for all to appreciate and the foremost concern was to be a neighbor. Businessmen resold the minerals and timber at a much higher figure, causing the destiny of the mountaineer to be controlled by men who lived far away and seldom saw the mountains.

The mountaineer has been characterized in many ways, usually negatively. Most early mountaineers had a preference for being fair, honest and personable. They became victim to many outsiders who took advantage of naivety. Eyes opened wide when fast-talking people flashed money before him. Had they learned to be more diplomatic, perhaps conditions and consequences would have been different. This awkward approach to business created a long-term curse difficult to break and a lack of success in his offspring as well. This pushed them into a corner, causing much of the religion, music, and conversation to become fatalistic. That is not to say that all of their religion and music was futile, but rather they failed to discover the fact that these can hold more optimism. They failed to learn that religion and business can be compatible.

Instead, for many there was nostalgia for the former things. There was a fascination, either for a time when things were fresh and abundant, or for a better afterlife. There were, however, a few who looked beyond the mountains with hope for the future, but few ever achieved their dream.

Up until the turn of the 20th century, the Appalachian mountain chain was a sleeping giant, except for the robust nature and surging springs seeking sunlight, only to meander downward. For centuries, plants graced her glades and mountainsides, beautifying and emitting aromas to the heavens. Animals, some now extinct, moved with pride following olden trails, balancing nature, then one day returning to dust. Lone pioneers made little imprint as they blended their lives into the process in hopes of escaping pressures known elsewhere, but that was to change.

As with every culture, change had to come. The mountaineer truly hoped for change, but found it difficult to pull himself up by his own bootstraps. The changes that came usually were not the changes that the mountaineer had hoped for. Change would be forced upon him. Outsiders moved in and the sometimes naive mountaineers moved on in hopes of finding a more prosperous life. If unable to move, their option was to step aside, adapting to the influence of another. Many looked back and longed for the "good ole days." Whatever the case, change was inevitable.

In this novel, we will return to Appalachia and explore life at the turn of the 20th century. On the frontier, the James Gang had wreaked havoc in Southwest Missouri, the Earps had their shootout at the OK Corral and General Custer had fallen prey to the Sioux at the Little Big Horn. Hidden from the headlines was Appalachia, having her own troubles. Nestled away from the New York newsmen was a land rich in frontiers, though lacking the romanticism of the western cowboy and the cattle drives.

I wish to leave the reader with the good and bad of living and traveling with the Appalachian. It is my hope that you may better understand the folkways, the mores and the character of these people. They often had less schooling and were less refined, causing their roughness and sometimes crudeness to surface. They were survivors, making the most of what they were able to carve out. They moved to the region because of freedom, land, or hunting opportunities. They fought their own battles, cared for their own, and in the words of Teddy Roosevelt were "rugged individualists." When confrontations arose, they simply took matters into their own hands and were sometimes compensated with sour consequences, as portrayed in this book. This is indeed a saga for survival.

CONTENTS

I	YOU SHOULD HAVE BEEN THERE	5
II	THOSE WHO DARED THE ALLEGHANIES	11
III	INVESTIGATING THE GAP	18
IV	OLD HOPEVILLE, THE HUB OF THE COMMUNITY.	22
V	IT'S FINALLY SUNDAY	30
VI	THE MOUNTAINEER	37
VII	THE HOPEVILLE SCHOOL	41
VIII	A VIEW OF APPALACHIA	47
IX	APPALACHIA IN THE RAW	56
X	THE RIGHT TO MAKE "LIKKER"	61
XI	PERILS OF MOONSHINE	65
XII	CONTROLLING THE "MASH MAKERS"	71
XIII	WINTER ON ALLEGHANY	80
XIV	AT THE SAWMILL	86
XV	LOGGERS AND LOGGIN'	90
XVI	LIFE ON THE FORK	94
XVII	ROUGHCUTS IN THE APPALACHIANS	104
XVIII	HANDCUFFS - FREEDOM	112
XIX	NO BEGGING FOR LIFE	119
XX	THE TRUTH TALKED ABOUT	132
XXI	HE'S NOT A RELIGIOUS MAN	143
XXII	APPALACHIA'S HEART	148
XXIII	CATCHIN' TROUT	157

XXIV	ARE THESE PEOPLE REALLY THAT LAZY?	164
XXV	THE COUNTRY FOLK	168
XXVI	THE ACCUSED	176
XXVII	THE GAP'S HAINTED	190
XXVIII	THE REFINED AND THE NOT SO	196
XXIX	LONG HOLLOW BURYING	204
XXX	LONG HOLLOW INQUISITION	211
XXXI	THE TALK AND HEARING.	218
XXXII	THINGS SEEM TO MAKE SENSE	226
XXXIII	THE WATER FLOWS ON	230

PROLOGUE

This narrative is set in the early nineteen hundreds in the rugged Appalachian Mountain area of West Virginia, but can easily represent many areas along the Appalachian chain. The Appalachian Mountain chain extends fifteen hundred miles from southern Quebec to northern Alabama. The term Appalachia is reserved for the southern region, pronounced "Ap-pa-lacha" by locals.

Nowhere along the Appalachians has the term been applied to describe the area so much as in the central states, namely, West Virginia, Kentucky and Tennessee. The term conjures certain characteristics of poverty, economic depression, and ruggedness.

The Allegheny Mountains (this novel uses an older spelling, "Alleghany") are on the eastern side of the Appalachians and are some of the most rugged mountains in the East. Early in our nation's history, this area was a barricade to settlers moving westward. As an example, West Virginia has ninety percent of its land with slopes of more than ten percent grade.

Locally, the Alleghenies were given distinctive names originating from their characteristics or owner. Stretching across the sods on the mountain are: Roaring Plains, Dolly Sods, Rohrbaugh Plains (an older spelling is "Rohrbach"), Cline Place, Boar's Nest, Flat Rock Plains and Stack Rocks.

The Alleghenies further determine the Eastern Continental Divide. The crest of the Allegheny Mountains, where the Pendleton-Pocahontas County line lies, is the "Birthplace of Rivers." Those draining to the East flow to the Atlantic while those to the West flow into the Ohio drainage and ultimately the Gulf of Mexico. Here streams begin their descent, forming the headwaters of many rivers. Flowing from Spruce Knob are the Cheat and Tygart Rivers to the Monongahela, then on to the powerful Ohio, where once Lewis and Clark and The Corps of Discovery sailed into history. To the Southeast flows the Jackson and onto the headwaters of the James to the historic heartland of Virginia. The beginnings of the East Fork of the Greenbrier, Gauley, and Elk flow South and West out of the Alleghenies, from mountain swamps where balsam fir thrive, to the Kanawha, where they lose themselves in the New River near Hinton, West Virginia.

The distant fountains of the North Fork of the South Branch of the Potomac originate here as well. To the East rushes this untamed water as it cuts through mountain canyons, to be joined with other streams before making its way past Harpers Ferry, Mount Vernon, and to the Chesapeake Bay. Along its meandering journey, it has made a massive historical impact. Over thousands of years these rivers and tributaries have hewed out deep gorges, leaving many large exposed boulders and steep ravines.

About twenty five miles down the North Fork of the South Branch of the Potomac River, and flowing out of the Alleghenies, is a creek called "Jordan's Run," historically spelled "Jordon's," and pronounced "Jurden's" by some. It is normally about twelve feet wide and flows to Hopeville where it empties into the North Fork of the South Branch of the Potomac. Jordan's Run collects water from a confusion of sources ranging from Brushy Ridge to the Laneville Road. Three primary tributaries feed Jordan's Run: Laurel

Run, Ikes Run and Gap Run. This water system drains Dolly Sods, Cline Place and Rohrbaugh Plains. Two smaller mountains form the final waterway for Jordan's Run before it empties into the North Fork. These are Scrooges Knob and Cave Hill, both extensions of New Creek Mountain - a mountain which runs parallel to the Alleghenies. Some of the creeks draining the area west of this system are Samuel Run (known as Manuel Run), Broad Run and Moyer Run.

The North Fork River drains the Eastern Spruce Knob area, and twists its way around rocks and crags before making its way to the Atlantic Ocean. Jordan's Run and North Fork converge at the western end of the New Creek Mountain. New Creek and the North Fork Mountain run parallel for a short distance. One may think that historically they were part of one system except for the offset where they bypass one another. These twin mountains average about thirty-five hundred feet high and are almost perpendicular. Capping the top is an exposed ledge of Tuscarora Sandstone extending their entire length. This rugged land has been home to the Seneca Indians and early white hunters. Eventually, homesteaders sprinkled her mountain sides with homes.

Directly under the Alleghenies are a series of smaller foothills called the Foreknobs, known historically also as the Four Knobs. These knobs are quite large and attach to the Alleghenies in succession. Situated at the base of the mountains is a community called "Hopeville." Here resides the heart of our story. There is no record of anyone by the name Hope living in the area, or that it was named for anyone, so we can assume that the area was viewed with hope or optimism for earlier inhabitants.

This project utilizes the beautiful backdrop of the Alleghenies blanketed with steep moss covered slopes, swift and cold mountain streams, vibrant vegetation, and animals in native habitats, to unfold its story. Portraying a large cast of mountaineers are men who react to problems with their homespun wisdom. "Pap" embodies an appreciation for life, a rich source of information to the young and often marches to a different drum. His typical small farm lies against the side of a steep mountain where he hews out a living. "Martin" portrays those who love the mountains but acknowledges the many barriers and wishes for better opportunities. Appalachian culture is painted with live accounts of everyday activities: logging, farming, social activities, religious functions, and whiskey making, which is the cause of two killings in this novel. Examined is the mountaineer's dilemma of dealing with the outside world and changes on the horizon.

    This novel will provide a view of the people and obstacles that shaped some of America's most unique citizens. It portrays the vernacular and archaic language brought with them. In being loyal to articles and historical spellings, the original spelling(s) have been retained. Being indigenous to the area has qualified me to know first-hand the struggles and joys of mountain people. Join those who ventured into this unsettled land filled with many obstacles as you become immersed in this novel.

— I —

YOU SHOULD HAVE BEEN THERE

Saturday, May 7, 1921, Roxie, makes her way up the Gap road - a road that nobody knows how old - away from civilization.

Scampering out of the way on the obscure road a Fox Squirrel hurries to get the last bite of a White Oak Acorn. Buzzards bask in the morning sun and dry their putrid wings. High above a Bald Eagle rides the air currents in somewhat of a holding pattern, looking for prey. Her mate sits nearby, keeping watch over the nest.

Strapped to Roxie's back is a worn saddle whose pommel displays tattered rawhide someone wound there years ago. Sitting atop and braced against the wooden stirrups is Bibs, a man with an uncommon fear - a mysterious uneasiness that something is wrong.

I awake from my daydreaming and sit a few seconds before making an attempt to straighten my legs. The long crouched position causes much discomfort to my sore joints. My emotions soar as I ponder the events of that miserable day. Sitting mesmerized by the surroundings, thinking, looking, I try to relive what had happened. As I close my eyes again, I can almost feel the soft rain and hear the hoof beats of the horse as she finds footing among the rocks. My mind races on to relive the day the thunderous shots echoed off the canyon walls to race down the gorge, followed by a trail of blood and the problems to ensue.

Reaching for a small sapling, I pull myself up and stagger to gain footing. A needling sensation follows as blood rushes to fill cramped veins, but the long seated position prevents any sudden movement.

The crows' cawing high in the trees interrupts the stillness and pondering. To the west, the sun slips behind the ridge and dew forms on the moss-covered rocks around me. The creek streaming from the Four Knobs is ice cold and quiet while steering its way over the many rocks and fallen branches. Our mountain vocabulary does not contain adequate words to convey the feelings that wrench my heart. It is hard to believe that men would allow bitterness to lead to this and be a part of a cold, calculated murder.

My mind drifts from one scene to another as the evening wears on. Realizing the roadway will soon become dark, except for the flickering light the moon provides between the trees, I figure I had better skedaddle. Crawling and sometimes sliding from the ledge makes me think of those who have pioneered places much more renown, but I am not a pioneer in the classical sense. I simply enjoy uncovering the past, although it causes a pit in the bottom of my stomach and my heart to feel heavy. It is not a morbid thing, just a desire to get to the bottom of events.

This trip has done much to recreate that numbing day in history, but I need this experience and many more to help me understand the killing and these people.

I moved here some time ago to enrich myself and to enjoy this wild beauty, but I've come to find more than I had expected. Actually, I feel as though a part of me has always belonged here. In a sense, I am like the poet Thoreau, a naturalist who "wished to live deliberately" and to determine the most important things in life. I am not here to look on as a spectator, but to merge with these mountain people I love and become a part of their culture. I have been fortunate to weld my way into their acceptance and create an enjoyable life.

The sacrifice to protect my pencil and pad causes my elbows and backside to take quite a mutilating as I miscalculate the steadiness of a rock. A look about quickly reveals no life-threatening wounds, albeit greenbriers and thorns make their presence known. Surviving the spill at the creek urges the demand to move on, lest I become a victim of further injury with darkness quickly falling.

The walk out of the Gap is as lonely as the dickens. As I near Hopeville, I see no one to talk to, just a brief glimpse of Maynard over by the cave. I had hoped to see Pap or some of the others who frequently meander there. Nearby is old Ped Rohrbach's house, Charley Hankse's house, the old school which also serves as our church and the store where customers can also pick up a hint of groceries.

These are near the mouth of Jordon's Run, where it empties into the North Fork. Here it splashes into the river at a right angle, very turbulent. The cold mountain water sends a horrifying chill to the larger body of water, but a welcome sensation to the native trout and minnows that swirl there.

A mile walk west takes the traveler to Amos Dolly's farm. He has one of the nicest farms in these parts, including use of the sods on the mountain. Amos fits into the lineage of Johann Dahle, a Hessian soldier who at the end of the Revolutionary War settled in Pendleton County. Dolly is the Anglicized version of the German name, Dahle. The family began making use of the sods on the mountain to pasture their sheep and cattle; hence the name Dolly Sods.

But as I see it, there are those who oppose this naming

since many families used the sods as much as the Dolly's. The Macksville section of our local paper recently stated, "Many large herds of cattle have passed through here the last few days, the owners taking them to the grazing farms in the Alleghany Mountains." The lush green grass all along the mountain is a delight to hundreds of sheep and cattle.

This rich wilderness has had its share of suffering. Dolly Sods has been burned time and again. It is said that confederate spies once allowed a campfire to get out. The biggest reason for fires, however, has been that of poor logging techniques. Since spruce is the most valuable to be cut, and most of it even-aged stands, the loggers generally end up leaving very few trees standing. The tops of the trees are left in a tangled mat of slash piles, which makes for a perfect fire. Many fires begin when sparks from steam engines and aerial skidders quickly ignite and spread. Little effort is made to stop the blazes, with the destruction often spreading to adjacent areas. Many mountainsides have repeatedly burned, including the humus, until no new growth of trees can possibly come back. This particularly damaged spruce since it has no taproot.

Once out of the Gap my trip is level, making my aching legs feel good after the rugged venture. No wonder God created our precious horses and mules with strong backs and weak minds. The poor creatures pulling farm wagons up that awful road through the Gap have to strain with every step. I wonder if those "new-fangled" horseless buggies will ever travel these roads to help these folk. Then to think, if they ever make it, will these roads be passable? How will these lives change?

As dusk settles over the mountains, I am careful to watch my steps while traveling the bridge crossing the run. Often, boards spring loose and leave ends turned up, waiting to trip the unwitting traveler. More than one soul has fallen headlong into the creek, or worse yet, has broken through and had the misfortune of scraping the shin and lodge about the knee.

Upon reaching home, I pull the yard gate shut and to greet me is my dog Blaze, who nearly knocks me down. He is a big, hairy, mixed breed that wandered into my place one day. Looking poorly and orphaned, I threw out some leftovers, which coaxed him to remain here ever since. He's become one of my best friends and is nearly always by my side. I ordered him to stay around home today to keep an eye on things.

As habit would have it, the first thing off as I step on the porch is my checkered wool hat. The exposed rafters are filled with dozens of nails to hang things I need handy, such as hats, ropes, buckets and sundry items. To one side of the porch is a large stack of wood stored there out of the weather. On the other is a bench and splint-bottom rocker. Glancing there reminds me of work for a rainy day; the splints are in need of repair. Today it's too late, plus the fact I'm tuckered out and in need of rest. The more urgent chores include tending the fire, frying some deer meat and finding my feather tick.

Hearing the noise of the clock sounding nine dongs reminds me of one last thing to do today and that is to wind it. About every eight days, I find the key in the bottom of the case and slide it over the pegs, turn one clockwise and the other counter clockwise. Having done that, I restart the pendulum with a soft nudge from my index finger.

Long after the clock sounds ten dongs, I linger at my ole desk with the flickering lamp recording the day's activities in my journal. Through the open window comes the short yelp of a fox, which I hope my dog keeps out of the sheep. On the other hand, a couple creatures in my flock have settled more than one score.

I can see in the distance the mysterious stars high in the night sky and the lonesome rims of the mountains around my little cabin. High on North Mountain, I hear the melody of dogs as they trail a bear, which has one thing on its mind. The few houses in the distance have now blended into the mountainside as their dim coal oil lamps have been snuffed out. Off in the coldness, an owl sounds a lonesome cry. At last, I bar the door and reach for the bedstead where awaits the feather tick.

– II –

THOSE WHO DARED THE ALLEGHANIES

The morning stroll takes me around Wildcat to see if I might learn anything more of the killing. News of this sort is big here, because there is a general concern for the welfare of others.

Wildcat lies at the base of New Creek Mountain, an area of rattlesnake infested rocks, brambles, vines, ferns and ledges here and there, yet people have built dwellings along its ancient trail. Obviously, these were pushed into these hollows and ledges because they couldn't afford a sensible place elsewhere. Enormous rocks have been exposed as a result of upheavals and floods. They look small from my house, but that deception is uncovered when close.

Wildcat was named for the frequent sighting of wildcats that like to hide in the rock ledges. These wildcats come from different species of the lithe-bodied cat family - the lynx or bobcat and the panther. Another common term, catamount, is used to describe various wildcats.

The road could not have been made down in the valley because the river hugs Wildcat and curves around and under the Hanging Rocks. It is pretty clear that the river forged paths while high and settled there, shifting from one side of the valley to the other over the years. Occasionally, we boat around the rocks, but it is less troublesome to walk over them.

The Potomac River is what it is today because of what has happened along its banks for eons. There are wider, longer and swifter rivers, but none with a personality, habits and the ability to rearrange geography and real estate as this. Rocks, small and great, have rolled down its bed over the centuries until they are smooth as anything you will see. The chiseled valley has caused her to rise above her banks and hunt a new bed, all to the expense of rearranging corn fields, houses, and forest. In a short time, it destroys farms, barns and boundaries. In time, it returns to the old and reestablishes wherever it wishes, even if others have taken up residence there. It has no respect for persons or property. No one can tame it, not stone dams, politicians or farmers. What it has destroyed would humble the banker in contemplating the costs.

Mud Hill is the western entry of the Wildcat road and ascends at about a forty-five degree grade. Teams with empty wagons struggle as they labor under this pull. Animals pulling loaded wagons can be heard for some distance as their nostrils widen to suck air. Loggers hauling crossties to the train depot in town find it necessary to hook two teams to pull the wagon, or chunk the wheels often to let a single team rest. Those who come off Jordon's Run must leave the evening before and use two teams until they pull Mud Hill. They let the wagon sit until the next morning and return home. Before daybreak, they bring one team back to take the load on to town.

It is said that all early wagon masters worth their salt soon learned valuable tricks. They always stopped for the night on the far side of a river to place a flooding river behind them. If it should rain during the night, the far bank would become slippery and difficult to ascend. Also, teams will rarely pull as well in "cold collars," that is, when fresh geared - as opposed to a warm up. Some have been known to drive a circuit before facing a heavy pull in the morning.

Living on Wildcat is an old couple, whose house sits at the turn where the road rounds the bend over the Hanging Rocks. We affectionately call the old man, Pap, and his wife, Mom. Pap is worn with age and toil. Years of work behind the plow and in the woods has formed huge calluses on his broad hands, making them feel like tree bark. Carving out a living in these mountains has been his passion.

His thin gray hair is swept aside under a brown slouched hat. Beneath his hat is a line-etched face that depicts a lot of winters - a kind face where time has plowed many furrows that run deep, illustrating mountain anguish and labor. A face that has labored with disappointment and grief, usually covered with a day or two growth of beard. A closer look reveals pride of birth and pride for the culture into which he was born. Another view reveals the work of a sculptor who wished to achieve a look of wisdom, yet accessibility, a spark, yet wear.

Beneath shaggy brows are piercing blue eyes that express intellect and captivate audiences in a way as to look beyond the person and into the heart. From his slightly stooped shoulders hang his ever-present Uncle Ben's overalls from which emerges a chain attached to a cherished pocket watch. Concealing his arms from summer's heat and winter's cold is a long sleeve shirt.

He is never distant from these mountain people because he is one of them. He displays the presence of someone sent from God to assist. Under his exterior lies a heart of understanding and wisdom. Never does he speak without first considering the impact. I have seen him frequently open himself in words of direction and discernment. I suppose his most famous byline is to refer to "over there," which he uses to make reference to Heaven, where peace will replace sorrows and questions will be answered. Yet, now, he provides a great deal of joy to these mountain people and regularly finds humor in the most complicated circumstances and has learned to find good in the bad.

Living such a short distance from Pap gives me opportunity to visit often and hear stories of these mountain people. They provide a living history of the people and mountains here. Every once in a while a new incident is revealed, although I enjoy the old ones as he repeats them with new enthusiasm. He must think I am foolish to cherish hearing about those difficult times. I love to see his repositioning as he takes a deep breath and moves into another line. We sit on the porch for hours, he in the rocker and I on the tongue-and-groove oak boards. I treasure the evenings when we can watch the twilight as it settles across the narrow valley, talking of hobbies, chores and incidents of the past. Pap's delivery is oratorical in its own way, as he has the habit of closing one eye and leaning toward the listener.

Mom is in her early eighties and has been like a mother to many, far and near. From time to time, she and Pap have taken folks in to care for them. They have just one of their own. Maynard, as Pap puts it, "is not right in th' head." He gallivants all over New Creek. It's a wonder a rattler or copperhead doesn't take hold of him. Sometimes he stays for days on the top of New Creek in the Willard Day Hole, named after an old man who hid there from the law for making moonshine.

Mom takes the best care of Maynard that she can, but he is always tormented. It's like there is another person inside him, wishing to control. Sometimes he can be so docile, and other times he goes into a rage that most better avoid. His strength is valuable when Pap can direct it to good use. He has an understanding way with the animals and can carry rocks that would break most men down. His hair always unkempt and his clothes, being hand-me-downs, never quite fit. Often Pap has to return an item Maynard has stolen and folks know it's not the fault of the old folk, but Pap repeatedly apologizes.

Oh, they had more children. Mom and Pap often sit on the porch overlooking the graves out in the meadow, surrounded by a split-rail fence, broken only by a stile. Recently I sat with Pap as he spoke of the others.

"There was others," he said as tears flowed across his cataract-covered eyes. "Ove' yonder," he waved a long arm, pointing a finger to the apple grove which shadows the graves. "A fever come through - our young'ins couldn't fight 't. One by one we laid 'em t' rest. Maynard's left, sech as he is." Tears broke over his eyes as a strange mixture of sorrow and confidence sounded in his voice, knowing God does all things well. He then pulled the horsehair bow across his fiddle to the tune of "Amazing Grace." Having stroked just a few bars, Mom sang softly, "Thro' many dangers, toils an' snares, I have already come", then Pap, with an outburst of a broken voice joined in, "Tis grace hath brought me safe thus far, And grace will lead me home."

Mom is notably heavy, always wears an apron, and constantly thinks of others. Her hair is swept back away from small, discerning green eyes that are set in small openings inviting a conversation. Her most noticeable feature is the lines that etch deep in her face and crisscross like a map reflecting stories of past events. That is not to say that beneath the facade there is not a smile available. A few ladies at our functions have maintained a look of always being cared for and having never gone through a problem, but Mom wears evidence of having her share. She has anguishes because of the inconsideration of others or her worry for them. Any needing prayer or comfort call on her. Many nights she sets up tending the sick or bereaved. She has created some of the most beautiful quilts eyes have ever seen. Usually the patterns are of a simple variety, but when time permits, mountain art comes to life. She prepares one of the nicest baskets at our church functions. When the lid opens, saliva begins to flow as the aroma of fresh pie and baked beans emerge.

Their house sits on locust posts and against a rock ledge overlooking the North Fork and Hopeville. It looks somewhat unstable because of its precarious perch, but has withstood the test of winter winds. There's no underpinning beneath the house so their old mongrel finds shelter there, and an occasional bewildered chicken. Periodically, Mom steps out with the broom to scatter all the unwanted loiterers. As with so many houses, siding from Boy's lumber mill covers the veneer. Oak and chestnut boards run vertical with strips covering the cracks to help keep out the weather. A few windows line the side toward the Fork, providing a view of the road and river. The board floor shows through the worn carpet where she spends the most time in front of the range, preparing food for Pap and anyone passing. "Th' latchstring's alw'ys out," proclaims Pap in hospitality, knowing Mom always has something cooked up.

Christmas comes to their house, not so much with festivities, but with the smells of baking. Aromas originate in the kitchen as whiffs of apple pie drift through the doorway curtains to the sitting room. Pies made with the best Granny Smith apples and covered with a browned flaky crust melt in your mouth. Mom gives each one her signature touch as she takes her thumb to imprint the edges and a fork to emboss the middle. A helping of rich cow cream on top seems to place one in another world. Pap forever reminds me that rich people eat no better nor have better company or view, as we look out the windows that open to North Mountain and the Sods.

The luster of Christmas comes from Pap's fiddle as it sounds out melodies such as Silent Night, Joy to the World, and others. The extra apples and pears for visitors add brilliance to celebrate the season.

One of the most enjoyable activities at Christmas time is "Belsnickling." Folks dress up in all kinds of crazy outfits and cover their faces to conceal their identity. Upon approaching the houses, the crowd begins yelling, "Let th' Belsnicklers in." With that, faces begin appearing as curtains are pulled aside to investigate the commotion. Children inside usually run to hide. Soon the door is opened, allowing the Belsnicklers to move in to be guessed. There is a smile of victory for the one whose identity is hidden the longest. Before going on to another house, candy or an apple is given to the unexpected guests.

— III —

INVESTIGATING THE GAP

I arrive at Pap's place as he folds his sheep in another pen for the day. He opens, "What a ya doin' on th' road s' early?"

"I'm on my way to the Gap to look around."

"Wait a bit an' I'll keep ya comp'ny. I was a figurin' on goin' up m'self," he replies as he lays the last chestnut timber in place to contain the sheep.

We push up Weese Hollow, past the sputtering artesian well and atop Cave Hill, where we stop to catch our breath. Not being a native, or all that knowledgeable of the culture, I figure an agreeable subject will be our surroundings. You see, I still tread a little lightly so as not to provoke any unnecessary offense.

"God sure expressed some of His best handiwork when He made this place. When He looked down and called creation good, He surely must have been looking right here: the panorama of Hopeville, the sunlit and shadowed trails that follow mountainsides, leading to remote feeding grounds and homes, the swift and cold trout streams, the stands of virgin oak and....well, it's almost Heaven!" I sense enough, for I lost my audience; however, I knew I'd struck a chord with the old mountaineer, but his response wasn't what I had hoped.

After a pause, "It's that way, fir them that don't know," he stated gruffly. "Fir me, it don't matter much, but fir th' young, there's them who..." He lifts his head, as if someone tugged on it with a cord, and cups his hand to his ear to get a better reception of the sounds below. He pauses again, "An' boy, I'll tell ya 'nother thing, it ain't Heaven! There's beauty here 'lright, but t' equal this place t' Heaven shows yer ignerance, ya gone an' stretched it a might too fir! This land has 'lways give me a whole lot, but ya need some schoolin' on Heaven!"

The long silence breaks when he checks to see if he's been heard or ignored, then follows, "Boy, boy, are ya a listenin?"

Slow to answer, I respectfully respond, "Yes, Pap, I'm listening."

I'd angered the old timer and know I'd better keep my mouth shut. I came to learn that he is a man of propriety, but uncomfortable there. He is suited to dress in homespun clothing, being a heavy linsey shirt, bulky trousers and a round, flat, wide-brimmed hat from which he can peer out of the shade into the far distance. I came to learn that he is a man who enjoys knowing what lies ahead with a passion for fact. He steers away from gossip and leans toward subjects dealing with things and ideas.

Echoing out of the Gap are voices of other bewildered searchers, having the same idea as ourselves. We follow the steep descent into the Gap to where folks are mingling. An almost vertical trail, or horse path, descends through Mountain Laurel and Bull Pine for those approaching from Weese Hollow.

As we arrive, someone asks if they had caught the killers. There are suspicions as to those who committed this evil, but this sort of thing opens up a lot of possibilities. The probable cause is moonshine, but most who engage in the trade have conflicts.

We talk about the cold still body of Harness Bibs lying in the road, with a khaki colored blazer pulled up over his head. Dried blood remains to stain the trail. There stands Thaddeus, a young lad in bibs and a felt hat, who had driven the matched, sweaty, dapple-gray team as it came to an abrupt halt that day to where Bibs laid prostrate. Thaddeus's dad, Milt Cornshakle, stands talking to some townspeople who had come to investigate. He had walked behind the wagon that day and had summoned the Coroner. He feels more than a little important since he was the first adult to come upon the corpse. He's not to be outdone by the highly mannered investigators from town, whose little derby hats, clothes and speech reveal they are from beyond these ridges. Tied off to the side of the road are some of their high-stepping horses and a carriage or two. Most of the locals had walked, but a few had brought their road wagons and teams, and an array of riding animals.

We linger for some time talking about all the possible gunmen and other matters, such as farming, the weather and people. Pap and I talk at length to Martin to get his take on the event. He, like everyone else, is not sure but has a good idea as to the guilty parties.

Eventually, Pap gets around to ask in a euphemistic way (there is often more to his questions than the surface reveals), "Martin, 'ave ya got a chance t' see that Sara Jane lately? If I'm not a mistakin' I seen 'er over 't town with that town feller, seems he's 'bout t' beat yer time!" All the while, I knew Pap was interested in Martin's reaction. I also knew Pap had not been in town for months. She is the prize passion of every young man around.

Suddenly, Pap's many good-bye conversations are interrupted when he senses commotion and Maynard crouching down behind a buggy. Pap yells at him, realizing he had thrown the mule manure that now resides on Sheriff Kimble's dude suit. Maynard had been loitering behind the spotted mule waiting for it to defecate. The manure hadn't time to totally harden when he scooped his hands full and hurled the stink at the suits.

Kimble had just poured Prince Albert tobacco in waiting thin paper when manure targeted his back. From fury, his derby hat and tobacco soared to the air as eyes turned toward Maynard. Partially digested weeds stain the once pressed suit.

Pap moves with an apology, "Mr. Kimble, I'm sorry fir what Maynard has gone an' done, but, but Mom 'll sure 'nough clean it fir ya." Pap soon senses the apology is too inadequate to calm the situation. Each party tenses and is helpless to do anything to prevent further embarrassment. The townspeople realize they are outsiders and better not move toward simple-minded Maynard. Fortunately for Kimble, the creek is handy, so he sets to cleaning the manure. Any move otherwise will mean a fresh bath, compliments of Martin. The only incident happened when some slender, fair-skinned, "greenhorn' from town, was scared into his buggy, when he spouted off about the 'backwoods' ignorance and killing.

— IV —

OLD HOPEVILLE, THE HUB OF THE COMMUNITY

Hopeville is where Jordon's Run and the North Fork Pike converge. It is a community of about fifty people, the nucleus having a store and schoolhouse, which also serves as our church. It sits in a clearing where the Jordon's Run spills into the North Fork of the South Branch of the Potomac. Lying outside its cluster of pine buildings are small farms and gardens, and an endless forest beyond. A well-worn road straggles in from the East, and two beginning toward the West, one not much more than a bridle path going up the Gap. Here school convenes during the week and church is held on the weekends, or sometimes more often when there is sensed a need for a spiritual refreshing.

It is difficult to say which is the most popular, as both occupy a commanding position in the community. In light of city functions, there is little concentration of energy, a mere dot on the map. However, nearly every time I venture up there, someone is milling around, since these buildings sit at the crossroads of either going up the Gap or up the Fork. It doesn't take much of an excuse to stop off and talk.

THE HUB OF THE COMMUNITY

What the club is to the city man, the store is to the country folk. The store serves as a gossip center for those who may otherwise feel convicted of gossiping in church. In the center is a potbelly stove with a pipe that runs across the room and exits out the side of the building. The door handle droops from frequent opening and usually left that way so visitors can spit into the blaze with little effort. Around the stove are a few chairs someone has crafted, a bench and kegs to sit on. Off to the side is a checker board mounted on an old nail keg, sandwiched between two chairs, usually occupied. Lining one side of the counter is butter, a basket filled with eggs, a weighing scale and containers of candy. Crackers and Longhorn Cheese sit on the counter to make a quick snack.

A string hanging from the ceiling drawn through a system of pulleys is used to wrap purchases. Sugar-cured hog hams and a few sides of bacon hang from the ceiling that patrons have bartered. Also, suspended above are some peltries, ginseng and venison hams. On display are yarn stockings, maple sugar, homemade clothes, crockery, tin and hardware. Open kegs lining the front of the counter are filled with oats, corn, potatoes, tobacco, gun powder, coffee and farm supplies. Behind the counter are some wooden shelves displaying medicines, for both human and animal ailments. Added to this assortment are a few horse collars, shovels, pitchforks, coats and a catalog where patrons can order things not in inventory. Pap said, sometime back, the store displayed corpulent jugs of whiskey for sale.

A small section over in the corner of the store, about five feet square, is the remainder of what was our Post Office, now covered with dust. A spider has spun an intricate web that connects an old set of deer horns to one of the top pigeonholes. The central figure is a long worn out office chair that has been off limits to everyone, except Amos. During his postmaster days, he reigned supreme and still does when he is here. Anyone sitting in the chair kindly gets up and kids know to vacate the chair when he visits. The oak table sitting in the corner once provided an area for writing and postage preparation. The front is greatly worn by the constant leaning forward of Amos' portly frame. Rats have made many meals on one leg in attempts to salvage salt and grease drippings that ran from Amos's pork broth. Above hangs a roughly divided pigeon-hole sorting box. There are no names to indicate where patron letters went but Amos had a system. He seemed to have a slot for each. I guess it made his job more official.

Leaning forward on my oak chair, as we sit around the stove, I ask Pap about the history of the post office. "I don't 'ave that infirmation, but Amos 'll tell ya. He's 'bout due t' come any time now t' catch up on th' news. I thought I'd seen his buggy pull 'cross the creek a minute er two ago – he'll soon be 'ere."

The screen door opens to the store and Amos enters. First, a loud screech, then a slam, as if someone thought he was tightening a fiddle string when installing the spring. The barefooted kid occupying the broad barrel-back postal chair vacates. Amos says his "howdies," and sure enough, the old timer waddles over to the old chair and abruptly pulls it to a comfort zone. He settles back, flips his suspenders and reaches for his mail.

Amos is busy reading when I make my way over to the old desk to interrupt. "Amos, I know the post office is used now as a drop off point, but what is its history?"

As always, he is glad to share the past and begins searching through some papers to get the facts. After digging for some time through the drawer, he comes up with some scribbling. In his shirt pocket he fingers his taped glasses and sets them on his broad nose. His shirt buttons tighten as he rears back in the chair to get comfortable. I declare, if one should break loose with all that force against it, surely it would be fatal! A button screaming like a bullet across the room could cause some unfortunate soul instant blindness!

He squints as he begins to decipher the past. I listen as he reads, stopping him from time to time for a better understanding. He begins: "The Hopeville Post Office"[1] was 'stablished October 20, 1868, t' serve th' early settlers jist after th' Civil War. William Lentz was granted th' first contract t' be Hopeville's first postmaster. It was t' be ten miles from Luney's [Lunice] Creek, t' th' east, and t' have mail delivery once a week. The next office t' th' west is th' Mouth of Cinica [Seneca], fourteen miles away. Th' contract states that there were eleven families within two miles of th' Hopeville Post Office, an' twenty-four families within one-half th' distance t' th' Mouth of Seneca office. James Lambert assumed th' office of postmaster on January 24, 1870, an' remained in that position 'til it closed on June 7, 1871, causing people t' meet th' mail carrier on th' road going to Mouth of Cinica, er pick it up here."

He goes on. "That wadn't t' last long because on th' cold day of February 19, 1872 th' doors were reopened t' serve th' locals. Th' new postmaster was Andrew Awers, who filled th' office 'til June 12, 1884, when Mrs. Christina Awers took over th' duties. She held th' position 'til June 29, 1897, when Cal Awers assumed th' office an' preformed th' duties 'til January 8, 1902."

Amos finishes the reading and looks up from the notes with pride and removes his glasses to return them to their case and to his shirt pocket. "Fin'ly, I was made postmaster. Many a mornin' I tended this place, an' took stuff t' people who couldn't git here, as part of m' duty."

Pap says, a position Amos performed religiously until its final and official closing as a Post Office, September 15, 1911.

Not far from the store sits the Hopeville School, serving also as the meeting place for the church. The building is covered with pine clapboard lumber, which is typical of schools and churches. There are four windows along each side and one at the front to provide ventilation for the minister or teacher, depending on the use. Standing seam metal covers the roof, which accentuates the sound of rain when a downpour comes. Red Oak and White Oak boards run horizontal on the walls to line the inside. In the center stands a buckeye stove, which does a swell job heating those who sit close to it. Coal oil lamps mounted on the walls bring light to the dark oak. Teeth marks line the short benches that line each side. The young have either used these to cut their teeth or were bored and needed something to chew. Some benches in the rear have initials expressing someone's love. This building houses the majority of the community gatherings and is the hub of much of the activity. The log building that preceded our new one sat on the property owned by one of Godfrey's boys, Lee, who is said to be one of the best workers and farriers in the country.

Worship service is a very important part of mountain lives. We are fortunate to have Sister Dolly as minister of our church. Her husband, Minor, has a farm up the river, so she is able to minister nearly every Sunday. Occasionally we have others drop by to speak, or set up a tent for meetings, which may go on for weeks. Some are ever so diligent in their labor that their shirt becomes entirely soaked with sweat as if they have been hoeing corn all day. Their philosophy is that one should be as excited about serving the Lord as anything they do. Many work a regular job because most churches cannot support them. It has been said that these rough backwoodsmen have no use for a "preacher that can't shoot without a rest." They want someone who has the same rugged spirit as themselves. They demand preachers who have as their primary theology, "The Great Commission" and the imminent return of Christ.

Some leave lasting positive results and, as Pap says, "kin preach a purty fair sermon" but others are mere illiterate preachers who shout backwoods scripture colored with their private interpretations. It is common for them to read a text from the scriptures and not look at a piece of print from that point on. More likely than not, they begin with a crescendo and continue that pace throughout the service, except for stopping to remove an overcoat, or to slap gnats and mosquitoes. It can be stated that these believe the Holy Ghost informs the heart rather than the mind. From time to time, members of the audience get so emotionally involved that they shout, dance and even roll on the floor, hence the name "Holy Roller." Worshippers sometimes get so happy praising God and feel so secure that they go home and forget a sleeping child on a bench. Recently, Brother John began dancing and shouting so ecstatically that he lost his false teeth in the aisle. He hardly missed a stride as he stooped to pick them up, stuffing them into his shirt pocket.

Of course, not everyone takes part in these revivals. Drunks have been known to disrupt them as Elias Rohrbach did some time ago. He was arrested for "disrupting a place of worship." Some drunks have thrown tomatoes or snakes wrapped loosely in sheets into tent meetings to disrupt the service, causing everyone to scamper to safety until peace was restored.

Not far from here, a preacher has been known to wear a "Leg Iron" to protect himself and the congregation. People like this caused Francis Asbury, the early Methodist bishop, to note in his journal, "there were so many wicked whisky drinkers who brought with them so much of the power of the devil; that he had little satisfaction in preaching." Asbury, the horseback riding circuit rider, has been described as carrying a rifle under his shroud-like cloak and a Bible stuck under his coonskin vest.

It is said that some members of one early Appalachian church placed loaded rifles in the gun rack near the door to be used, should they need protection from hostile Indians.

The women and children sat in the balcony, while the older boys and men sat on the benches on the ground floor.

Since early times, efforts were made to spread the word of God in the mountains by itinerant preachers who were sent out by various denominations. Some chose to live in communities, and others traveled about, holding revivals, hoping a permanent congregation would result.

Pap tells a story of one "Circuit Riding" team. "Th' two preachers went 'bout, but had only one horse. They had a "ride an' tie plan." One rode a ways, tied th' horse by th' trail, an' started walkin', th' other caught up t' th' horse an' rode 'til he come up t' his friend ahead, who was a walkin'. That way both rode some, an' walked some."

At first, services were held wherever there was a shelter, tent, or out in the open. Common to the tent service was the "sawdust trail." Preachers always gave an invitation for salvation and asked those who wished to be saved to come forward. They did so by moving to the aisle and walking to the front on a path of sawdust, placed there to dry up the mud.

It was soon discovered that mountain people were more suited to a less formal style of worship rather than those with a liturgy - not "the religion of the gentry," as some have been labeled. Part of the theology is the preaching about Heaven and the deliverance from the drudgery of hard work, escaping poverty and the assurance of a better world. The preaching of "Hellfire" and the need to follow God's call or suffer the fate of fiery and eternal damnation is prominent.

In a way, it seems ironic to use something so terrible to cause one to escape mountain hardships. But most mountain people have had a glimpse of Hell in their tribulations and they sure wished to avoid the real place. We can still see that type of preaching around Hopeville. It's evident that this preaching moves the people at least for a while. Someone has said, religion is for those who are trying to avoid Hell and spirituality is for those who have experienced some Hell.

In the mountains there is an alliance between holiness and poverty. Jesus spoke much about riches, causing mountain folk to equate all material wealth with worldliness. They have interpreted these principles literally, when, in fact, riches are not the problem, but rather, where they are placed in the relationship of man and God. Another weakness in their worship is a reliance on God when all is going badly, but declining to do so when all is going well. Or, if God doesn't meet their needs when and where they expect, they sometimes throw in the towel.

It is difficult, if not impossible, to determine all that is accomplished in their worship; only eternity will tell. One thing for sure, they come to worship and feel better afterward. The services allow them to forget the hardships of living in these mountains and gain the needed strength to face another week. Throughout the week, they can reflect on Sunday's sermon and fellowship to provide encouragement. They have learned one important thing. The only way one can make sense out of a man's reason for being and the purpose for trials is to see an eternal purpose in them. For that reason alone, it is a workable gospel.

— V —

IT'S FINALLY SUNDAY

It's Sunday and time for service. Everyone around Hopeville plans to be there to worship and to learn more of the terrible incident in the Gap. Pap started out early this morning as always to allow time to stand outside before service to talk. Mom cannot always attend because of ailments and the long walk. Lambing obligations caused me to be somewhat tardy, but after saying the usual howdies to everyone, I slide in on the bench with Pap and Maynard. Folks that had not been there for some time come today to hear the lingering gossip about the killing.

As a surprise to everyone, Sara Jane rides up in her buggy. She is not only the finest specimen of God's creation in these parts, but so is her Morgan, a sorrel gelding. The rhythm of his trot makes a melodious sound as if he is a part of an orchestra. He is well muscled and fills out his harness as well as any horse that had ever worn one. His barrel-chested breath and strength is endless, providing the ability to pull the steep hills on the North Fork without a rest, especially Mud Hill. Sara's gelding gleams as if he had been bathed in oil. The leather harness and buggy glisten, except where hoofs and wheels splashed a smattering of mud. That doesn't deter from the beauty that sets on the rig, holding the reins so gracefully, yet with all the assurance necessary. Every young man has his eyes fastened on her, as well as some jealous ladies.

She is one of those rare young ladies whose appearance words will not do justice, having an aristocratic quality and a confidence that make her worth envying - perfectly proportioned, sharp-witted and yielding a disposition that attracts folk. Full lips highlight her irresistible smile, creating small arches at the ends. Complementing her glow are whitened teeth that display impeccable beauty. The most charming sparkling eyes radiate character that speaks of a good heritage. Encapsulating her beauty is brown flowing hair, making her enviable throughout the mountains. She is breathtaking in every way, but not seductive.

Oh, some of the local girls would have their bragging rights if privileged to set before a professional photographer. He could take their best pose, showing off their most prized qualities. If only they had the luxuries offered to others. Without a doubt, a store-bought dress and cosmetics would level the playing field. Actually, there are many inequities: intellect, skills, talents, environment, beauty, personality, etc. It would be interesting to see what would happen if folks had the opportunity to trade places. But then we are simply responsible for what has been handed us and will stand before God with that in mind. I wonder, too, how many unsung persons have been on the planet, not having their attributes discovered by those in the media.

Coming from town has provided privileges not known to country folk. Sara is forgiven because of her unique form of meekness. Her dad is well respected in these parts but also understands how to charge patients, thus providing well. It is not uncommon that Sara should be schooled in the best manners and speech, or that she should have the latest of antebellum fashions. To wear a handmade dress would be unmentionable. They're the kind of people who drink tea when those around Hopeville drink cider.

She steps down from the buggy and in a school girl whisper confides to a friend that she had told her parents she was going to visit relatives. It is said she has as much interest in a certain young man as everyone seems to have in her. Some of the local girls brush off her presence while the young men only desire the opportunity to get a glance. Everyone looks around for the reason she must have come this distance, but the terrain that young Martin must traverse gives reason for tardiness.

Worship begins with familiar songs as everyone takes on a different demeanor. During an interval of quietness, there is heard the sound of metal striking against rocks, and the whinny of Martin's fine strawberry roan as he is tied to a nearby apple tree. Steps soon creak under the weight of a well muscle-toned young man. The door is pushed open sufficiently to allow Martin's entry.

Pap likes to boast that the door, "Is wide 'nough t' 'low any red-fleeced sinner er white-fleeced lamb t' enter!" Everyone looks around to see who is entering, as is the habit.

Entering as quietly as possible, Martin finds a seat spared for "late comers" and sits where he can see Sara in full view. She delicately turns to see him and smiles ever so slightly, enough to cause small crow's feet to form at her temples. Fitted over Martin's athletic frame are clothes his mother took great care in pressing. From head to toe well groomed, unlike most of the locals, who believe that running their fingers through their hair is good enough. Even though the ride here is long and jostling, he looks refreshed.

Sister Dolly steps up to the hewn pulpit that some of the men had cut from a black walnut log years ago. It was sawn to height with a crosscut saw and crudely carved, possessing marks the adz left behind. The top slopes at a slight angle so as to display the Bible. Fastened to the side is a wrought iron lamp holder someone forged. The pastor's suit is pieced together with the best that mountain gifts can afford. Her hair is grayed from years of caring for the people and toil to make a living in these hills. The knees of the long dress are well worn and her black faded shoes turn up at the end like sled runners, formed that way from time spent in prayer. The tattered Bible falls open to a familiar passage, half quoted and half read.

The text, Lamentations 3:22 & 23, "It is of the Lord's mercies that we are not consumed, because his compassions fail not. They are new every morning; great is thy faithfulness." With that she begins her sermon. Knowing the events of the past few days, she speaks of how vulnerable we are to the elements and people who would prey upon us. "It's 'cause of God's mercies that we ain't consumed. He sometimes 'lows us t' be stretched t' th' limit in order t' test our faith. When things go wrong, when ya see no way out, God is faithful. He'll never allow ya t' be tempted beyond what yer able t' bear!"

Momentum picks up in her voice, urged on by an occasional amen or shout. The conclusion isn't as dynamic as some, but the seriousness of her voice gives assurance that there are eternal benefits for those who are faithful. She closes her Bible and walks to the aisle, convincing men in bibs and women in their handmade dresses of God's love and faithfulness when they don't have life's answers.

Today will be special since we planned dinner on the grounds. Folks brought an assortment of food - chicken, homemade bread, pies and other staples. The pies are especially worth looking forward to. They come in all shapes and varieties. My favorite is the huckleberry cobbler, with an added feature of cream poured over the helping.

The huckleberries are picked on Dolly Sods along about July. They thrive in that environment and are so plentiful that a good picker can pick a five-gallon bucket full in a day. They are the, sometimes, reward for a land heavily logged and in spite of fire.

I love to go up there with Pap to pick berries, where it is customary to stay the night because of the distance. A novice may become lost, but not the native. The terrain and the direction the limbs point on the evergreens guide him. The terrible western winds have prevented growth on the western side of the trees, providing direction to the traveler. While much of the terrain may look the same, Pap has learned the subtle art of discerning the lay of the wilderness. He knows the woods like some men know their office or sitting room. He can discern the twitch of a deer's ear among mountain laurel, or distinguish sounds unique to game. In my opinion, he's a genius of nature. It holds few secrets or obstacles from him. In a sense, Pap is like the old western trapper, Jedediah Smith, who was deemed half preacher and half grizzly. I wish I were like that.

It is no small experience to stand dwarfed among the giant Spruce that haven't yet been touched with the axe or fire, and to be surrounded by the numerous Beaver Dams along Red Creek. Beaver cuttings are abundant where they have downed a tree to make an addition to their house or dam. When surprised, they make a thunderous smack on the water with their tail, then dive to safety.

No doubt the prettiest scene is that of a wood duck with her ducklings swimming on the backed-up water. Their colors glisten as the sun shines through the evergreens. Every color of the rainbow is seen as they display their feathers, much like our wild turkey. Those that survive the harsh winters display the most fascinating array of colors depicted by the boss gobbler who struts proudly prior to mating season.

Our fall season is marked with the fellowship dinner that provides one of the last opportunities to feast before severe weather sets in. Also, this allows time for healing wounds and settling some confusion in the community. The Jake Hausshalter family is disheartened by the murder and made the journey off the mountain. Old man Hausshalter boasted, "I'd like t' take a hold a th' man who killed ole Harness in th' Gap." If there is a man that would fight the killer, he would! Although older, he yet prides himself in his ability to stand up and fight.

Arlie Hawkins, standing nearby, spoke of Big Jake's former years." "Ere, 'll back ere on th' moun'ain, if he wadn't fightin', he wadn't happy." He believes that Jake's vast experience fighting qualifies him to do the job. Although much gossip and speculation flows, it is still uncertain as to who did the killing.

Most stay until mid-afternoon, catching up on the latest news and talk of tomorrow's obligations. Many walked, but some rode their farm animals. I take time to watch one family as they board a huge draft horse. Children line the back, from neck to tail, with their homemade clothes and nearly white hair. From the back they are indistinguishable. It would be unthinkable to go to the barber, so all look essentially the same. Each child knows the routine, where to sit and how to behave.

Sara Jane knew her parents would be expecting her return soon and left at the earliest convenience, but not before talking to Martin. Some in these parts believe that one should not spark or marry out of their class and go to great measures to prevent it. Sometimes young people are sent away or disciplined to avoid embarrassing the family. But that doesn't prevent couples from sneaking around to get together.

Sara's hand glides over Martin's as they take the last few steps to the rig. The big Morgan takes a step backward. Martin grasps the reins in his strong hands, assisting Maynard who had been holding the bridle. Maynard's enthusiasm to assist Martin is apparent as he hopes to get the slightest attention from Sara. She steps gracefully aboard. Martin watches as the buggy rounds the bend and heads back to town. The tearing in their hearts is evident as they wave good-bye to each other. Always realizing their difficulty of ever being together, they must rely on their thoughts and infrequent meetings such as this to suffice for now. Perhaps someday they will be unrestrained. Martin gives Maynard a pat on the back, prompting Maynard to say, "She's a purty thing, that Sara Jane." Martin laughs, "You ornery ole rascal!"

To those who responded, today's service met all kind of needs - spiritual, social and the meal providing natural food. Folks around here look forward to these meetings. They come to sing, worship and to learn how to better serve our Creator. The daily struggle of living here in these mountains is lessened when they can socialize and feel God's presence. This gives reason to living.

— VI —

THE MOUNTAINEER

The mountaineer has a strange dichotomy of character. In some ways, he can be seen as a backward individual who would rather avoid any communication with the outside world, yet some possess the components that equip them with enough independence to live anywhere. We often think of backward individuals as those who are dependent on governments, and there is a move in that direction, but the Appalachian pioneers were independent. The last thing they would want is governmental control. They not only came across the Blue Ridge Mountains of Virginia, but conquered. Many mountaineers can be seen as rugged independent individuals, who can survive on their own and need no one. This self-reliant and independent spirit was further forged on the anvil of hardships and the rugged Alleghanies.

The mountaineer's dislike of control cultivated an independent spirit and skepticism. Yet, socializing is of utmost importance at our Hopeville functions, albeit unique. At a reunion or church dinner, it is customary for the men and women to segregate while talking. After the meal, men make their way out under a shade tree to discuss hunting or things pertaining to farming, almost never any other subject. Kids are shooed away anytime elderly people are conversing. This segregation is seen at other times as well. In most mountain churches, men kneel on one side of the altar and the women on the other. The custom of a husband and wife sitting apart at church is also practiced.

They are "person-oriented" individuals. They are concerned with having or gaining approval of their group. They wish to be liked, accepted and sometimes noticed as it relates to the group. They will never do anything to provoke jealousy. They often allow another to have a foreman job so friendships can remain. Business and friends are sometimes seen in conflict. Most mountaineers would rather sacrifice the opportunity of making money rather than to lose a friend. They never wish to be viewed as a "tightwad." Pap has a few identified, however. He says one ole miser squeezed a penny until "In God We Trust" was left imprinted on the palm of his hand.

A friendly relationship is priority and usually involves "setting a spell." That explains why our local store, "Jake's Store," has benches pulled up around the stove. Hours are spent talking while chores wait. One of the unique positions to assume is to hunker down to talk - sometimes for an hour! Try that if you think it's easy! I've seen men talk for hours while their wives wait patiently. Schedules and agendas are secondary.

Some familiar faces that can be found at the store are: Pap and Maynard; Amos Dolly; Boy Awers, a man with a legendary gift of wit and candor, even at another's expense; and Milt Cornshakle, a true patriarch of the Four Knobs, known for his unique accent nurtured out of habit. Coming out of the Gap is Harry Hanks, who would rather be a neighbor than anything else. Adept to tell a story or two are the Hawkins brothers, who work here and there, wherever they can land a job. Ped Rohrbach perhaps understands more about farming than most and has crops to prove it. From up the river is Godfrey Stats, a man with focus and community respect, who would rather own a business than manage another's. Also, from up the river comes Ocie Fields, one who would rather mind his own affairs, but can hold his own and spin yarns with the best.

Big Jake Housshalter sits heavily on the bench, a man with a round face and a larger stature than heart. It seems as one of God's rare pranks to make a man so large. There is always the discomfort of fitting into ordinary chairs, clothes, and such. Other true-bred mountaineers visit from time to time and not to be overlooked are wide-eyed kids hoping for a piece of store-bought candy.

I recall a spell-binding story told recently by Godfrey about a hunting venture. He had gone behind his farm on North Mountain to tend his cattle and was returning when he spotted a Chicken Hawk perched high in a giant Sycamore. A great dislike had grown because of the thievery they engage in.

He began, "Th' hen was a settin' high up in th' growth of a big ole Sycamore, real proud, lookin' m' meder an' animals over. Sittin' there like a statue, with her ole head shinin' in th' sun. I brung m' gun t' m' shoulder, but ere a bead could be drawn, she swept from th' perch an' sailed t' m' hen house. I said, there goes th' thievin' devil! In spite of 't, I let fly a wild shot at th' robber. I walked a ways down th' ridge, an' low an' behold she'd done circled t' where she started, an' 'bout t' lite, but 'stead dropped like a leaf t' th' ground. I come up t' her, only t' see her dead as a hammer. I looked over t' th' side, an' a weasel, all torn an' bloody, was a crawlin' off in th' weeds with a broke back. I set m' heel on its head t' put it out of its misery.

"Couldn't figure what happened, but got t' lookin' an' seen where th' weasel had managed t' reach its head back under th' killer's wing an' eat a hole in th' hawk's heart. All I could 'clare was, one thief gittin' even with th' other!"

The "goal-oriented" person has goals and everything revolves around them. He may step on people to reach them. His goals come first and persons second. He is concerned about things, such as a bank account or his status. The mountaineer is first of all concerned with his acceptance, and subordinate to that are his goals. This orientation may not predict all behavior, because the mountaineer may like or dislike a person when objects intervene, but when treated fairly, he likes nothing more than to be a neighbor. The person who cheats, lies, or takes unfair advantage of another is "marked" by the Appalachian.

The mountaineer is an unpretentious individual. He never pretends to be something that he is not and may even play down his personal attributes. His appearance is not nearly as important as the degree to which he fits in a group. His first choice of conversation is to talk of an event, such as a hunting trip; second to that is to talk of people and lastly, to talk of ideas. He may allow someone to talk for some time about a method or procedure before eventually responding. The response may be in agreement or may not be. He does not always respond with an answer as rapidly as an outsider, causing him to be viewed by some as ignorant. That is his way of being polite and a way of giving the outsider every opportunity to express himself. All the while, the mountaineer is amazed at the sometimes ignorance.

— VII —

THE HOPEVILLE SCHOOL

"Standing in the corner were some hickory branches and they were put to use," boasts Pap, as he reminisces the past, while we talk on the school steps. Well, today the branches are still here and so are the benches that are used by kids and worshippers alike.

I look down from the school steps from where we sit to the barren ground to where someone's horse has grazed too close to a rosebush. Hovering nearby is a colorful yellow humming bee sucking nectar out of a flower. Today we enjoy smelling the sweet perfume of the Lilacs. Looking toward North Mountain, we see buzzards swirling above taking aim on a dead animal - no doubt a groundhog. Kids have attended from all directions, some from Wildcat, some from up the Fork, and some from the head of the Gap.

Schools serving this area are the "Rohrbach School" at the head of Laurel Run, the "Open Ridge School" further West on the Alleghany Front near the Cornshakle farm, and "Brook Side School" near the Jordon's Run store. Just west of here is the "Long Hollow School," and another just beyond the county line. Our school here at Hopeville is one of the largest since it sets at the crossroads of lower Jordon's Run and the North Fork. While some may see just clapboard buildings, each have unique characters, from giant rocks or puncheons that provide firm foundations, to metal clad roofs that provide character.

The schools as well as the teachers who serve our children are special. Teachers who dedicate their time to serve in this remote place deserve respect. It is the ambition of all of them to see these children learn so they can have an opportunity to resurrect from what is perceived as poverty. Teachers, indeed, see all types of emotion as they look across the room at faces and into the eyes of these rural children - eyes that express fear because of the new environment or that of older boys who would much rather be fishing or hunting. They almost wish they could be free to roam like Maynard, who sometimes is seen through the schoolhouse window as he passes, on his way to nowhere. The young have up to this time hidden behind their mothers's dresses and have been sheltered, as an eagle, which for the first time makes its flight from a high branch. The older boys reason, "Why do I have to be here? I'll never need this!" Perhaps they will not need most of it. Teachers rationalize, if only some of the material will sink in, then perhaps a better quality of life will ensue. The teachers have a standing contract, but soon move on to better jobs. Subsequently, our school has a different teacher every couple of years.

Most children come with a respect for authority because they have learned it at home, but not necessarily a respect for teaching. Girls are obedient. They may not see a value in learning some of this material, but at least they respond to discipline. Added to the problem of teaching, and perhaps worse, is the inadequate learning environment at home. Parents are often without formal education, and for that matter, could care less. It is a common saying, "Ya don't need that ol' book learnin!" This can heighten the difficulty of teaching to impossible levels.

The boys sit on one side and girls on the other, all arranged according to grade. It is an artistic balance of attention, trying to deal with so many grades combined with varied learning styles. It is like a doctor, lawyer, or other professional having twenty-five patients at once, all with different problems, expecting a diagnosis particular to the individual. To add to the problem is the lack of pay. Teachers often get room and board and just a few dollars for all their service. They can easily be attracted to better conditions in town.

The Hopeville School sits by the North Fork and in the shadow of New Creek and North Mountain. In the fall and spring, a gentle breeze passes through the valley and windows that line each side of the schoolhouse. The community gets together nearly every spring to whitewash the sides. The inside is lined with oak boards covering everything from floor to ceiling. A portion behind the desk is painted a dull black to provide the needed contrast with the chalk.

Families attending our school are the Paxtons, Awers, Hawkins, Waldrons, Turners, Cornshakles and Hankses. There are about forty kids, ranging from the first to the eighth grade. The study habits vary, depending on the home, interest and family obligations. Those traveling the furthest are those from off the lower end of Jordon's Run. The schedule runs from late September to the first of May, and is usually interrupted by snows that prevail which may hinder the opening of school for days at a time. Often the trails cross the creeks several times making travel difficult - if not impossible.

Pap, in his reliving the past, recounts a prank. "We'd git th' biggest charge out a dippin' a girl's pigtails in a inkwell. If she was a studin', er th' prank wadn't done fir a while, it was easy t' pull off." Pap said, "The kids were purty much behaved, but that don't stop th' orneriness."

I listen intently as he moves into some stories. "We had a lot of fun times at school, least from th' kid's point of view, sech as times playin' 'Annie Over,' 'Baseball,' 'Marbles,' er 'Hide an' Seek' in th' cave."

The following are some general rules for the game of

marbles. If just two are playing, the game can be played as follows: one places a marble to the ground, which provides a target for the opponent. The opponent tries to hit the marble by throwing a marble of his own. They alternate doing this, until one succeeds. He then gets to keep the marble. When played by a group, a circle is drawn in the dirt or gravels. Everyone places a number of marbles in the circle and each takes a turn to try and knock the marbles out of the circle using various techniques to flick the marble forward. A person continues playing as long as he is knocking marbles out of the circle. The person holding the most is the winner and is allowed to keep them.

No doubt the greatest commotion at the school is when a rattler or copperhead pushes their devilish heads from between the moss-covered cracks in the rock foundation. Mountaineers show no mercy, knowing the damage snakes commit. They prey on birds and other varmints and people. If not properly cared for, their bites can certainly be a messenger of death. The only thing keeping this number low is the fact that the rattler sings prior to striking. Pap declares, "I knowed different ones who've fell t' th' pisonous creatures."

Another reason mountain folk in these parts detest the snake, and not soon to be forgotten, is the way it was used to impersonate Satan in the Garden of Eden. This last acknowledgment is apart from the few in southern Appalachia who use snakes in their worship, and do so to prove that God can protect them while handling the dangerous reptiles.

The rattlesnake is by far the largest and most dangerous of all the reptiles in these parts. Men have killed rattlers nearly six feet long and a foot in circumference. These snakes are of three different colors: one is almost black; another, which generally grows larger than the black, is spotted with yellow diamonds; and the third is a dirty brown, nearly the color of dirt and never grows to a large size. This last one, Pap declares, "It's s' wicked it 'll run after a man an' 'll strike soon as it gits in reach."

Not to be overlooked is the lethal copperhead, which has a diamond shaped head and gives no warning. They could be mistaken for some of the common grass snakes if it were not for the head, being much flatter than the non-poisonous snakes.

Many stories are told around the store of the rattler. Some love their story so dearly that it's not uncommon to hear them more than once. Pap's favorite story is of a prize cow that was bitten.

Pap begins, "M' ole milk cow was a grazin' when she walked up an' scered a rattler. A second later vicious fangs sunk int' her nose." Pap straightens from his leaning, adjusts his galluses, pauses to make sure all ears are tuned and every wide-eyed child attentive. "I happened by when I took notice of 'er actin' strange, 'lmost like she'd got in a hornet's nest. I soon closed in, grabbed her halter, an' quieted her. Leadin' her back t' th' barn, I noticed right away she was a havin' trouble seein'. It was then I knowed a rattler had pisoned her! All a sudden, her nose began spoutin' like a sieve. Ole bossey's head swelled t' th' size of a whiskey keg!"

He has told the story so many times he knows when and where to pause. He takes a sip of coffee and tilts his head to the side, indicating the great taste, then continues. "If a bidy could see jist her head, they'd sure 'nough wonder what kind a animal they's a lookin' at! Her breathin' was s' fierce that it could be heard over t' th' next ridge! Caused her t' die a awful death, in th' greatest agony! I wouldn't wersh that on anybidy er anything, fir that matter, poor soul."

Other stories are told of snakes swallowing birds, squirrels, rabbits, mice, chickens, etc. Arlie, although known to paint some of his tales with a broad brush, describes a most enormous prey that a hungry rattler ingested. "Back 'ere on th' moun'ain," he begins, as he drops one shoulder and gains an earnest composure, "me, Pete an' Jeb Arbas seen a old rattler tryin' t' swaller a whistle pig, ere a groundhog. It laid there fir nigh a week 'fore it got 't down. The funny thing was t' see 't try t' crawl off with that hog in its belly!"

He went on to tell of a man, who hated the rattler so fierce that he skinned one alive. Taking out a pocketknife, which all mountain men carry, he cut a ring around its neck and skinned it like an eel. Arlie said it was the weirdest thing to see the varmint crawl off, still sticking its forked tongue out seeking vengeance. Dry weather brings snakes down to the creek, but the older boys or someone at the store soon makes short work of the creatures.

However, once in a while someone is bitten. All the old people have a list of remedies that they have known to be effective. Pap says, "Cut where th' person got bit, an' rub th' place down, allowin' th' pison t' run out." He carefully lifts his shirt sleeve and motions as if he's going to cut an area with his opened pocket knife and then rubs with his hand in a downward motion to demonstrate this method of removing the poison. Others say one should cut the flesh around the bite, which prevents the poison from circulating in the blood, then place a caustic upon the raw flesh, or if that is not available, fill the wound with salt. After that is done, take a dose of sweet oil and spirits of turpentine to defend the stomach. Still some have said that pokeroot boiled into a soft poultice is a cure. Others say "gather th' weed called Boneset, or St. Anthony's Cross, boil a handful of 't in new milk, drink th' milk an' bind th' weed on th' wound." Some say you can drink a pint to a quart of whiskey to deaden the poison, or you can use turpentine on the wound to draw out the poison and bring a cure. Pap demands, "Th' best thing t' do is t' not git bit, an' thats t' wear high boots, or 'leggin's.'"

All snakes have a subtle nature; however, the rattlesnake possesses a rattle. This prevents many people from getting bitten. This always leaves a lasting effect upon everyone. The threat they impose causes mountain people to hate them.

— VIII —

A VIEW OF APPALACHIA

The autumn sun climbs up over the horizon where North Mountain and New Creek slide together. This valley looks as if the Creator made it with the deep slash of an ax-bite. Daylight causes my rooster to wake the valley as he rears his ugly head to crow. Just to make sure everything is working after the night in the tree, he lifts one of his knotty feet, then the other. He forces a fresh supply of blood into his battle-scarred wattles to enlarge them to full capacity in hopes of making him look fierce. Finally, jumping down from the giant Shagbark Hickory, he takes a few steps and shakes the night's dew from his plumage. Wings beat furiously in the wind, scattering everything not nailed down. After all this display, he composes himself so as to show who is boss of the barnyard. About every five minutes, he pushes out his chest, which causes feathers to ruffle, arches his back to give the appearance of might, then sends out another war whoop echoing up and down the valley. Not to be outdone by any of the rest, soon neighboring competitors sound off.

    I thank the Lord for the good night's rest and get ready for another day. My feet hit the floor to the same worn spot made by another, now gone on. Grabbing the pump handle to draw some morning water gives time to plan all the important chores that need doing since taking off yesterday. The wood box is piled high with plenty of kindling and pine to start the morning fires in the Home Comfort. The flame died during the night to just a few embers but is sufficient to get a fire going. A few pieces of pine laid carefully on them soon burns with a blue blaze as I lean to the firebox and blow softly on the remaining sparks. When you do this every day of your life, it becomes routine; even when that doesn't work, we have instant combustion from a stick. Earlier pioneers had to rely on flint and steel, the punk and tinder.

Leftover side meat from the cellar soon falls victim to the heat and begins to fry, followed by two large brown eggs in the grease that had been rendered. Grease has splattered against the warming closet, leaving me with some battle scars as well. In another Griswold Skillet, I watch the spuds begin to brown as a whetting aroma fills the kitchen. "Cat Heads", that's what we call our biscuits, are in the oven from another meal. Coffee is coming to a boil. Saliva has already prepared my digestive system for the tantalizing experience of breaking from the night's fast. This will stick to my ribs today!

Most men around here are not overweight. The thousands of calories are burned and converted into sinew and muscle. Housewives often do not get outside exercise and are forever working with food, causing them to become rather fleshy. That is not to say they contribute less, but their tasks are unlike swinging a grain cradle! My day's schedule will more than exhaust the calories I'm taking in.

Nearly everyone lives on a small farm in these mountains, and by some standards aren't worth the time. These are sandwiched between ledges, boulders, and trees that were too large to move, and creeks that run at will, cutting away and carrying precious soil along the watershed and on to the Atlantic. It is like we watch our livelihood go down stream.

We slash and burn, preparing the fields, to build the soil, and then have it taken away. Farms are splattered with an outcropping of rocks. Springs burst indiscriminately out of the ground. It all makes sense when a plow sinks into soil, sod that has not felt the plod of horse hooves or the tip of iron. One begins to understand why people settle here.

With the inside chores done and milk bucket in hand, the open door welcomes in an uninvited brisk air to shock my face. The frost on the ground causes a crunching sound as I go to milk. The stubborn grass snaps under my boots as I walk the old path to the barn, made by one who built the place and had no doubt operated pretty much like myself. The sun has gotten in full view, but isn't adequate to penetrate the cold.

The lowing Jersey greets me with that look of disgust as she bellows into the freeze. I grab the milking stand and bully my head into her side as she steps backward. I remember the days when she was not as obedient. There used to be a need for kickers and a halter, but now she seems content to accept her role in life. The biggest concern is the calf we're trying to wean. The plans are to give it most of the milk and save a little for myself. The way I've got it figured is I'm the one who sees that mom gets enough to eat and a place to sleep!

I think of the day's activities as I milk, and cup my chilled hands to her udder, trying to find some warmth. She stands munching on grain as slobbers string out both sides of her mouth - retrieved with the next bite. In the feed-way, the cat sits patiently awaiting her portion to be poured into a bowl. With that completed, I return to the kitchen to strain the milk through cheesecloth to be stored in the springhouse for later use.

The paper didn't waste any space describing the weather, just "cold and rainy," but, of course, we knew that. Gazing toward Dolly Sods in the West, I can see a heavy overcast and it appears that a cold rain has set in, accompanied with occasional sleet. My neighbor, Boy, has smoke billowing skyward and I don't have to wonder what he's up to -- he's not one that will allow a little inclement weather to stop him! Anyway, there's been some frost, and that seems to launch the season to butcher. The hogs no doubt are wishing for last spring.

Boy always keeps the fattest hogs because they range on acorns all fall and are finished off with corn. One year, he made the mistake of telling this novice to buy a hog for him. I will never forget him declaring, "That hog didn't have 'nough fat on its rear end t' fry its ears!"

I'll have to make my way up there directly to help. That is one sure way to get a good meal, because it's always the best of the year. Some save the tenderloin for themselves, but he cuts the best for those who have done the work, and work it is. He butchers a half dozen hogs to provide food throughout the winter. Then, too, others will bring hogs of their own to butcher since everything is ready and there's lots of help.

Farmers either raise pigs or swap another animal to have hogs at butchering time. Life here in these mountains is what some might call a vicious cycle. Really, the cycle is not vicious; it is just the way we live. It's true that we take from the fields and woods, but in return we make life better for all of God's creatures by balancing them. Animals are well cared for and people survive. It is demanding, but we understand nature. The trees are cut to provide housing and fuel, and make way for younger ones. We sow seed and await harvest to provide food so that we can tend things in our care. We are stewards of what we have been blessed with. Farmers raise crops to feed the hogs, and the hogs to feed his family, and the meal leftovers go back into feeding the soil, that in turn feeds the crops, that is if nothing fails. Only a few have a surplus of goods to sell at town, enabling them to buy things not grown on the farm.

A VIEW OF APPALACHIA

"How ya doing, Boy?" I ask.

He'd been back at Davis, a lumbering town near Whitmer, working timber and had come home for the winter to tend things. Davis is a community, back of the mountain, having more than one logging camp. These drafty camps possess a hard-core, calloused lot. These camps house men that have harden muscles caused by the labor of swinging axes, handling cant hooks, crosscut saws, and toiling behind horses and oxen.

A place where every man has a pecking order - a peg for his hat, an earned seat at the table, and these are off limits to another without a fight. Meals of Cat-Head Biscuits, gravy, spuds, beans and hog meat provide fuel for early and late hours. Buckeye stoves, bed bug infested beds, bibs, long underwear strung about provide less than a homey atmosphere.

Boy's darkened face looks up from peddling the grinding stone just long enough to acknowledge my presence and to spit a stream of Square Snuff in the direction of an inquisitive cat. Normally, we find a stump to sit and chat while he whittles, but today is business and there's lots of work to do. Anyway, I feel appreciated, roll the sleeves up on my plaid shirt and begin sharpening another knife. I hear the hogs in the distance waiting their morning feed. It is fascinating to hear powerful, turned up Yorkshire jaws crunch rock-hard corn from cobs that have been thrown aimlessly over the fence.

A characteristic of warm weather is a mud pit around the many turned up rocks. Today that is certainly not a problem, however. Hogs have no sweat glands to serve as a cooling system, so wallowing is important and they are usually accommodated by the trough. Boy keeps a trough made from a hollowed-out Cucumber log for slop and such. Without the rings in their noses, it is impossible to keep in place.

With all the preparations made, we make our way to

where the monstrous gluttons are penned. Their huge ears and noses are tuned to the usual feast of corn and Boy throws in a couple of "ears" to get their attention. He straddles the fence and slips alongside the largest sow, slides a rough calloused hand along her back to rest in a headlock position. Gripped in his right hand is his favorite kitchen knife, which inches to the predetermined spot and is swiftly gouged to the hilt. Some shoot their hogs, but Boy chooses to blind side his and plunge a ten-inch blade into the jugular.

He gives the knife a couple twisting motions as blood begins gushing, causing the sow to give out a horrendous squeal. She then gives a few grunts as strength exits, causing her to fall back on her haunches, then to her side. By the time she makes her last few kicks, we cut the back legs to reveal the ligaments and maneuver a gambrel between them. Some would view it as cruel that she should die this way, but Boy feels this method is as humane as any, plus we save a bullet. What is cruel is the way we have to chase hogs all over North Mountain after they have been roaming and feeding on acorns and chestnuts the past several months before they can be corralled.

The mule had been harnessed about daylight so he'd be ready to hitch to the "six hundred pounder." Up to this time, Boy's mule hasn't developed too many bad habits, but one never can be quite sure. Sometimes you can observe him standing around thinking about his sins! One farmer said a mule would work faithfully for you all his life just to kick you once! Folk around here have another saying pertaining to a mule, which may discourage anyone from criticizing another: "never kick a pullin' mule!" Many are convinced of the adage, "what mulish animals are mules!"

Boy, as his dad before him, has a fifty-gallon oak barrel laid against the end of the sled to slosh hogs in. The water must be just right and is tested by an old timer, who reaches his hand into the kettle. The theory is that if you are unable to immerse your hand three times in succession, it's hot enough! Time passed, the fire continually stoked, and Boy finally walks over to the kettle to stick his trusty hand into the foaming water declaring, "By gumbies, I believe that'll do it!"

Grabbing a bucket, I begin transferring the boiling water into the barrel. The sloshing begins and the constant up and down in the barrel makes it possible to scrape the hair off.

Martin came to help as he had promised. He's an imposing sort, but not in an arrogant sense. His slightly modeled face is set with frank cheekbones, shadowed blue eyes, a good straight nose, a well-chiseled mouth, and tapering chin. His thick dark hair is swept off his high forehead and brushed loosely over his ears. It's a sensitive face, yet with a set to the jaw. He's generous and seems to understand the important things and what he wants from life. He's very much appreciated today, strong as a young ox, mighty welcomed! He withstands all the ribbing about Sara Jane, in spite of it being almost non-stop. She is one of the town folk, and doesn't get up this way often, but sure has her sights set on him. Martin never minds too much either way - he takes it with a grin, and keeps working.

As the day wears on, we settle down to the more stationary tasks, that of cutting up meat, rendering lard, and listening to the fat as it is transformed to grease in the kettle. Conversation continues as I question Boy, "What about the killing?"

"I reckon ole Bibs got what he deserved!" Boy asserts.

"Well, if that be the case, there will be a lot more of it," I finish, while stuffing more sausage pokes.

Every time we spew out a big irregular sausage poke, Boy can't resist saying it looks like the arm of a certain heavy-set lady, and he is never reluctant to suggest the name. Actually, they do take on the look of skin packed with a heavy dose of cellulite.

"Take some home t' fry in th' mornin'," Boy urges.

"Don't care if I do," I quickly reply.

There's nothing like the mouth-watering smell of fresh sausage frying, or having hog meat hanging in the smoke house in the dead of winter to cut on.

Boy often gives a hog head to those who help. He says of one man, "Th' heads he takes always have th' longest necks!" Obviously, the man wants to get as much of the hog as possible for his contribution. We make use of everything except "the squeal." I might add to that the "lights," which are hung on a nail for the crows.

My porch step seems a little higher this evening, but I feel better after doing a hard day's work helping a neighbor - although I ache from head to toe. My back seems a few inches shorter, and my arms a few inches longer from wrestling the heavy meat all day. One thing I can count on is that I will get a returned favor when my hogs are ready to kill. Then I will have hams hanging in my smokehouse.

Settling down in my easy chair gives me time to catch up on some reading. Opening the paper, my eyes fall to the Hopeville section. The writer printed the usual gossip, which is always of interest, but his news of another butchering makes my job seem easier. He wrote, Mr. T.M. Rotruck, the manager of the Glebe, killed the boss hog last week. It weighed 528 lbs. net. I agree with the writer who states: "It looks as though there will be a good time among the Paupers when they devour a hog such as that!"

I am sure no one had to rock those butchers to sleep after the job of slaughtering that beast! Hams the size of a number three washing tub and tenderloin the length of a split rail raises the attention of any mountaineer!

Speaking of hogs, the paper states that E.M. Shears of Harman Hills "was seen passing here with a fifty pound hog on his back leaning homeward." The writer did a great job painting a mental picture for the reader.

A good thing about bib overalls is that they just slide off after a day like today. The sight and smell indicate they're about due for washing. I have noticed that most folk around here get at least a week of wear between washing. Interestingly enough, some of the men folk wear nothing under them in the summertime. That makes for an interesting sight as they try to maintain both ventilation and some degree of modesty.

After a good drink of spring water and some time for meditation, it is time to hit the hay. In seconds, the flicker of the coal oil lamp fades into darkness as I reach to the nightstand to turn down the wick. Lying in my bed, I can see out the upstairs window to the stars in the West. The view makes me contemplate the vastness of this world and my seeming insignificance, yet there must be some importance to my journey here. Above all, I want to be a blessing to those struggling in these mountains.

— IX —

APPALACHIA IN THE RAW

Vice is everywhere. It always has been. Here in the mountains the problem is not the abundance of brothels, back room card games, or the constant slaying of persons, although these exist to some measure. There are mistresses, gambling to some degree, and an occasional killing, but the major problem is that of making moonshine, which figures into the killing in the Gap.

Since early times it has always been around for medicinal purposes, but there is great addiction, and temptation to make it to sell. Good money can be made if one is courageous and creative enough to take all the necessary illicit steps. Men can get over a dollar a jug! That far surpasses the money one can earn doing other jobs. It would take months of working at the mill or on a farm to equal that income. It has been said that some got their start - or financial edge - and were able to buy a farm from money earned from its trade. That's called dirty money in the hills.

Distilled Whiskey is called by many names, including "Moonshine," "Branch Water," "Rheumatis Medicine," "Corn Squeezins," "Corn Liquor," "White Lighting," and "Bootleg Whiskey."

The most popular name, "Moonshine," was given to it because it is commonly made by moonlight or smuggled under the cover of darkness when there will be less suspicion. "Branch Water" originated from the customary places desired to make it - along a branch of water. "Rheumatis Medicine" comes from the belief that it can cure rheumatism. Other ailments it is believed to cure are: depression, cold, soothe teething baby gums, fevers, snake bites, pneumonia, food poison, etc.

Corn is usually the primary ingredient, hence the name, "Corn Liquor" or "Corn Squeezins." The clear natural color and the shock it sends vibrating through an individual prompted the name "White Lighting." The name "Bootleg Whiskey" originated from the method to conceal the drink. Men hide a small flask of whiskey in the leg of a tall boot.

It is strange to see some of the men around here take a big swig, make the most distorted face, then comment on how good it is! It has been said that some of it is so rank "it 'll make a pig squeal." Arlie Hawkins declares, "Ere, some of that stuff 'll make ya plum crazy, what it will!"

Most of the drinking is done out behind "the shed," or in the cover of darkness, and almost never in the company of women-folk. Some go on a binge and drink for days at a time. There goes the pride one may have had. This drunken stupor sometimes results in incontinent behavior and a general unkempt appearance. Families struggle to survive domestically and economically when plagued by this varmint. It has been said that a moonshine operation will demoralize a community for at least three miles in every direction. Professionals report that little boys, girls and mothers are sometimes brutally mistreated by a drunken husband and father, and struggle for the comforts necessary for life.

"Moonshiners" and "Revenuers" create a lot of news in the hills. Moonshiners are trying to make a "run," and Revenuers are trying to put a stop to the trafficking. There are some contrasts that need to be made between the two.

Moonshiners look like any other mountain person. Most wear bib overalls or wool trousers with a long sleeve linsey shirt, shielded in the winter by a denim coat, referred to as a blouse. Flax and wool are raised, then spun and woven into linen and linsey by womenfolk. After hours of toil, these take shape into garments. All must guard against wearing garments that are easily ignited by open fires or wood burners, as cotton is.

Pants worn by the mountaineer are rather bulky. They never have a pleat and reach to just above their boots, which are a little higher than the ankle. If a man wears high boots, he is considered a gentleman, and if a lady has on a pair of calfskin shoes, she is declared a belle. Mountain clothing is much simpler.

He would never think of going without a head covering. The most common wear is a round felt hat with a turned up brim, usually dilapidated. Because of no dental hygiene, seldom do the older people have any large quantity of teeth. Usually the remaining few are not side-by-side and are normally tobacco covered. It is jokingly said that you can tell if a mountaineer is level headed when tobacco juice is seen running out of both sides of the mouth.

Most Revenuers come from the outside and therefore have a different appearance. They seldom wear bibs and if a hat is worn, it is always felt. Their mannerisms and speech are difficult to disguise. They don't have "the mountain accent, nor the idioms in their language." Any mountaineer can tell them from a mile away. But if the Moonshiner has no "lookout" or becomes too lax, which he sometimes does, the Revenuer can make his presence known while the Moonshiner is concentrating on the "run." The chaos and reckless activity that takes place when surprised by Revenuers must be a sight to behold!

The Revenuer is armed to the teeth, usually with Springfield rifles, known to carry an ounce ball a thousand yards. Among those who make "Corn Squeezins," he is the symbol of stern justice and not to be trifled with. He travels on horseback as far as possible; from that point, he walks. They must be ready to navigate terrain not fit for man or beast. He must travel through walls of Mountain Laurel, tiptoe along ledges, wade creeks and peer into caves where rattlers may be hiding. The Revenuer constantly must dodge tree branches and sometimes bullets. He needs to be on the lookout, not only for the still, but also for his own safety.

The Revenuer must hone skills necessary to track down stills. He looks for signs like a hunter. His horse hates the smell of the mash and is quick to stop. In contrast, hogs love the mash and can be seen hanging around stills. The agent's nose and ears become assets as he tunes them to the woods. A working still makes gurgling sounds and gives off an odor, sometimes like a bakery and at other times like a hog pen. The smell lingers on the leaves of nearby trees and drifts in the wind. The Revenuer looks for the "slops" that have been emptied into a stream, where dead fish turn up.

To hinder the Revenuer's efforts is the nature of the woods. Animals betray him as he sneaks along the ridges in search of a still. The birds have a language unique to calling their offspring when trouble is approaching and another call if she has a ready meal. Each has a call distinguishing distress or conversation. The barking squirrel's call announces visitors. The Moonshiner listens and is on guard for these unusual sounds.

Sources that benefit the efforts of the Revenuer are many. Customers who have been swindled, overcharged, or sold inferior moonshine may divulge information that may lead to an arrest. Women or mothers whose lives have been wrecked may wish to shut a still down. "Holiness" converts have been known to police neighborhoods. Other informers are motivated by money. Laws have been enacted to pay anyone to oblige information that leads to a still. That is more money than a man can earn in a week. It's been said that if some ever found one of these latter informers, they'd injure the informer in a way they may improve, but would never get well! Lastly, a competitor may be quick to turn another in.

If the Revenuer should find a still, it is not always certain that the "Mash Mixer" will be found. For curing reasons, it is not necessary that the still always be manned. Agents have been known to add a teaspoon of coal oil or small amount of salt in the vat to prevent the mash from fermenting, in hopes of catching those who attend the set. This is one sure way to catch the operators as they work, analyzing the problem.

The Revenuer has no problem with making and selling "Shine" as a criminal offense, but rather, because it is a tax violation. One may ask, "Why would one seek employment that stifles the income of poor mountaineers?" Some have declared they make it for medicinal purposes and income for buying food and clothes. The mountaineer rationalizes that this should be of no concern to anyone else. I suppose all have their reasons, some moral and some greed and some say that greed drives the economy.

— X —

THE RIGHT TO MAKE "LIKKER"

From early times, every man was almost a law unto himself in the remoteness of the mountains. He grew to hate and even rebel against laws that were regarded as unfairly enacted against mountain people and the fruits of their labors. The supreme example is the distilling of moonshine whiskey and the deliberate effort to escape the excise tax.

Throughout history, there have been efforts to tax and control. I Kings 12 records a story of hatred toward obsessive control. Here Israel stoned Adoram who was in charge of the forced labor. Jesus addressed governmental authority in Matthew 22:21, by stating, "Render therefore unto Caesar the things which are Caesar's; and unto God the things that are God's." As a result of studying his teachings, I believe we must be obedient to civil laws, except where they violate God's laws.

Tax was not new to Appalachian minds. Alexander Hamilton had a $21,000,000 war debt he wished to liquidate, so he imposed an excise tax on all spirits. The Whiskey Rebellion came along in 1794 as an outcry against taxation. The tax was repealed in 1802. Later, Lincoln applied a tax that stuck, a part of which created the Internal Revenue Service. There was substantial profit if one could escape paying this. Some have evaded paying this tax, but have drunk up the profit.

In looking at possible profits, men can make money if they avoid the tax. Most earn $1.10 to $1.20 per gallon for the sale of whiskey. If a still turns out 80 gallons, they average $92.00 per week. Twenty dollars will need to be subtracted from this for supplies, which nets $72.00 profit. That's a lot of money, especially if he can avoid taxes.

It was felt that the mountaineer should have the right to make moonshine without governmental regulation. The Germans and Scotch-Irish brought with them to America the skill of making whisky and the hatred of the tax. Where a means or road to transport grain to market was poor or nonexistent, it was often easier to convert the corn crop into liquor than to haul the grain to market. The only exception was that one must be on guard against getting caught.

Any decent mule or horse can carry four bushels of corn in the husk, or carry the equivalent of twenty-four in liquid form. Looking at the economics another way, a wagon and team can haul twenty bushels of corn to market, earning $10.00, or haul one hundred and twenty gallons of whiskey at a much higher profit. This came to be known as "Whiskey Farming." Others bartered their corn for whiskey to a neighbor who had an operation, the exchange rate being three bushels to one gallon of whiskey.

But the state doesn't share any sentiment to allow moonshine to be marketed as any other commodity. The only sympathy is to allow one quart per month, a far cry from the free use and transport law that has been in effect in West Virginia. Our local newspaper, the Grant County Gazette, ran the following article on May 11, 1917:

THE RIGHT TO MAKE "LIKKER" 63

"Quart A Month Law Effective"

"Man Now Has to Confine His Importations to One Quart in Every Thirty Days."

"The new amendment to the prohibition law limiting to one quart a month the amount of liquor that one person can bring into the state, became effective Tuesday, May 1st. The new prohibition commissioner states that the law will be rigidly enforced and that violators will receive no mercy.

So it is one quart every thirty days now, henceforth and forever, or so long as the present statutes are permitted to hold sway. The penalties for violations are very severe. For the first offense, a person convicted of violating the law will be fined a sum not less than $100 and not more than $500; and he will be sentenced to jail not less than two months and not more than six months. For the second offense, the penalty is very drastic. The second offense constitutes a felony and the offender will be compelled to serve a sentence in the penitentiary, the lowest term being one year and the highest term being five years. There is no alternative for the courts to follow; the penalties and sentences are fixed by the law, and the offenders will be dealt with very severely."

West Virginia now has one of the most drastic liquor laws of any state in the Union. Legislatures believe the present severe statutes should act as an effective deterrent to bootleggers. Confronted with a possible penitentiary sentence, they certainly will hamper business, but after living here, I can testify that they must be dreaming if they think laws will stop it. These people have been making "shine" too long to stop soon. They can make quick money in spite of the risk.

While digging through some old papers, I ran into an article dealing with the age-old problem. Where there is money to be made and a thirst to be quenched, moonshine will be around. Appearing in our weekly paper, the Grant County Gazette on August 5, 1921, was the following. It outlines the facts that Bootlegging has been around a long time in our state.

"Bootlegging is An Ancient Art"

"Bootlegging is not a new art developed with the coming of prohibition. County Clerk Charles A. Johnson of Charlestown discovered this fact a few days ago in casually looking over old records in his office, says the Farmers Advocate.

Way back in May 1802, the year after Jefferson County was organized from a part of Berkeley, the old records disclosed that one John Whitlock was indicted for selling one half pint of whiskey to one Richard Crow, without the formality of taking out a license for the purpose. Whitlock could not have profit and a motive for the sale, because wet goods were so cheap in those days that a quantity as small as a half pint could not be said to have any value. A gallon was worth only 50 cents or less.

Some time later in the year, Whitlock was tried after pleading not guilty. The sentence against him was that he be confined to jail one day, from the rising of the sun, to the setting of the same."

– XI –

PERILS OF MOONSHINE

The following poem outlines the perils of the mountaineer caught in the grips of moonshine.

"Your Humble Servant"

You've set an' wondered, dear sir,
'bout this 'n that, as a bench-legged cur;
Why th' trouble an' all th' strife;
Why th' waste of a precious life,

Th' pastures now quiet, in peace they graze,
Jist a few milk cows, yonder in th' haze;
Lyin' there on th' ground, a youthful form,
Drunken, skidded, but blood beatin' warm;

Manhood crushed an' left miserably meek,
A good heart, but will an' courage weak;
Seems as tho' th' gable end blew out of hell,
Wrecked its damage on he that fell;

Cain to Abel, are we his keep,
Ask th' Shepherd, who folds th' sheep;
Lays fresh of mind: respected sir,
You asked th' question, an' that'd be her.

It is almost hilarious to see Maynard imitate the drunks, although Pap has warned him to never go near the stuff. He's handicapped but manages to convey their awkward walk and slurred, stupid speech. The added attention and laughs make him do it all the more. Pap and I often see an old hermit along Wildcat in a drunken stupor. He remains wherever his final drink overtakes him; his judgment impaired, pride gone and disowned by family. Added to this pathetic state of sickness is his decrepit look and urine-stained pants. Pap says, "He looks like some buzzard layed 'im an' th' sun's a dryin' 'im out."

In addition to the known ingredients, which have either been placed in the mash or have fallen into it, there are other possibilities. Since a working still sometimes sounds like a beehive, insects add themselves to it. Added to this concoction are maggots: opossums, foxes, chipmunks, and other creatures that eat away and sometimes become trapped.

Our paper confirmed the belief that much of it may be poisonous. The Grant County Gazette, on March 3, 1922, ran this article of the findings by the prohibition commissioner.

"Poison is Found in 98 Per Cent of Bootleg Whiskey."

"Commissioner Haynes Adds New Facts in Amazing Rum Traffic Regulations."

"Washington, D.C., March 8 - Perils besetting the imbiber of bootleg whiskey were forcibly demonstrated today by a statement of Prohibition Commissioner Haynes, who told reporters that only two percent of the liquor analyzed by chemists of the prohibition forces is found to be drinkable. The other 98 percent is poison.

Of course, the poison runs from the deadly type to that which is only temporarily injurious. But in the thousands of gallons of bootleg whiskey seized by prohibition agents, the general average is only two per cent liquor that may be taken without harm.

'The poison contents of bootleg whiskey cannot be too strongly emphasized,' Mr. Haynes said today. 'Continually we find whiskey brought in after raids which would be deadly if taken in sufficient quantities.'

In Washington there is a prohibition department storehouse in which there are hundreds of gallons of whiskey, bottled as genuine whiskey should be, but which are only bootleg preparations and which contain wood alcohol or formaldehyde or large quantities of fusel oil.

An interesting antedote is told by Commissioner Haynes to illustrate what the bootleg whiskey drinker may expect.

A group of agents raiding a still in a mountainous section not far away from this part of the country. They got plenty of mash and plenty of alleged liquor. One of them, officers, on examining the liquor said to the prisoner; 'Great scott, man, do you drink this stuff?'

The manufacturer was shocked at the question.

'You bet your life I don't' He replied in disgust. 'This is made to sell. I wouldn't risk my life with a drink of it.'

This case, according to prohibition authorities, is not exceptional. It is typical of the manufacturer of bootleg poison.

In Washington, what the officials of the health department are marveling at is the fact that only five died during the year of 1921 from drinking poisonous liquor or whiskey with a denatured alcohol base. Why more deaths did not occur is regarded as miraculous.

A casual survey of local hospitals shows that virtually every hospital in the city has treated large numbers of alcoholic cases cause by inferior liquor."

This small number of deaths may result from inadequate records. First, the survey was casual; secondly, there are few hospitals, and most cannot afford to be admitted. The causes of deaths are often obscure or deemed "God's will." Another reason for inadequate documents determining one's death is that up to this time, folks were simply buried with no death certificates, making it unclear as to the cause of their death. Only recently did a law pass mandating that a burying permit be obtained. These permits should help maintain more accurate records and causes of deaths. Our Grant County Gazette on August 5, 1921 published this article. The law reads:

"Must Have Premit [Permit] to Bury Dead."

"...the dead body of no persons shall be interred, deposited in vault or tomb, cremated, or removed without a permit, from the local registrar of the district in which the death occurred or the body found. One must obtain a death certificate of Vital Statistics, then the burial permit shall be granted. Undertakers have a large responsibility for this, but where none exist, the friend or neighbor who acts as undertaker is subject to the same fines and penalties. Fines shall range from $1.00 to $5.00."

Distillation may be as complicated as one's desires. It can be defined as a technique to cook ingredients, collecting the vapor, and changing this back to liquid again by passing it through a pipe emerged in cold water, leaving the impurities behind. Centuries ago, alchemists, physicians, and interested individuals experimented with ways to create intoxicating drink.

Regardless of the problems associated with it, there are plenty of operations in these mountains. As some say, "these hills reek with it." Every hollow that has a spring has a story to tell. It would be too obvious to make it along a major river, so men set up at a spring where they can see for some distance, or have a sentry and/or a warning bell. The size of the operation will determine the equipment. The mere necessities are a cooking pot, a coil of copper, an oak barrel, corn or bran, yeast and water. Many Moonshiners have their own formulas and methods of brewing, based on his preferred ingredients.

The process takes a great deal of work. Moonshiners need to be on guard so as to not attract attention and always be on guard for betrayal. They have to transport equipment and materials to the crudest places. There is the need to haul bushels of corn up and down mountainsides and the finished product to where it can be sold. Long and damp nights are spent in a lean-to. The hard work has caused more than one soul to declare, "It's th' hardest work I ever done!"

An observant traveler may see the evidence of a Moonshine Still when one buys an abundance of sugar, ground mill or jars. A well-traveled path into the woods may also be an indication. Smoke itself is adequately concealed by beginning fires before daylight, or in a hollow too rough for most to travel. The cave at Hopeville, according to legend, was used as a hideout to make moonshine.

It's a risky business, but the lure of money causes plenty of men to take the chance. Once a person feels he is far enough from the law, there is little to do to be in business. The supply of corn, sugar, and water provides the necessary ingredients. Many hollows have an operation, a lookout, and a system to get it to market. The problem arises when there is competition or jealously.

Many scuffles have erupted as a result of conflict with buyers. If there is not a direct conflict, there is for certain indirect ones. It often makes the ruffians around here feel they are a better man than nature dealt them. I have seen some pretty good men take on very different characters, or some puny individuals think they could take on the world.

Not that Jess Bass is puny, for he can shoulder a log

like nobody's business and is feared by many more than the Almighty. But one drink makes him do some foolish things. He often speaks of sparking Sara Jane, even though he would have to deal with Martin. It's pretty much held in this community that both are as tough as leather. Jess's friends usually uphold his brags, but not when encountering Martin.

Jeb Arbas, in his drawn speech, said, "Ere you'll 'ave yer hands full if ya take on Martin 'out some 'f us t' hep." Jess has the opinion that he could beat any man in these hills, and some believe it. It is a well-known fact he's more of a man of muscle than mind. Someone said Jess shirt collared Jeb for saying such a thing.

Imagine his slouched body being lifted off the ground and straightened from the constant slagging and his galluses stretched to new lengths. He didn't let this incident spoil their friendship for long, because his type can't be particular when it comes to the choice of friends.

There is no doubt that moonshining figures into the killing of Harness Bibs in the Gap. He had lived on the Four Knobs with his wife and was known for making moonshine. Problems had been escalating between him and a couple of boys, actually young men - Arnie Cornshakle and Wilbur Hawkins. It is generally believed that they had something to do with the killing up the Gap, but the investigation is still ongoing.

Who knows? Maybe an outsider killed Bibs. After all, peddlers come through the area from time to time. It is a known fact, too, that some never leave these mountains. Then perhaps, Bib's death may have stemmed from woman problems or from running his mouth too much to the wrong person.

— XII —

CONTROLLING THE
MASH MIXERS

We learned just the other day about the Revenuers raiding a still on Cave Hill. Aus Stats and Cal Turner were making a run when agents outside the camp began firing, causing poor old Aus to lose a thumb. Both escaped to a place higher in the mountain until the Revenuers left. Cal escaped unhurt, but Aus's son was nabbed, then turned loose. I remember Pap chuckling when he told me about the raid. Aus, too, will always remember it when he tips a jug to his mouth and sees that missing thumb. Axes had no mercy on the old still as it was smashed beyond recognition by Revenuers.

News travels fairly fast in the mountains, especially when moonshine and the law are involved. More than one incident has taken place in neighboring Randolph County, which shows some of the seriousness and sentiment of the whiskey industry, as was seen in Whitmer.

Whitmer is a twin to the lumbering town Horton, which prides itself with one of the largest sawmills east of the Mississippi. It sits at the base of Spruce Knob and is in the heart of some of the best timber country around. In 1894, the mill was equipped with a Stearns single band saw, circular saw and a gang saw and shipping over one hundred thousand board feet of lumber per day. A few years later, both the band saw and the circular saw were replaced with more efficient band saws. At the peak of production, the mill operated with an eight-foot, double cut softwood band saw, an eight-foot, single cut hardwood band saw, a circular resaw, and a complete planing and dimension mill.

    Where there is a mill of this size there are sure to be problems. The Grant County Gazette, April 22, 1921, carried this article describing an incident illustrating a zero tolerance to moonshining. The writer pointed out the many sides of this issue, the intolerance, the bravery, and the craving.

"Bootleggers"

"Caught at Whitmer - Whiskey Emptied into Gandy Creek."

"Whitmer, March 2 - Since the "Big Raid" on bootleggers almost two weeks ago, our little lumbering towns have settled down and become very quiet and peaceable again, not a bootlegger to be seen and it began to look like our citizens must surely go dry once again, but such a state of affairs for Whitmer is almost too good to be true and when the evening train arrived at the station Wednesday, three big husky young men alighted on the station platform accompanied by a large, apparently heavy looking suitcase as baggage, and we at once decided from the label pasted on the side that it contained whiskey and that bootleggers were again in town.

    After lifting the heavy suitcase to the shoulders of one of their number, the march up street to "Hotel Alpha," began, and we noticed the Eagle Eye of Chief Police G. E. Bond carefully watching them and we at once decided that something would be doing soon.

Soon as the supposed bootleggers entered the hotel, people began flocking there just like little "Ducks to Water," until Chief Bond entered the hotel, arrested the bootleggers and come out driving them at the point of his big 44-calibre Smith and Wesson and with the suitcase in the other hand, landed them in the lockup.

The suitcase was opened in the presence of Mayor Hedreck and several citizens that had already assembled at the Mayor's office and found to contain 19 quarts of whiskey and 4 quarts of alcohol.

The bootleggers were then at once arraigned before Mayor Hedreck, charged with bootlegging and carrying intoxicants into dry territory. The leader was fined $20 and cost and his assistant that carried the suitcase to the hotel was induced to give up $10 and cost while the third man claimed he was not implicated with the other two, but also handed over $5 for cursing the officer.

Mayor Hedreck also ordered that the whiskey should be confiscated and Chief Bond carried it to the banks of Gandy Creek and, amid the cheers of more than two hundred people, emptied every bottle into the stream.

One of our people - an old familiar figure that has lived here for a number of years, and it is said that several barrels of whiskey at least has gone down his throat - lay down and drank from the stream just below where the bottles were being emptied. He was promptly arrested for disorderly conduct and fined $5 and cost which he handed over without much objection.

Chief Bond says he intends to arrest everyone caught in the town with intoxicants, if he even makes Whitmer so dry that the church people have to use coffee or water to administer the sacrament.

County Sheriff Marstiller was here yesterday, giving out printed invitations to 40 of our hard working citizens to come to Elkins, our county seat and give evidence before the grand jury on March 8th. This trip to Elkins will be an expense of $6 in cash besides a loss of two days work at $2.25 per day, or a total of $10.50 to 40 working men, which means a loss of $420 to the citizens of Whitmer, and not counting the heavy loss to the mill people on account of part of the lumber mills being shut down for that length of time, all on account of the bootlegging business."

Whitmer is also known for the lynching of Joe Brown March 19, 1909. He was a white man from Kentucky and considered a labor agitator. It seems he wanted laborers to join the union and if they did not do as he ordered, he would riddle their dinner pails with buckshot and shoot hats off their heads with rifle fire. On a couple occasions, he shot pipes from mouths in his reign of terror. Brown was locked up and released. In George Nethkin's saloon, he demanded his two revolvers to be returned to him. In the contest, he shot chief of police Scott White. Brown escaped into the mountains, but was captured after having an arm shot nearly off. He was then returned to the Whitmer jail. That night, a masked mob drug Brown from the jail and lynched him. The rope used was pulled through a pulley and tied off. The pulley was secured to a rope strung across the street from the store to a telephone pole. Since the knot was across Brown's nose, his death was slow. Throughout the night he squirmed with pain, was kicked, stoned, spit on, and nearly stripped, until a woodsman's sock was rammed down his throat with a stove poker. Brown, in fact, hung until dead, rather than the usual expectation.

White survived the ordeal and no one was ever convicted of the hanging crime. Later accounts related how the woman who made the masks for the lynch mob "went crazy." A prognosticator proclaimed: "Them that done this evil 'll die with their boots on!"

MASH MIXERS

Our paper, the Grant County Gazette, on August 5, 1921 carried the story stating West Virginia's new position on bootlegging. Since the prohibition law passed by the recent session of the legislature went into effect Wednesday of last week, West Virginia possesses one of the most drastic and far-reaching anti-liquor laws of any state in the union. The bill, which is known as the West Virginia prohibition law, includes federal and state constitutional amendments and the acts of Congress known as the Webb Kenyon Law, parcel post regulations and the amendments passed by the legislature of 1921.

"New Prohibition Law"

"For West Virginia Most Drastic of Any State in the Union Says Experts."

"The law absolutely forbids any person possessing at any time liquor of any description whether it be for medicinal purposes or otherwise. This drastic legislation is fully covered in section 34 of the prohibition law."

"Section 34. It shall be unlawful for any persons in this state to receive directly or indirectly, intoxicating liquors from a common or other carrier. It shall also be unlawful for any person in this state to possess intoxicating liquors, received directly or indirectly, from a common or other carrier. This section shall apply to as well as for otherwise, and to interstate as well as ultra state shipments or carriage. Any persons violating this section shall be guilty of a misdemeanor and upon violation shall be fined not less than 100 dollars and not more than 200 dollars, and in addition, thereto may be imprisoned not more than 3 months; provided, however, that druggists may receive and possess pure grain alcohol, wine and such preparations as may be sold by druggists for the special purpose and in the manner set forth in sections four and twenty four." (Amendment of second extraordinary session of the legislature of 1915).

Without a doubt, the most drastic part of the new law is that contained in section 37, which says that the finding of any liquor in the possession of any person other than commercial whiskies which were purchased when it was lawful to do so, shall be prime evidence that the same is moonshine. It goes further and says that it is unlawful for anyone to have in their possession moonshine liquor, so that the mere possession of any kind of liquor after July 30 will be a violation of the law and will subject the person. If found guilty, to a heavy fine or imprisonment, or both.

This section in part follows:

Section 27. It shall be unlawful for any person to own, operate, maintain, or have in his possession, or any interest in any apparatus for the manufacture of intoxicating liquors, commonly known as "moonshine still" or in any device of like kind or character. For the purpose of this act any mechanism, apparatus or device that is kept or maintained in any place away from the observation of the general public, or in any building, dwelling houses or other places for the purpose of distilling, making or manufacturing intoxicating liquors or which by any process of evaporation, separate alcohol liquor from grain, molasses, fruit or any other fermented substance or that is capable of such use, shall be taken and deemed to be a "moonshine" still shall be guilty of a felony and upon conviction thereof, shall be fined not less than $390, nor more than $1,000, and be confined to the penitentiary, not less than two nor more than five years. Any person who aids or abets in the operation or maintenance of any "moonshine still" shall be guilty of a felony and upon conviction thereof shall be fined not less than $500, and confined in the penitentiary not less than one nor more than three years.

"Any person who has in his possession any quantity of moonshine liquor shall be guilty of a misdemeanor and upon conviction thereof shall be fined not less than $100 nor more than $300, and confined in the county jail not less than thirty days nor more than ninety days, provided that if any such person shall fully and freely disclose the name or names of any person or persons from whom he received said moonshine, and give any other information that he may have relative to the manufacture and distribution of same and shall truthfully testify as to any such matters of information, he shall be immune from further punishment; and provided, further, that the finding of any quantity of intoxicating liquor in the possession of any other than commercial whiskies which were obtained at a time when it was lawful to do so shall be prima facie evidence that the same is moonshine."

Just North of Whitmer, Morgantown seems to have similar problems. The Keyser paper, "The Mountain Echo," May 14, 1921, reported heavy sentences given to men who were found guilty of possessing liquor.

"Judge Bears Down On Moonshiners."

"Heavy Sentences Given Men Found Guilty of Having Liquor."
"State Police of West Virginia continued to round up moonshiners and liquor law violators during the month of May, records of the Department of Public Safety show. Heavy fines and long jail sentences were imposed by the courts, following the establishment of guilt."
"Two men, ages 35 and 40, were arrested at Morgantown, on charges of transporting liquor into the state. Both were fined $100 and sentenced to the county jail for four months. Four gallons of alcohol were confiscated and upon order of the court, turned over to the custody of the sheriff.
Two other men were taken into custody on the charge of operating a moonshine still, when officers seized the still and four

gallons of moonshine in Ohio county. The court ordered the men to pay a fine of $300 each or serve three months in the county jail. Appeal from the hearing was taken and upon furnishing bonds, the men were released, the case going up to the higher court for trial.

Possession of a moonshine still drew a fine of $100 and a jail sentence of two months when two Kingwood men were arraigned on similar charges by the court. Another was sentenced to jail for 60 days when arraigned at Williamson on the charge of having a gallon of moonshine whiskey in his possession. In another case, at Williamson, a man was ordered to pay the costs of the case, amounting to $4.60, when arraigned on the charge of possessing a pop bottle full of moonshine."

We haven't had too many seizures around here. Perhaps it's because of our remoteness or the efforts of the Revenuers are needed elsewhere. Then too, most of the Moonshiners here have a fair support system. When anyone strange comes into our area, he is noticed and his presence is broadcasted quickly. Whitmer is different in that they have many strangers. The mill there brings in a greater number of outsiders looking for work, plus they have a well-traveled rail line, having a rail spur that connects to the line that stretches from Elkins, West Virginia to Cumberland, Maryland. Those who have had problems with Revenuers often could have avoided it if a disgruntled neighbor or jealous competitor had not turned them in. In time, that may bring the plague to a halt. The threat of the Revenuers sure isn't working!

— XIII —

WINTER ON ALLEGHANY

It's again time to gather for a shindig and the schoolhouse is the perfect meeting place, since it is the largest building around. Locals will be there with a "five-string," a guitar and a fiddle or two. Since I live closer than most, I don't mind to go a little early to get things ready. Martin and his gelding join me as I make my last few steps to the shindig. Martin hopes that by some miracle Sara Jane will find an excuse to attend and the Lord knows the rowdies will be there as well.

The night air sends chills to my face as I make my way to the school. It's an unwelcome change from all the comfortable fall temperatures that have been gracing us, but they must come. Solomon said, with everything there is a season - birth, death, sowing, harvest, and so it goes. A full moon blooms overhead, providing some much needed light to guide folk over the trails and across the ridges. Opening the door to the old school is always followed by creaks and sounds long familiar to the traveler's ears. More eerie sounds come as I make my way across the oak floor filled with knots and darkened nail heads to start a fire in the Buckeye, taking a path worn by earlier contributors to these events. With the fire rekindled and the coal oil lamps flaming, I begin to tidy up a bit. Soon footsteps, animal sounds, and the rumbling of wagon wheels catch my attention. The door opens again and again as friends enter.

Martin walks to the window to see if there is a hint of car lights coming around Wildcat. Eventually, through the darkness, headlights break the darkness as Sara Jane rolls up in her dad's Model T. Martin anxiously heads toward the door as Sara brings the car to a stop.

Hand in hand they enter. Fit as a fiddle; everything just perfect, as if she was going to a Southern Plantation Ball. Her large blue eyes match her starched dress that sways with intention. Long brown hair has been disciplined to curls that bounce with every step. Her cheeks are as rosy as the most beautiful flower of summer. To lighten the evening, she displays a charming, irresistible smile. What a beautiful couple. The strong love they have for each other is evident as Martin holds her close.

Everyone gets into the swing of things and displays an uninhibited spirit as they enjoy the evening. Pap, with his arm garters forming the most perfect Bishop Sleeves, gets things rolling. An announcement is made that no drinking will be tolerated. But, sure enough, Jess, Jeb, and Pete enter the building with the smell of moonshine on their breath. The craving for another drink draws them outside from time to time. They have no inhibitions with their drinking. Some have gone so far as to measure a man's strength and vigor in terms of the quantity he is able to eat and drink. An early Egyptian is said to have consumed five hundred loaves of bread, a whole ox joint per week, and to have drunk ten jugs of beer each day!

Martin steers clear of Jess, knowing his cockiness, and not wanting to upset Sara. The musicians move to their corner as everyone finds a partner and begin enjoying the music. Pap pulls out his fiddle and breaks into his rendition of "Sweet Liza Jane," causing everyone to grin from ear to ear. Providing his contribution to the festivities, he once again stops to define the difference between a fiddle and a violin.

"Well ya see, a fiddle ya curry in a salt sack, like mine here, an' a violin, well ya curry them in a store bought case."

The room fills with laughter. Pap then invites everyone, in usual mountain hospitality, to enjoy the pies, cakes and apple cider.

Throughout the evening, Jess passes jeering remarks to Martin, only to be ignored. Periodically, he strokes his heavy mustache to assure its best-groomed position. Martin has other things on his mind this evening and certainly doesn't want anything to deter his hopes of sparking Sara. Undoubtedly, Jess's drinking has clouded his thinking, causing him to flirt with some mighty big trouble, or underestimate his prey.

A century ago, Meriwether Lewis stated that he would rather fight two Indians than a grizzly whose feet measured nine inches across the ball, had seven inch nails and took nine bullets to bring down. Anyone around here in a sober mind would rather take on the grizzly than Martin! He's the kind of person who, when provoked to fight, is determined to win or lose his life in the attempt.

The festivities continue as some of the men suggest to Jess and the boys that they find another place to have their fun. As they step outside, they run into some folk who are not so kind. They know the reputation of Jess and his rowdies. Just a few remarks need to be exchanged until threats are made. Jess, being mad already, bumps into Russ, who is the smallest of the clan. That's all it takes to cause Brose to step up to defend. He bares his huge chest and arms, conditioned after years of hard work, and declares, "If ya want t' pursh somebidy, pursh me!"

Jeb and Pete, came to Jess's rescue, making the excuse that they had better get back to the mountain because of earlier commitments, only they didn't use that word. They said

WINTER ON ALLEGHANY

something like "meetin'."

Jeb and Pete scurry to get away, but are delayed since some prankster hobbled their ride. They work furiously to get him untied and straddle the good size dun mule to dart off. It takes to the Gap like a frightened fox with a hornets nest tied to its tail! Everyone knows the real reasons for leaving so soon, that of their moonshine and the huge possibility that they would get a "thrashin'." Russ pipes up as the rowdies are in the distance, "Brose could throw ya an' hold ya, er fix ya so ya don't hav't be held!"

Jess, not so quick to get pushed around, stands off to the side near his charcoal gray gelding running his arrogant mouth. He takes his time placing his left foot in the stirrup and to grab hold of the pommel to swing aboard. He nudges the horse fearlessly toward the gate. Once by the porch, he meets unwitting Maynard, who steps up to pat the horse. Jess places a foot against Maynard's chest, unmercifully knocking him to the ground. In no time, Brose is beside Jess's horse with a vice-like grip grasping Jess's belt and his other hand on his shirt collar. With brute strength, he hoists the backwoods giant off his horse and throws him against the wood shed, among some blackberry vines. Brose bends over and picks Jess's treasured wide brim hat off the ground, grabs it with both hands and shoves it over the mountaineer's head. Brose finishes, "That ought a keep yer teeth idle fir a while!" Brose straightens himself and leads Maynard back to the school.

After some time, Jess comes to his senses and steps aboard his light-footed horse once again. "There'll be 'nother day," he demands. Looking directly at Martin, he yells, "An' as fir you, one a these days I'll have m' way with that Sara Jane!"

The horse is now turned toward the split-rail fence, which presents little problem. Jess kicks him in the flanks and gives a tug on the reins. The gelding lifts his front feet to the air and arches his neck. Rear quarter muscles push with might and with grace, the load is lifted over the fence and headed toward the Gap.

Big Jake's one time friend, Ocie, had walked down from Long Hollow. He came, for the same reasons as most, to catch up on the news as much as anything. Many times during the course of the evening, their eyes meet, causing Ocie to quickly look the other way. His short stature generally enables him to hide in the crowd, unlike Jake, who stands head and shoulders over everyone else. Jake makes no effort to conceal his dislike, because he has a reputation to uphold, and a score to settle with Ocie.

The earlier scuffle with Jess and the boys on the mountain causes everyone to be out front talking. Finally, Ocie and Jake must face each other. Here piercing eyes lock in a stare. Jake forces his shoulders somewhat wider and focuses his eyes, cold as steel, onto Ocie.

Ocie's uneasiness causes his hand to move ever so subtly beneath his bibs to rest on his peacemaker. Ocie remembers Samuel Colt's motto, "God created man and Colt made man equal." For the sake of friends and family, each figure it is better to move on to other company. Eventually, Jake, along with a crowd, goes up the Gap and to the Four Knobs, and Ocie back to Long Hollow.

About midnight, the locals begin leaving. No one is in any great hurry to leave because the "doin's" means so much. The road lanterns are relit one by one to melt the darkness, as each begins their separate journey home. In the distance, there is laughter and talking as folk travel. Just to the side of the school, I see Martin and Sara Jane. They make the most of this fortunate opportunity to embrace. She expresses her desire to be with him, never to part, and someday bear his children. She goes on to convey her love and the prohibitions of her father. Martin wraps his huge hands around Sara's perfectly proportioned waist as he looks into her eyes and comforts her hurt.

Aware of the hour, Martin helps her into the car and walks to the front reaching for the crank. With one swift turn, the engine fires up. Sara would have driven him home, but the Fork is the only road that a car can travel. Plus the fact, there is one conniving farmer further up the road, which makes quite a bundle pulling cars out of ruts with his team. He pulls the cars out for the enormous sum of five dollars. If need be, he goes out during the night to recreate ruts and add water to worsen the conditions so his enterprise can continue.

Martin struts off like a proud peacock as Sara speeds down the road. He has every reason to be proud; otherwise, there's not a big feelin' bone in his body.

I had traveled just a short distance when he caught up. He speaks of their desires - that of opportunities away from these mountains, a place where he and Sara could be together unhindered. Martin fantasizes of a place where there are more rewards for a man's work, espousing, "If only I could git beyond th' trap of poverty that holds us here, then there's my folk t' care for. It jist seems these mountains have us hemmed in. Every time I go t' th' top of one of these mountains, I kin see in th' distance a land of opportunity. I have folk tell me that away from here land is measured by th' section. They say, it's nothin' fir a man t' have a thousand acres. Here a man is fortunate t' have fifty acres. If he has a hundred acres, he's rich, an' ya know, much of that ain't worth nothin'. Traveling salesmen tell of other places, where people have good jobs and fine houses, an' such."

I listened patiently as I believed Pap would have, only I didn't have the answers as Pap. I just thought that someday Martin might grow to appreciate this land as much as the older folks, but then maybe not.

— XIV —

AT THE SAWMILL

Much of the employment is at the local sawmill. Pap says, "Once ya git sawdust in yer hair, ya can't git it out!" There is a great satisfaction in logging. In the woods one can experience the beauty of the forest, wild animals in their habitats, watch the crashing of giant oaks through the undergrowth and the straining of the huge horses and swaying oxen as they pull against singletrees. There is excitement to behold the symphony of veteran lumbermen who guide logs down the skidway where they are seized by dogs. The clicking sound of the pawl as it ratchets against cogs and the pull of the wooden lever to set the depth of the saw is all coordinated by the sawyer. These men love the smell and sounds of the steam engine as she builds steam. Another lever is pulled and the prostrate log inches toward the waiting sharp teeth. Soon the smell of sawdust pours from the saw. Distant markets await this transformation of boards to be molded into furniture and houses. These have made indelible impressions on mountaineers

Wintertime means much preparation for the months that lie ahead. All the men at the local sawmill know they had better work hard now before the woods fill up with ice and snow, causing difficulty for loggers to feed the mill, but that

AT THE SAWMILL

doesn't stop things from going haywire. There are too many variables and parts that can fail.

Things are going well when Martin rolls a big Red Oak down the skidway to the waiting carriage. Pap pulls back on the smooth oak lever that engages a system of pulleys and belts, then finally the carriage. The huge log soon rides on its way to the anxious saw propelled by a huge head of steam. About halfway through, the rawhide laced belt tightens and governors respond. The engine strains with all its might, crying for more power. Suddenly, the worse happens when a knot catches the saw table, throwing the carriage off its rails. Metal begins to twist, pieces fling through the air and men run for cover. Pap shields himself behind the single board plank nailed vertically where he stands.

As I replay the incident through my mind, it all seems like slow motion, but was, in fact, over in a few seconds as the engine sputtered to a halt.

Repair gets underway to rework huge timbers and massive iron rails supporting the carriage. The crew works well into the night, dismantling mangled parts. At daybreak, the crew is ready to reassemble everything. Mid-morning, Jeb and his team pull up with a trail of logs. Jeb sizes up the new twenty-foot iron rail that must go in place. Ole "goggle eyes," Pete Arbas, also works at the mill. As soon as their eyes meet, they are up to mischief. Jeb swings the team around the skidway to where the logs can be rolled up on the head blocks. The stomping hooves of the big drafts come to a stop.

One can scarcely see Jeb's face because of beard as he saunters with an awkward pace to where the men are studying the matter. He takes his cruddy hat off to reveal unkempt hair and uses his stained sleeve to wipe sweat from his forehead. First thing out of his mouth: "Ere, if Jess was here, he'd shoulder that rail an' curry 't in place, what of 't Pete?"

Pete ejects a barrage of tobacco juice from between his

few teeth, "Err, it's a might heavy, but he might. I wonder if Martin might take a hold of 't? I'll bet if he did, Jess 'uld stay his distance fir good!"

With that, Martin's ears perk up. The men encourage him. Martin reasons, *if I lift this rail, I might be free of being bothered by the likes of them.* The young giant steps over to the rail, which weighs several hundred pounds and lifts one end. Walking to the middle, he places his six-foot frame under the massive load, engaging every muscle in his body. Muscles and veins bulge as he heaves it, swinging it around toward the mill. Eyes bulge all around as he finds footing over the rugged bark and debris to carry it to its destination. A horrendous thug vibrates along the machinery as the rail is pushed from his shoulder to the skidway timbers. Everyone is stunned - especially ole Pete.

Pap declares, "Ole Pete's eyes are as big as lard buckets!"

Immediately, Pete and drop-jawed Jeb begin conniving. Pete exclaims, "I would a bet nary a man could curry that iron!"

For a moment, Martin thought he could trust them, but soon learns of their intent. Jeb swings the pick to knock the Jay Grabs out, gathers the reins, and blurts to Pete, "Jist wait 'till Jess finds this out!"

Martin mutters, "They're no doubt th' sorriest critters in these parts!"

Looking sternly in their direction and with anger in his voice, he demands, "You've lied an' deceived s' much it's a wonder ya don't have t' git somebidy else t' call yer dogs!"

As Martin turns his attention to other duties, Pap can only say, "Bless God, what a man! What a specimen. I don't believe he knows how strong he is! My, my, my, I want t' be on th' good side of a bidy that kin handle weight sech as that. I swear there's nary a man 'round that could a done that!" Then with a mischievous twinkle in his eye, "Any you boys want t' go a round with 'im?"

AT THE SAWMILL

In time, the fifty-two inch circular blade is sent singing through timber, having no mercy on anything in its path. The only stopping is to sharpen and set the teeth. That is often when cutting hardwoods and when frequently hitting dirt and rocks imbedded in the bark.

Back on the Sods, men are cutting to fuel the mill back at Laneville. The Shay geared locomotive has a spur that runs the Four Knobs. When loaded, it chugs to the Sods, then makes a switchback and on to Laneville. These are capable of pulling heavy loads up steep slopes. The Shay has extremely good traction because all of the engine's wheels, including those under the tender, are drivers with no dead weight riding on the un-powered wheel trucks.

Getting the timber out is yet a problem. The snow has already set in, which brings a whole new level of difficulties. A few years ago, trees had been cut during the winter snows, causing the stumps to be several feet high, being revealed when the spring thaw occurred.

Our mill saws orders depending upon the customer. That ranges from timber of many kinds: pine (white and yellow), many types of oak, curled birch, cherry, spruce, popular, black and white walnut, cucumber and chestnut.

We still have some huge virgin trees off the Sods, but none is reported to match a massive white oak cut in Tucker County. It was thirteen feet in diameter. It was said that someone turned a team of horses on the stump. Yellow Poplars on the headwaters of Elk River have been reported up to eight feet in diameter and one cut in Tucker County filled an entire log train when hauled to the mill. The mill at Laneville can handle the giants we have to let stand for den trees, but that serves a purpose as well.

— XV —

LOGGERS AND LOGGIN'

Timber has been king and employer in many communities. It has been said that proper maintenance and respect for the forest is more important to the industrial base than any other industrial activity. There is all too often an abuse of the rich forest Appalachia has to offer. When not cared for, it has been said that there is also a breakdown in living standards and in social and economic institutions.

To think of Spruce Knob is to think of fresh mountain streams and timber - lots of timber. Timber was harvested to the north until the best was worked over. Timber entrepreneurs began looking south to Spruce Knob. Rails were laid from Thomas to Davis, along Canaan and on to Dry Fork. Here supply trains were loaded for distant markets. The tracks continued to Elkins, where trains crawled on to Durbin to extract timber from mountainsides.

Years ago, a stage had hauled passengers to serve this area. From Elkins, the stage continued to Huttonsville Fork, from there it followed one of two routes. Here it could have gone up the Tygart River to Valley Head and Mingo. The other trail followed the old Staunton-Parkersburg Pike over Cheat Mountain, across Shavers Fork and into Durbin. About half way over Cheat, the stage changed horses to continue to Durbin and to Travelors Repose, where one could spend the night before continuing to Staunton and on to Marlinton. This was the first stage west of the Alleghanies.

How Cheat got its name is unknown, but knowing the weather conditions and the scars she imposes on men and horses is reason enough to blame her for the years she has "cheated" men. This part of Spruce is wild with game and covered with a dark canopy of forest. It has been said that a squirrel can live forever in its tree tops by jumping from one to another without ever returning to the ground, except for water. The forest is so dark that one can scarcely see a hand held in front of one's face. The good thing about this darkness is that rattlesnakes must have sunshine to survive and for that reason are not found in the heavy woods.

Along the rail line, one traveler counted forty-five sawmills in the space of not as many miles. The major mills are located at Whitmer and Big Run. Companies either bought thousands of acres or obtained options to buy what they could not get their hands on readily. Italians built many of the rail lines and developed their own settlement above Horton called "Little Italy." They labored around and across Spruce to the drainage of the North Fork of the South Branch of the Potomac River.

These railroads require one hundred thousand feet of timber to build each mile of line. Each car holds about three thousand feet of logs and it normally takes six or seven logs to the thousand. Generally, ten carloads of lumber roll out of Horton each day, loaded with ten to twelve thousand feet of lumber each. To give one a rough description of one thousand board feet of lumber, you may imagine a stack of lumber approximately three feet high, three feet wide, and ten feet long.

In getting lumber out of the mountains and supplies back to mills and the people that operate them, some have been known to "pour the coal on." Tradition says that Booker, a logging boss, instructed one engineer to "open th' throttle, whistle once fir a cow, twice fir a man, an' three times fir God 'lmighty, an' if they still don't move t' run over 'em !"

Many areas on Spruce cause one to step back and take a second look and the Sinks are no exception. They captivate the eye with high plains, many species of wild flowers, rhododendron, mountain laurel, and a prolific growth of evergreens, beech and birch. The only man-made sites are an occasional Moonshiner's cabin and the train tracks that wind across the Sinks down onto the East Fork of the Greenbrier River to hook up with the Staunton-Parkersburg Turnpike. Perhaps the most exciting spectacle is the stream that winds through hemlock, past feeding deer, to sink into the earth and exit the cavern a few hundred yards to the east. Spotted, red-bellied trout flourish and can be caught with zeal.

To cut the vast timber, the six-foot, Raker Tooth Simons Cross Cut saw is sharpened to needle sharpness. One man will notch, two will saw and fell the tree, then help limb or trim the tree. Men carry axes, one cross cut saw, a measuring pole, felling wedges and a maul. Kerosene is also needed to rid the pine pitch as it accumulates on the saw.

Now and in the past it has been ball-hooted from mountainsides with cant hooks or skidded with oxen and horses. From there it has been driven as cattle on the Greenbrier, Blackwater and other rivers of size. Where there is not a river capable of floating logs, spurs of rail line are built deep into the forest.

To build access into the forest, immigrants of many lands spiked the rails -- Irish, Italian, German, Austrian and Russian. They endured many winters in their huts along the lines. The dollar and freedom forced them to stay, in spite of the snows deep around them. The logger followed the tracks into the woods. His bright shirt stood out with color against the background of green. His saw and spiked shoes brought new sounds to the forest. Then his patient horse and huge engines came to awake the woods from slumber.

To the farmer, the forest provides materials for fencing and buildings, but also sees grazing and meadows as important to him. To burn the land off means little if it gets away, except to burn another person's crops or buildings. To the logger, there are those in distant cities needing lumber, and that means employment.

But harvest has its unnecessary casualties. Fire takes its toll around sawmills and logging camps as steam engines spew and workers become careless. Other fires destroy the forest along the train tracks as locomotives belch out embers. A not so obvious effect of the many burned areas is the streams that have dried, causing fish to die and wild game to disappear as can be seen on the sods. Also, the Ledgerwood steam-powered aerial skidder rips the mountainsides to shreds because the ends of the logs drag the ground.

Pap declares, "As people conquer diseases t' he'p everbidy live t' be older, may he also learn t' control fires an' be stingy when cuttin' timber."

— XVI —

LIFE ON THE FORK

Down in the valley, families settle down to less activity. Except for feeding the sheep, a few cows, hogs kept over, and chickens, much of the work is done. The winter wood has been cut and the pantry is full of cans. My house on the Fork is pretty well winterized and I've been able to purchase some winter reading material. We can always rely on the daily mail, that is, if the weather doesn't prevent travel. Jake's store provides winter entertainment and news. Most Saturday night schedules find several men and boys huddled around the stove.

Midweek brings another winter enterprise for Pap and I as we think of the Sods. With much effort, we head for Red Creek and the beckoning glades of Blackbird Knob to secure some venison and to trap. With all the supplies loaded on our horses, we take to the Gap and on to the Rohrbach Trail - that takes the better part of a day. Soon axes go to work to build a lean-to and prepare a mat of pine needles on which to sleep. It is venturesome to spread my bed with the wild creatures out under the canopy of heaven.

Dusk comes and time to check on the deer population close by. I take Blaze beyond the first horizon, keeping him by my side until I give him the signal. My gun is carried in the crook of my muscled arm with a primed finger arched by the trigger. We stay to the leeward side of the knoll to conceal our scent. Stunted apple and pine trees stand scattered among the now dormant blueberry bushes. A deer soon comes in view. For a second, he fills up my sights as I level on him, but that is not to last long. My gun belches smoke and a deer for our supper is wounded. Immediate death would be the case if time were on my side and the shot not so distant. Blaze uses that as a sign to charge. The tracks make a huge circle before he pounces on the exhausted deer. He fastens on the throat and drags the victim to a quick death. In camp, we hang the deer to a scrub pine to be cut as needed. Before we leave, there will be several more to pack off the mountain to our smokehouses and cans. Another deer will be killed tomorrow to bait our bear trap. Honey will be our primary bait, but a deer carcass always helps. We hope to have some bear meat to pack off the Sods as well.

Wild animals have odd innocent ways. They are vulnerable when all is quiet, and some have features much out of proportion. Sometimes they can be the most trusting of man, and at other times, they are afraid of his very smell. But their Creator has endowed them with abilities to survive most adversaries. The Indians have a saying: When a pine needle falls in the woods, a deer hears it, a turkey sees it, and a bear smells it! An optometrist friend, having given the art of turkey hunting and the turkey's eye much consideration, stated, "I declare, if they could smell, you'd never kill one!"

The wild turkey was once nominated to be our national bird, but was eclipsed by the Bald Eagle. The turkey is a complicated species. To some, it seems cunning, clever, cautious, wary, suspicious, and leery and the most distrusting of all of God's creatures. Although challenging, the skilled hunter can outwit them. The turkey has many traits to guarantee survival, but stealth on the part of the hunter can level the playing field.

In some ways, they appear stupid: they announce their position as they travel, constantly chirp, strut, gobble and rustle leaves while scratching for food. They walk for great distances along a fencerow looking for a hole, instead of merely jumping over it. It is not until the hunter moves and becomes unique to the woods that the turkey is alarmed. Acute eyes mounted on a snorkel-like head picks up the slightest abnormal movement. Then, in a split second, their defense system goes into action. Legs immediately charge to put great distance between danger and themselves. I have the opinion that if they were like the bear and deer and kept their mouths shut, they would be camouflaged in the wilderness and the hunter would scarcely see one.

We look for muskrat and otter slides where they have displayed their musk to mark their territory. To appreciate the few warm days of winter, the otter appears on the ice to play. He dives under the water and catches fish while they are stiff with cold and can't escape. We set our traps, placing a small one about two inches under the water where they slide down the banks. Care is taken to place them exactly where they enter the water so they can be caught as they place a foot in the trap. I watch as Pap demonstrates the importance of fastening a rock to the trap chain, which causes them to drown. He explains that if this is not done, they will gnaw their foot off to escape. The trap is set with the rock on a nearby log that extends out over the water. As soon as the animal begins kicking, the rock falls in the water and causes the animal to drown.

To trap a fox or cat requires another level of expertise. Those of the cat family are dastardly cowards, unlike the bear who will fight with little coercion. The sole way to trap either is to feed them for a few days, then plant a trap in their path, baited with a deer carcass. Hides bring a fair price and greatly supplement one's income.

As we pack to head off the Sods, we can say it has been good. Another mule or horse would come in handy. The bear we so proudly harvested greatly rewards our venture.

Services continue to be held at Hopeville. Attendance fluctuates because of the weather and sickness. Most of our illnesses are cured with our home remedies, but occasionally, someone must call for the doctor. His services are not cheap and most cannot afford them. It seems there is always someone that needs help of some kind in the winter. The nights are long and the days short as the sun loses its power. Plus, this valley is sandwiched between North and New Creek mountains, shutting out much of the morning sun. That is a benefit in the summertime, but now we could enjoy its warmth during the long winter months. The wind howls as it descends down the valley from the Alleghanies and usually brings with it flurries called the "Alleghany Gnats."

Ole man winter seems to find entry, although I'm fairly certain all those holes last summer were filled, so this evening

I must bank the Buckeye Stove a little tighter. Thank goodness I have plenty of comforters to pull up over me. When I lay down between the feather tick and the comforters, I feel like a newborn cradled in its mother's arms. There is no need of an alarm clock with my faithful rooster. Last night I threw an old comforter over the chickens to prevent their combs from freezing. But that extra darkness doesn't seem to confuse their time clock.

As morning breaks, I open the curtains to discover new snow, which should measure an accumulation of about sixteen inches. The fresh, still, soft, flakes of snow and Red Birds fluttering here and there trying to find morsels are incredibly peaceful. The cows and the horses are all patiently looking toward the barn, waiting to be fed. It's amazing how their winter coats can provide enough warmth to prevent freezing. As soon as they get a full stomach, they will be fine. It's important to have a big breakfast myself, knowing the uncertainty of when I'll return. With the household chores done, I pull my five buckle Arctics on and set about to shovel a path to the barn.

Each night, the wind blows the path shut, but if it stays open for a while, it will be easier walking. Kicking snow and frozen manure off my boots, I climb the steep ladder to the haymow to throw down some hay for the animals. They gore and butt each other until they get settled in their pecking order to find a place to eat. There is no begging to get them to eat today, because of the ground cover.

The sheep didn't come in. They no doubt stayed over in the pine patch to be sheltered from the weather. It seems I hear a faint sheep's bell sounding in that direction. They can browse on the undergrowth there until I can see about them. Their Creator did a fine job designing their coat. As long as they have something to eat, they're snug as can be. I have come to learn that not everyone can be a shepherd. Although not as adept as some, I have grown to understand quite a

LIFE ON THE FORK

bit about the nature of sheep. I believe it is an innate love for the animal that you must possess. You must appreciate their habits, and in time they will obey you as their shepherd and with proper care you may see a profit. If one succeeds - in spite of all the obstacles - there are two possible profits: selling wool and eating mutton.

Pap declares, "Sheep come int' this world lookin' fir a way t' die," and I believe it! They have so many enemies ranging from sickness, to animals and birds of prey. Once a bear develops an appetite for sheep, he is hooked and keeps it up until men with their hounds bring him to bay and kill him. Sheep run impulsively from dogs only to agitate the chase, and as soon as one gets the taste of blood, there is certain death. The only way to wean a dog is to kill him. Over countless generations, sheep have loss most of their natural instincts to defend themselves.

I have seen sheep do some of the most stupid things, such as running headlong off cliffs, or become frightened easily to the extent of trying to cram through a barn door designed for just one, only to get their sides torn. From the time lambs enter the world, one has to teach ewe ownership and that lambs need to suck to live. Some say no other creature is so dumb, or perhaps better stated, dependent. Sickness is a constant battle. They need to be inoculated to eat and to not overeat. If a sheep should get under a shed, it cannot retreat to free itself. If one should get on its back against a rock, they cannot get up, also causing death.

This example of their helplessness, no doubt, is the reason Jesus used the analogy of sheep and the shepherd to express His relationship to dependent mankind. Although the independent person may take offense to this, there are so many ways that we need God's guidance. He spoke of Himself saving just one sheep and that they can know their master's voice. An interesting thing about a flock is that they tend to follow a leader, sometimes a ram, an older ewe, or shepherd. If that leader is reliable, all is well.

The almost romantic picture depicts Pap with his cane quietly leading a small flock down a country path. That can be done and is done, but our mountain grazing often shapes another creature. We sometimes cannot tend them or see them every day, causing them to be somewhat less than tame. Sheering, doctoring, and lambing time causes us to gather them from hundreds of acres of hillsides. Their free roaming and lack of shepherding causes them to be as wild as deer. Their breath is endless as they dart from one steep cliff to another. Their wool becomes shaggy and filled with burdocks as they graze on whatever is available. Pap is one of the few farmers having a split-rail fence around his pasture and a sheepfold. This enables him to tend his sheep close to home. This can cause a relationship to develop. One can see leadership and obedience.

After five months of gestation, lambs are born. All shepherds, at one time or another, have had to pull one from the birth canal. They can be particularly fun to observe and have an innocent jubilant nature. Once they survive the first few weeks of life, they are most interesting to watch as they play. They remind one so much of children as they play tag, climb rocks only to jump down, and agitate their mothers. During their three months of sucking, they are interesting to watch at feeding time as they jar ewes off the ground in hopes of a larger meal. Ewes can be amazing to watch as they seem to ignore all that is around them while grazing, perfectly happy chewing cud. Bucks, on the other hand, are unquestionably masculine. Their heads are built for butting. The fact is, when they are secluded from the ewes for a while and feel mischievous, they have set men on their backsides!

While working with them, I often think of King David as he watched his father's sheep and protected them from the adversaries. And to think, all those experiences educated him to pen the 23rd Psalm. In it he states, "The Lord is my shepherd, I shall not want . . ." I'm not sure of the environment David was accustomed to, but I like to envision him in these mountains while writing. He no doubt had a good relationship with the sheep and grew to appreciate the experiences. He is seen leading and guarding them. In youth, he was a great example of what a shepherd should be. In the same way, God wishes to be our Shepherd.

Some pastors attempt to be Chief Shepherds rather than pastors; in doing so, they have manipulated people and hindered personal growth. Some have even misled and abused souls. Rather than point people to God, they set themselves up as the final word of authority and begin cults. Eventually that causes people to be scattered abroad to the wind and hurting.

These mountains bring many obstacles, hardships, and good times, but whatever the occasion, some of these people seek God as their Shepherd. Sister Dolly preaches the message of the Great Shepherd with such conviction. We all have responsibilities here and are shepherds in our own right. God wants to be the Chief Shepherd and guide the path of each one. We are like sheep without a shepherd, bewildered and lost, if we fail to look to Him. With His abundance, we do not really need to desire other guidance. We become discontent because of selfish reasons and go our own way.

Looking from the haymow door, I notice that the Fork is frozen, which means two things. I can gather ice for the spring house to keep things cooler in the coming months. The added blessing of the ice on the river is ice fishing. Today will be a good day to gather ice, since I am caught up on my other chores. With the team harnessed and the saw sharpened, I'm off. The Belgians are so obedient; they never say no. If only people could be that way in time of need. I try not to ask too much, such as pulling something impossible or working too long in inclement weather. But they sure know how to get under a load. They get down on their knees and pull, causing muscles to bulge, forming riffles that remind me of the ocean's waves. The ice is not heavy. It is actually worse on me trying to manhandle it. The tongs help to get it loaded and stacked in the ice house. I had gathered sawdust earlier to pack around it.

It is dinner time and we're loaded. A couple more like this and the spring house will be filled. I am blessed to have one of the greatest springs around. It gushes out of New Creek and is most refreshing. It flows through the trough in the rock house, where I can keep milk for days, but the ice helps when the weather turns warmer. I have constructed troughs on either side to store crocks of cottage cheese, butter, and fruit. Eggs are stored on a higher shelf. They will eventually be traded for flour, sugar, or coffee.

Tomorrow should be a good day for ice fishing. I've got a craving for some yellow suckers. Who knows? We may snare a Carp and have the joy of pulling it in, although they're no good to eat. One of the old-timers told of the way to eat a Carp, "Ya lay a Carp on a slab, scrape th' scales off, then eat th' board!" Nonetheless, they race up and down the river and they're a thrill to snare because of their size.

The sun is high enough to hit the sun side of the mountain, signaling the time to make my way toward rounding up a crew to go to the ice. One can usually find willing persons at the store. With little effort, some of the boys found some snares and axes. There are a couple of long, calm holes close by that make good sucker holes. One is down from the hanging rocks and another around the bend where Manuel Run feeds into the North Fork.

A daring soul ventures out on the ice first to test it. Holes about one foot square are cut in the ice across the river. We drag brush out to the holes to lie on and assume a prone position with a submerged cocked snare awaiting the fish. After some pounding and stomping from side to side, Pap, with his keen eye, yells "Ere they come!" Anticipation soars as the hog-nose yellow suckers come in droves and snares are guided over them to their gills. With that, the jerking begins and onto the ice are suckers, flopping, in hopes of returning to the crisp water. Quickly, another snare is dropped into the hole to await latecomers.

After many frigid hours stomping up and down the river, Pap looks up from his hole shivering, "It's 'bout supper time, ain't it?" With that, we divide the suckers. I throw mine in a sack I had brought along for the purpose and head home. With only one person falling in today, we've had a good time.

— XVII —

ROUGHCUTS IN THE APPALACHIANS

A gentle breeze breaks across the Alleghanies with the coming of spring. Those around here know not to get their hopes up, because "Granny's Nightcap" is still hovering over the Four Knobs. That is that lingering frozen midst that canopies the Sods. Signs of spring are here when those low-lying clouds leave. We look for the spring thaw, then the first Robin's presence, and soon the first sprigs of grass begin making their way beneath cow piles. If one wishes for his pasture to grow, the animals must be penned and forced to eat stored hay. An animal will opt for the tender shoots of spring, alongside plenty of winter food.

Among many things, spring brings with it an opportunity to mend what winter has destroyed, and corn planting - the latter being governed by the Bumble Bee's presence. When they begin to fly, corn can be planted. Another method to determine the time to plant is to watch the White Oak leaves. When they grow to the size of a squirrel's ear, it's time to plant. The method to plant is outlined in the following poem.

One for the squirrel,
One for the crow,
One for the bad weather,
And one to grow.

Another version includes the phrases:

One for the dodger and one to feed,
One for "likker" and one for seed.

This spring brings business as usual, but also reminders of the trouble in the Gap and on the mountain. The trouble began back on the mountain as farmers were mending fence, so they could turn their animals out to pasture. The boys, Arnie and Wilbur, were doing just that, mending fence and tending the animals.

"They's ought'a be a better way t' make a livin'," Arnie said while repositioning a bib strap.

Wilbur reacted, "I hear tell ole Harness is a sellin' likker over 't town t' some of th' big wheels, mebie we culd git in on it."

They talked often about making moonshine to sell. It didn't take much to convince each other that the profit would be worth the risk.

Looking over the progress they had made, Arnie, realizing it is late in the day, states, "It close 'nough t' quittin' time, what ya say we leave early 'nough t' stop an' ask if ole Bibs 'll learn us how t' make shine?"

Wilbur stows the axes and sledge in a hollow tree and Arnie picks up the lines to drive the horse off the ridge. As they get closer to Harness's blacksmith shop, they hear the clanging as metal surrenders to the hammer. The high-pitch sounds ring throughout the countryside, bouncing and glancing as it goes. The metal succumbs to the anvil with each blow as it is molded. The only acoustics to the sounds are trees, a half shelter and a few meandering sheep. Harness doesn't really need to worry about the presence of a stranger anyway; most don't have the courage to travel these parts. The steep lonely trails and sounds of this untamed wilderness are not suited for the faint of heart.

Sure enough, as they pull up to the blacksmith shop, they see the works. The finishing touches are being made to repair an old still. Bibs is not alarmed because he had recognized them in the distance. The tall, lanky frame of Arnie and short, stocky Wilbur were unmistakable.

Arnie brings the horse to a stop close by a yellow locust post and flings the reins over the corner brace to prevent the hungry, tired horse from wandering too far. She immediately begins feeding on the nearby Orchard Grass shoots and dreams of home, the watering trough, and a pile of grain, the burden of the harness removed, and cooling under the oak where generations of animals pranced in the dirt. While walking to the shed, the boys watch a hen demonstrate to her chicks the way to scratch a meal out of the earth.

So as not to be too pushy, Arnie figures he had better begin with some light talk. He opens with the usual "Howdy, Harness! Purty day, hain't it?"

Harness looks up and adjusts his sleeves, which had been rolled up over his powerful arms to provide additional protection from the heat of the forge. The sparks are many, but the leather-tanned skin and the Esau-like arms aren't too much of a bother.

Harness says, "I see ya boys been a makin' fence t'day – splittin' rails 'll take th' wind right out a ya."

He picks up his pipe by the forge to take a drag, then rears back, putting one hand on his lower back to massage some aching muscles. Breaking a twig from a nearby branch, he holds it to the burning embers in the forge, causing instant flame. Bringing the small fire to his pipe, he draws the fire into the dormant tobacco. A few quick draws on the pipe causes the tobacco to ignite. Harness slowly exhales the smoke, both through his mouth and hairy nostrils. Meanwhile, the boys admire a hand-forged bear trap Harness recently made and farm equipment he has either created or repaired.

Wilbur rubs his calloused hand over the metal. Trying to be diplomatic opens, "What a ya doin' 'ere?"

Harness, in a backwoods manner and slight humor, "I are fixin' an old still, been lookin' fir some good hep."

That was the opening Arnie was waiting for and quickly cuts in, "We're not much at workin' metal, but we's a hopin' ya could show us how t' make some likker. Some say ya kin make th' best likker that kin ever be squeezed out of a corn patch."

He figures some flattery wouldn't hurt.

Harness smiles slightly, pauses a minute as he takes another drag, and watches smoke curl to the translucent sky. Arnie's proposition doesn't sound bad, knowing there may be some free help. The most it would cost would be a drink or two, and that would be expected.

He answers, "Be over t' th' big spring in Dry Holler tomorr' night. I are a plannin' t' run a batch off."

With that, Arnie quickly obliges, "We'll be there!" Wilbur grabs the horse's bridle and sets out with Arnie on the trail west to the Cornshakle place. They cross the streams that feed the North Fork, which wind their way through mountain laurel and rocks, eventually ending up in the Atlantic. They watch in the distance as a squirrel scampers to freedom, where, even in the mountains, wildlife lives on the edge. There is always the prey and the predator.

This is the opportunity the boys have been looking for - someone to show them a way to make some quick money, regardless of how dirty it is. Their steps seem a little lighter and their stride somewhat longer.

In the months ahead, Harness demonstrates carefully the craft of making moonshine, after the same general recipe taught to him and practiced by others in the mountains. Soon the boys bargain for a still of their own and waste little time putting their skills to work, figuring it would beat most jobs they have done.

Moonshining is viewed by many as any other job, and more particularly, a harvest job - something that needs done before winter; the mash doesn't ferment in the cold, tracks are too obvious in the snow, and transportation to market is much more difficult.

From the thick forest of trees, leaves are yet plentiful in the woods, and heavy on the trails that the boys must travel. They bury a barrel in the rich abundance of leaves, to provide insulation and concealment in the rocky hollow. With cool clear water running into it, they empty in selected corn to submerge. Now they must wait the necessary two or three days for sprouts to form to create malt.

Arnie reminds Wilbur of another tactic mentioned by Harness: "Some 'ave been known t' put th' corn in sacks an' place it under a manure pile t' hurry th' sproutin'."

As the sprouts reach a couple inches long, the boys place them in the full sun to dry. Bibs had instructed them, "Some time ya 'll want t' warm it by a fire t' hurry th' dryin', or t' hep if th' sun's not hot."

At the sign of all the moisture gone, the boys begin grinding the course meal into "corn grits," or "chop." Each scoop is placed again into an oak barrel to submerge in spring water and become "sweet mash" to remain three to five days. It then is uncovered to add warm water and rye malt to remain another several days to create "sour mash." Harness warned them to never place the mash in pine vats, because the alcohol would attract pitch and give the liquor a smell and taste of turpentine.

They work with the ease and skill taught from a master. Finally ready, Arnie hoists the mash sack to his shoulder and watches as it pours to the large copper kettle, situated on a stand about eighteen inches off the ground. Wilbur lifts the cap, made from a charred oak whiskey barrel sawed in half, and places it on the kettle. It slides perfectly into the barrel and stops within a few inches of the top. The boys set about to install the piping, which protrudes from the cap to a coil of copper. The piping routes through a trough running full of cool mountain water coming from a fresh mountain stream.

A gentle fire soon crackles under the pot. Harness had insisted, "A fire that's too hot 'ill scorch th' mash an' 'ill blow ya t' kingdom come!" The working still sounds like Harness advised, "Like rain on yer roof, er side meat a fryin'!" As heat surrounds the pot, steam begins rising. Alcohol vapor escapes the container to exit through the piping (worm) and condenses into the precious liquid.

Arnie reclines as he watches the "liquid gold" slowly drip into a half-gallon glass jar, later to be poured into a small barrel for transport. The boys observe to confirm what Bib's had advised, "Th' first run - or "singlin's" - is full of trash. Th' next run betters th' proof an' taste, an' ya call it, sloppin' back. Do it fir 'bout eight times, an' most say, th' fourth's th' best."

The boys recall the final procedures as the run is being completed. Bibs had taught them how to determine the alcohol content. He had stated time and again, "Th' way t' tell th' alcohol 'mount is t' catch a couple drops in a spoon an' empty it on th' fire. If it jist hisses an' gives off steam, th' alcohol's not there. Th' alcohol is low if 't burns yeller. If 't burns with a dark blue fire, th' alcohol is high an' ready t' be put in a jar."

Frost covers every branch and rock in the hollow. In the distance, the barking dogs sound a chorus above the hissing and gurgling of the water in the working still. At daybreak, they finish running off some of the smoothest dew that had ever spilled out of a petcock. Selling the product means a mere trip to town. Now money becomes available as never before.

In time, the paths of Harness and the boys would cross. Each party grew envious of the other. This conflict led to jealously and terrible feelings from both sides. Time after time, they warned each other to stay clear of the other's territory. Harness, being much older and perhaps wiser, figured that he could get rid of the boys by turning them in to the Revenue Agents for making moonshine. This violated the very agreement the three had made. Harness had said in the beginning that he would teach them how to make moonshine, provided they would never tell anyone. He went on to warn them not to break confidence and vowed that the one who did would be killed.

Harness grew increasingly bitter over the conflict and thought long and hard about his course of action. Rather than incriminate himself, he decided to report the boys to the Federal Officers for being "slackers." That is a term to describe someone who evades going to the service, as many do in these mountains. Bibs made a trip to town to notify agents that he had some information they may be interested in.

Winter was passing when Bibs pointed the agents in the direction of Woodrow Cornshakle's house. The boys are caught inside as officers sneak up to the house. Wilbur jumps out the upstairs window and is nabbed. Arnie charges out of the house toward the tree that hid a rifle, but had made it only several yards from the house when an agent levels his sights on him. The bullet traces its way to his left shoulder, causing him to fall to the mercy of the law. Blood flows freely as flesh is exposed. The rugged mountaineer fights to no avail. Suddenly, a Home Rifle explodes from the front door as Woodrow sends a bullet streaming overhead. Handcuffs snap as they close tightly in place.

Arnie demands, "Don't, Dad! Yer're no match fir these

cowards - yer're needed 'ere 't home." Another shot and the fifty caliber is returned to the forged hooks over the fireplace. Mom Cornshakle weeps as she tenderly cares for her wounded son.

— XVIII —

HANDCUFFS - FREEDOM

As though it were yesterday, I remember the boys leaving the mountain with the agents. They had been arrested for being slackers. A cool chill stirred in the air that April 1920, as Wilbur and Arnie journeyed off the mountain to begin their three-month stay at Fort Meyers, Va. During this time of the year, snow covered the ground, and ice blanketed the creeks and ponds.

I return to that winter day in my reminiscing as Alleghany winds swirl off the Four Knobs. The officers hurried on their way, handcuffs clanging and gun chambers loaded. Itchy trigger fingers waited with anticipation, just in case the boys tried to make a break. The officers rode horses, while the boys walk. All the way off the mountain, Arnie favored his wounded shoulder. Every step caused excruciating pain to surge throughout his body. Most of the blood had been cleaned at home, but in no time, the constant jarring caused the clean shirt and bandages to redden from the oozing fresh blood.

He would have given anything to relive the events of the day, for then he may have been in a position to escape. Another day, he may not have been in the house to be such an easy target. Given half a chance in the open woods would have made all the difference. The conditioning of the mountain work made them fit to take on any outsider in a fair fight, but this time they were caught empty handed and now disadvantaged. With the sling bound tighter to his side, he and Wilbur talked while walking. Anger and vengeance were heard in their voices as they fumed about the way things had gone.

By noon, they had walked the many miles to reach town. Once there, Arnie was allowed to see a doctor, who quickly redressed the wound. Soon thereafter, they boarded a train to Fort Meyers, Virginia. From there they were moved to Fort Jay, New York for an additional four months, all the while longing for family and the mountains. Still, they were verbal with their intention to get even. What began as a squabble over moonshine customers led to an ongoing bitterness, and now, likened to an animal that once was free to do as it wills, except for gathering food. Now they are restrained by outsiders and men who know little about mountain men and their manners. There were daily reminders that no one within the high walls understood the Alleghanies or her inhabitants. However, they had each other and that would have to suffice. The many months are spent doing meaningless tasks and filled with thoughts of the mountain. Each day brings them closer to when they will return and settle a score.

Finally, Thanksgiving Day, 1920 arrives when they board the train that will carry them home. The narrow steps leading to the passenger car are a welcome sight. Each turns to get one last look at the huge cut-stone walls that has held them. Shrill sounds echo as metal wheels screech along the iron rails. Thick black smoke belches from the stack, spreading soot particles to settle on everything exposed. The sun winks through the heavy growth of trees that overshadows the narrow rail line. If the rumbling of rail cars is not enough to disturb passengers as wheels roll over offset rails, the fierce roar from the whistle sounds to ward animals off the tracks. It sounds a lonesome cry along the remote tracks. If one closes their eyes and listens closely, they can almost hear it.

For great distances, the boys gaze out the window and see the North Fork of the Potomac River. Minds race back to earlier days when they fished the upper reaches of the churning water. Sometimes with poles and other times "finger fishing." Off in the distance they get a glimpse of familiar mountains. But the memories are not all good, for there is ole Bibs, the reason they were sent away. At least the boys are convinced he had turned them in and that put a price on his head that must be dealt with.

The freight pulls up to the depot at Cumberland, Maryland, where it screeches to a stop to take on water, fuel and forwarding passengers. A dark man with a shovel works vigorously scooping black coal into the scorching boiler, seeming like Hell itself as tongues of fire from the flame lick outward. A giant wooden tank rushes water into the train's reservoir. The last passenger boards and the engineer watches as steam builds. The huge locomotive hisses like a giant prehistoric dinosaur as it belches through valves. The gloved hand pulls the control lever causing steam to surge through a system of pipes and into giant pistons. Wheels inch forward on the seventy-ton Shay, causing each car to engage. A clanging sound rings as each coupler tightens against the next. Connecting first to the locomotive are several flat beds ready to transport lumber and crossties out of the mountains. Next, a supply car loaded with some miscellaneous supplies begins to move. Finally, the passenger car and the caboose feel a tug to go forward.

Sitting across from the boys are two gentlemen from Grant County who had been in Cumberland on business, Lou Burgess and Mace Stonestreet. Wilbur's broad body slumps by the window and Arnie commands the remainder of the seat, legs stretching fully into the aisle. Naturally, conversation comes up as to the reason for traveling.

Arnie asks, "Is ole Harness Bibs 'round up in th' country?"

Mace retorts, "As far as I know, he's not; he's 'fraid t' stay 'round up 'ere."

After coarse vulgarity, Arnie continues, "He better not stay 'round up 'ere er I'll kill 'im! I 'clare t' git even with Bibs fir turnin' us over t' th' law."

Mace sternly reprimands him, "Ya better watch yer mouth; that's pretty big talk t' have, that kind a talk 'll git ya in trouble!" Mace watches as Arnie's scarred, giant right hand tightens its grip on the seat support, causing knuckles to whiten.

Arnie pauses a minute and continues, "It might be big talk, but he'd better not cross our path er he'll not cross 'nother!"

Mace discreetly nudges Lou to observe the vengeful look on the broad, muscular face of Wilbur as he peers out the window. He looks long at the shining black and silver river as it rolls ahead, periodically disappearing into a dark green tunnel of trees.

The boys knew they had little sympathy on the train and that did not matter; they were committed to settle accounts. They had relived the events over and over again, while in jail. Had it not been for that, they could have been enjoying their life around Hopeville and on the mountain. There was little to do but stare out the smoky train windows. Once in a while, a smile broadens the lips of each boy as their emotions are stirred while thinking of going home, the sounds of animals and fresh mountain streams.

The train continues on into the evening until it reaches Petersburg. Far down the tracks that run along the river, curious individuals watch as the single light squints from the train chugging up the valley. At first very faint, but soon the headlight brightens the street, making the lanterns useless. Some yards short of the depot, the engineer shuts off the steam valve and opens the whistle for one last blast. Even before coming to a halt, passengers stand ready to disembark. Some will stay the night in a local hotel, but the boys waste little time heading for the mountain. Early morning will bring businessmen with their road wagons to be backed up to the loading dock to take on supplies.

Arnie and Wilbur pause to stretch and breathe fresh mountain air. Wilbur steps on the feed scale while walking across the wooden dock. Time in prison has caused Wilbur's stocky frame to fall under two hundred pounds, his usual mountain weight.

The walk home is of no consequence since they are anxious to be home. The twenty-five miles home seem short because the beautiful Alleghanies are in view. Just outside town, they see the very hollow where the Cornshakle home sits. Arriving home would mean celebration for some, but dismay for another. They knew Bibs had left the mountain for fear of their return. Sooner or later, he would have to show up, and they knew that.

The steep climb through the Gap and to the mountain takes them well into the night and into morning hours. Each house they pass has long snuffed out its light. Quick reminders come and go as each laugh of experiences with different households. Wilbur stops off at his home, while Arnie continues through the night.

In the distance, Arnie hears the barking of dogs near the Open Ridge School and the familiar sounds on their farm. There is a temptation to hurry the pace the last few miles, but the legs are just too weary. The family dog begins to growl; the growl turns to short yelps, and a curtain is seen pulled back as the moon shines its light through the trees. A friendly hand reaches for the pet. Mom Cornshakle, already to the front porch, has open arms awaiting her son. Even before the tears are dry and the embrace is over, she asks if he is hungry. That is a habit formed well before Arnie was born. The old man sets the kettle back on the warm stove to heat the coffee and questions him about the past few months. The moon has made its way well into the western sky when they finally turn in.

Soon the boy's threats ring out across the Four Knobs, "Ole Bib's 'ad better keep 'is distance." Although Harness has avoided his mountain home, he's not exactly a pushover. Soon their paths must cross. There is deep-seated hatred, but caution as to how the conflict will play out. The remoteness of the mountain provides a great environment for a cat and mouse strategy.

In time, Harness regains his nerve and returns. He had left the mountain because of all the threats and fear of the boys, but the weight of homesickness was too heavy. His return causes trouble's ugly head to resurface, and each party makes no bones about it. The bickering and the gossip escalate. New threats ring from Arnie, "I 'clare t' git that ole Bibs if it's th' last thing I do!"

"Their souls are eaten up with hate," I told Pap. "They can't let the thing go. Even though the boys feel sure Bibs had turned them in, they need to get on with their lives."

"Kinda 'minds me of sheep killin' dogs," Pap replied. "When they git on th' trail of a sheep, they can't quit. They's might have a good 'nough reason t' git Bibs, but they're not choir boys 'emselves. Like all of us have 't at times, sometimes there's more questions than answers. Sometimes ya jist have t' let it go! One thing fir sure, God made 'em good bidies, but th' devil give 'em a mean heart."

The means came to get Bibs when Arnie purchases a high-powered rifle. He selects a 303 British that can blast an acorn out of an oak fifty yards away. If ever fired on a man, there is little left to do but "send his saddle home!" To add to his arsenal, he adds a 32 Special.

It's not uncommon for families to have more than one gun and to prize them as one of their family members. The men folk always have a gun handy. Many times I open a kitchen door, which is the usual way of entry to the mountain homes, only to find a gun leaning against the door jam, staring me in the face. These normally aren't kept there for protection, but for hunting purposes. I often look out my kitchen window to see a plump groundhog munching on my vegetables. All I have to do is crack the door open a bit and lower the sights on the varmint.

Some of the men hunt so much that it seems they must think they are on a continuous vacation, while the wife stays home and tends the house and children. She accepts this role as a purpose she must fulfill. Sometimes the only rest she gets is when she is sick, and often not then. Although constant hunting may be viewed as an obligation, it does get the men away from many responsibilities, often tying wives down to household chores and children.

– XIX –

NO BEGGING FOR LIFE

Another long and tough mountain winter now has passed into history. The coming of spring has given farmers a break from winter activities and opportunity for warmer chores. This spring brings with it many things.

This Saturday, May 7, 1921, is beautiful on the mountain. The sun has just broken through the mist, but a chill lingers in the air. The horse exhales a heavy vapor as she lunges up the ridge in labor pulling out logs. Arnie and Wilbur sweat as they labor to split chestnut rails to place in the fencerow. The morning goes well, except for the usual hard work. From time to time, the subject comes up about Bibs. Anger saturates the air as each relives the haunting harassment he caused. The nagging effect of the time spent at the forts continues to haunt them.

Arnie opens, "Ever time I think of ole Bibs, I git s' mad I could kill 'im!"

"Yer're not by yerself," Wilbur agreed.

Work continues until about twelve o'clock when they decide to go to the house to eat. On the trail home, they meet Hense Cornshakle, Milt's brother. He had started the twelve-mile ride to Laneville about mid-morning and was delayed by people on the road who wanted to chat. Laneville lies across the mountain where the large lumber mill stands.

Hense sets slouched atop his horse like sitting on a sidesaddle, and he knows the boys well. After the customary greetings, talk of the weather and such, Arnie asks, "What's ole Elias Rohrbach an' Harness Bibs a doin?"

Hense responds in broken English, "Elias' not doin' ary a thing, an' ole Harness, he goin' t' town."

With that, they part company and the boys reason that this will be a good time to get Bibs. Arnie gets his rifle and grabs a bite to eat since it is ready and may have a long wait ahead.

Wilbur heads off the mountain with the 32 Special to see his folks and wait for Arnie. The 32 Special is a gun ideal for these woods. It is a short lever action and easy to maneuver through small growth and mountain laurel. When a hunter is following bear dogs to a tree through the brush, he cannot afford to be distracted with anything that may hinder progress. Perching on top of the once blued barrel is a set of Buckhorn Sights. These assure a kill when aligned on a target. Guns like this are the icon of the mountains. Until recently, men around here had only Home Rifles to hunt with. Lever-actions prompted Civil War General Mosby to say the enemy can load it on Sunday and fire it all week. The Winchester boasts the motto, "two shots a second." The best man with a Home Rifle could barely squeeze off two shots a minute.

Arnie sits down to eat with the old folks and a visitor, G. B. Cornshakle, who had taken his cattle to the Mosby place that morning. The usual conversation concerns the weather, what work they had gotten done and afternoon plans. Of course, Arnie is not about to talk of his intent. He slides away from the table, leaving the old people to continue their conversation. Sneaking out with his newly acquired 303 British and several shells, he heads off the mountain to meet Wilbur. Together they walk Manuel Run to where they tackle the steep pull that places them against the back side of Scrooges Knob, always under the cover of woods. They make short time traveling the few miles off the Four Knobs and will soon be in the Gap, often referred to as "Gandy" by the locals.

Arnie's 303 is a more serious gun. The locals call any gun close to this caliber a "high powered rifle!" It has some battle scars due to being carried by a former owner while hunting the Four Knobs. This bolt action is particularly good on the Sods where bear or deer are often a hundred yards or more in the distance. When the hammer drops on anything under three hundred yards, you can bet there will be "meat in the pot." The most interesting thing about the engineering of this gun is the magazine where the bullets are stored. Unlike other guns, manufacturers gave this an appearance of having coarse external threads on the forearm region. With the bluing and varnish well worn, this 303 is destined to propel yet another bullet, but this time to an infamous destiny.

Taking usual effort, Wilbur and Arnie descend into the Gap. As with all mountain folk, they are used to walking and these few miles are but a "Sunday walk." They walk east along the rim of Scrooge Knob to the gorge concealing the Gap road. The growth of pines along the top enables them to keep out of sight of the lone Riggleman house, until they are engulfed by the laurel in the Gap.

The Gap road is reasonably quiet as usual, just the rippling water, a few small animals, and talk of strategy. An occasional crow sounds from high on the canyon walls. Soon they eye the crevice where school kids slide off the steep bank, providing them a short cut to Hopeville.

Strapping their guns across their shoulders to free both hands, they begin to make the climb. There is very little in the way of assistance, just a few saplings to grip and a couple of footholds that were carved from years of use. To the right they recognize a good hideout for Arnie and about fifteen feet up above is another ledge to conceal Wilbur. Although there are dozens of places to hide, these provide decent views and an excellent escape route.

The afternoon sun hangs high in the heavens and is casting shorter shadows as it makes its way to the far ridge tree tops. Each listens as the other slides cartridges into their guns. The 32 is side loaded and the 303 is loaded into the bolt chamber when withdrawn. There is only waiting and anticipating. They had come too far to retreat.

Wilbur's nerves become fidgety.

Arnie demands, "Quit worryin', it'll soon be done an' we're free of th' varmint."

Wilbur questions, "Ifin he's not quite dead, ought we go t' finish 'im off?"

Arnie demands again, "Don't worry 'bout stupid stuff like that, when my gun cracks, ya 'll have yer answer! And I'd better hear yer gun crack er you'll git the same!"

Sitting among the amphitheater of rock-faced terraces rising one above the other, there is no need to fear being heard by travelers. The boys can detect anything on the road for some distance and if they are spotted, they can always say they're hunting. Between the dazing, thinking, and repositioning so their backsides won't become numb, they wait their target.

Harness left the mountain towards Petersburg early this morning on Roxie, his horse. He had ridden her many times to make the trip. Many of those after dark and lonely, but she knew the path like a book. There were many strange night sounds, but none stranger than the swishing of moonshine in the jugs strapped across her back. It takes about an hour to make the trip from the head of the Gap to town, but Harness and Roxie travel from the Four Knobs, which adds on another one-half hour. While at town, he stops at the mill to pick up some supplies, candy, and bananas. He hands Vick Shreve a silver dollar for some grain and watches it flow from the scoop to the wooden trough. He rubs his hands across Roxie's mane and is overheard saying, "That 'll be th' last time I'll be a feedin' you, ole girl." Mountain people believe in omens, and this statement is surely the reaction to one.

The tannery whistle sounds, indicating either 12:00 or 1:00 P.M. None has a timepiece so they are uncertain as to which whistle this is. Harness climbs aboard Roxie when he sees Harry and Abe, a couple of acquaintances riding out of town, and yells, "Hey, wait up, how 'bout ridin' with ya?"

Abe Turner and Harry Hanks have a bad feeling about the request. It is common for folks to join company to make the trip, but this association spells trouble. Those traveling these mountains have learned to obey their instincts.

They flick the lines commanding the one horse wagon to move as far and fast ahead of Harness as possible. They wish to put some distance between him and them. Often looking over their shoulder, they see Harness in the distance, trying to catch up. Just outside town, Harness comes alongside Miles Hausshalter who is heading to Mouth of Seneca. Miles has been riding alongside the Milt Cornshakle wagon headed to Jordon's Run, but because of the wagon's slow pace, Harness and Miles proceed to ride on ahead together.

They continue to ride into the mountains leaving Petersburg, crossing Big Spring about five miles from town where water spews out of New Creek by the barrel. Years ago, someone experimented as to the water's source. They dumped sawdust in the water up on Klines Gap and watched it appear two days later at the spring on the Fork side. The sawdust, in fact, swirled the many miles through the mountain.

Further up the Fork, the unshaven mountaineers, Abe and Harry, cross the cave spring, where they look back to see Harness and Miles rounding the turn on Wildcat. Here one can get a view of the Hanging Rocks and the road as it makes the turn on top of them. Another one hundred yards and they dip into the Jordon's Run. The dripping buggy lunges from the opposite side to turn up the Gap.

Back in the Gap, time slowly passes. The clock has ticked away a couple of hours for the boys. In the distance, there are faint sounds of hooves pounding the road. The boys quietly position themselves so they can rest their guns on limbs of proper height. Soon they catch glimpses of an animal through the tree foliage as a horse rounds the bend in the road, ready to make the steep climb up Gap Run. Wilbur lowers and readies his gun in anticipation of their target. Arnie, with the fierce glitter of his eye and iron steadiness of his arm, positions his gun. The sound of metal shoes ricochets off nearby rocks as the horse chugs under the labor of the small wagon and load. Each boy peers across their sights for the right shot. But sitting on the wagon seat are two burly, "tough as nails" mountaineers, Harry Hanks and Abe Turner. The boys recline to relaxed positions.

There's no Bibs, no horse trailing the wagon, no reason to shoot. The hammer on Wilbur's 32 is quietly dropped to its safety position. Arnie flips his safety on and begins calming nerves. Wilbur takes a deep breath waiting for adrenalin to settle and seats himself to blend in with the rock crevices. Any sharp-eyed hunter can see the killers if they merely look to the right of the cliffs. Prince, Harry's horse, with his acute eyesight, discerns their presence as he steals a look at them while making lunges in the harness.

Harry and Abe are engaged in conversation of how nervous Harness had been in town and how he wished to ride with them. They talk of his apparent efforts to catch up with them. Also capturing their attention for the last half hour is the watching of the rear end of the horse as he flexes hindquarter muscles to stretch the leather harness, and sidestep rocks to pull the load.

It wouldn't have mattered, however, if Harry and Abe

had seen the killers. They had no quarrel with them. Arnie and Wilbur knew that few would sympathize with Harness, regardless of what would happen to him and this was reason enough to encourage them to proceed with their ordeal.

Soon Miles and Harness descend Mud Hill, discussing the growing season and conversations in town. All too soon Harness knows he must break from his company and go it alone. Under most circumstances, he wasn't afraid. Soon they will be saying their last words as Miles continues up the Fork and Harness turns to go up the Gap on the road leading deeper into the mountains. Harness and Roxie have traveled these trails so many times that he allows slack in the reins. But something just doesn't feel right today. If only there was some certainty that lurking up ahead awaits Roxie's ominous killer and that of her master, then he could wait until nightfall. Reluctantly, Harness parts company with Miles at Hopeville.

Miles turns toward Harness with, "I'll be seein' ya, ya ole moun'ain goat."

With a forced grin, Harness returns, "Yea, nice ridin' with ya," then swallows hard to suppress the lump in his throat. With that, he eases Roxie into the creek, kicks her ribs, and turns to the gap. Arm muscles harden and Harness grips the saddle horn tighter as Roxie goes into a slight trot, knowing she is heading toward the Four Knobs and home.

They go about one-half mile where they round the bend to go up Gap Run. This is where Gap Run feeds into the primary water of Jordan's Run.

To go on up the primary course would mean running into a twenty-five foot waterfall. The Gap has three waterfalls - small ones about twelve feet high at the lower and upper ends, and the formidable "High Falls" in the middle. Early pioneers had hewed the road out, choosing the course of least obstacles. They were able to go around the lower falls, but needed to go up Gap Run to avoid the middle falls. It is especially notable to realize the wearing on the rocks at the higher falls. It takes water untold years to wear the gully to its present form. The creek has made its way from one side to the other as it capsizes down the gully. The natural running water and massive floods roar down through the canyon, leaving their mark. Anything in the water's path gets swept away as it rushes to lower lands. The story is told of a cow that washed over the high falls to incredibly live afterward! But I cannot imagine most are that fortunate.

The road is extremely rugged and was formed out of the ledges. Where the ledges could not be cut, men with scoops attached behind teams hauled rocks to fill the roadbed. The first one-half mile is pretty good, but when the road rounds the bend to go up Gap Run, it takes on a different nature. The mountain ledges become quite narrow, not leaving much room to make a road. For obvious reasons, the creek is not as wide, but swifter. The walls are a mere twenty feet apart, providing the creek just enough space in the low water season, but not during flooding, requiring constant repair to the road. There are horrendous boulders on each side, leaving but a channel at places.

This Saturday is not much different than any other in the Gap. The creek is ice-cold and birds give no detectable warning signals, just their normal frivolity. In Harness's heart, there is uneasiness. Some may call it a sixth sense. Thoughts race through his head of his wife, children, life on the mountain, the day's activities, and conversations in town. A little rain shower begins to fall. Pap would say, "Th' heavens are weepin'," realizing the rain and knowing Harness's inner feelings. Roxie chooses her footing carefully. Nervously on her back sets her rider and master for these many years.

Bibs inches into the deepest part of the Gap, away from civilization. He cannot escape the thoughts that have invited his latest trouble with the boys.

He reasons, "If I wouldn' a turned 'em in, I'd have a

better feelin' inside. I'd love t' be at peace with these people."

The trouble on the mountain had now culminated to this. However, knowing that Harry and Abe had gone through the Gap just a few minutes before provides some consolation. He hopes their presence cleared the Gap of all potential enemies; then again, these men had no quarrel with the boys.

Harness peels a banana and lifts it to his mouth to enjoy in an attempt to calm his nerves. Bananas are real treats in these parts. The refrigeration methods are springs or ice houses and do not allow for many imported perishables. In his pocket is some sucking candy for the kids at home. Luxuries such as these are few and far between. Normally, the only sweets are made from Maple Sugar in the form of small cakes or pulled taffy. Tied to the saddle is a sack of oats he had purchased at town. Folks in these parts believe in taking good care of their animals. The oats are to be Roxie's treat for her labors. Just ahead looms men between the rocks, who have aligned their eyes across Buckhorn Sights and the sight at the end of their guns.

Harness comes into view as he rounds the bend to climb Gap Run. Here the road clings to the hillside because of the ledges. Occasionally he is camouflaged with foliage that lines the road. Suddenly, Roxie lifts her head, causing Harness to scan the hillside for trouble. A few more steps and the cold, calculated bullet will thread its way down the forty to fifty yards to Harness.

But for now, there is the agony of hearts pounding, as if to explode. Wilbur knows he must get hold of himself and does so with a whisper, "Arnie, a few more steps and let th' lead fly!"

Finally in the clear, the hair trigger that signals the fatal bullet is squeezed. The heavily loaded rifle belches forth fire and brimstone. The trajectory had been calculated to zero in on its target. The perfectly smooth bullet slides through bear grease, providing little resistance as it begins its journey.

Once out of the barrel, the still air and lack of trees provide little opposition to the thunderous bullet as it swirls to race to its destination. In seconds, time stands still.

Harness hears the crack of the rifle and feels a jolt in his neck, and then nothing. There is no begging for life, no surrender, no opportunity to fight it out with fists. Just as other mountain men, he wouldn't have begged anyway. If given the opportunity to fight, the story may have been told differently. Harness was use to work: handling fifty-five gallon barrels, wood, axes, working the forge, anything and everything that builds strength. Seconds later, Harness slumps off Roxie and onto the ground, as the death-messenger is sent violently through his brains.

The brain is the control center of much of the intricate and delicate activities of the human body. Making sense of the brain's complexity isn't easy for experts. What we do know is that it is the organ that makes us human, giving us the ability for creativity, language, moral judgments, and rational thought. It is also responsible for each individual's personality, memories, movements, and how we sense the world. The brain is extremely sensitive and delicate, and so requires maximum protection, provided by surrounding the skull with three tough membranes. The spaces between these membranes are filled with fluid that cushions the brain and keeps it from being damaged by contact with the inside of the skull. All of that could not help Harness.

This brain contained memories of childhood activities and the Alleghany wilderness. It housed the genetics to perform the responsibilities of fatherhood. It imagined the vision to live independently and hue out a living on his beloved mountainside. Finally, it ordered the skills and steps necessary to build and maintain things for survival. Now, thanks to a single round lead ball not much bigger than a pea, Harness is dead.

Another exploding bullet causes Roxie's powerful hindquarters to impulsively charge with energy. Like a shot out of a gun, she bolts up the Gap Road. Seconds later, a volcano of shock waves echo in her ears and out of the hollow. Harness lays in the road with his head in the wagon tracks; his feet are sprawled against the bank, hands up to his head, and the khaki colored jacket in disarray.

The same gun that provided meat for families on the mountain now enters history as a murder weapon. It is a perfect illustration of how something good can be used for something bad. Ants quickly make a mad rush to the fallen banana peeling. Blood flows down the wheel track, stretching for several feet. Suddenly, another shot rings out and a bullet that enters her girth strap stuns Roxie. For an instant, she humps up as muscles contract to ease the pain. Inflamed with agony, adrenalin fuels her to race on. Blood streams down her side to the stirrups, covering her stomach. A further five hundred seventy three feet up the Gap, she stumbles out of the road and into the creek, with blood oozing out of her left nostril. She quivers involuntarily until her last ounce of energy is drained. She did nothing to deserve this – just an actor in this terrible theater.

A shot, a short interval, another shot, another interval, then two shots in succession roar down the Gap. The sounds of shots cause folk in hearing distance to wonder. Ped Rohrbach's work mare comes to an abrupt halt as her ears twitch to each shot as it thunders from the gun, causing him to look up from the hillside plow. The Hanks family at the head of the Gap and sitting on their front porch is interrupted from conversation and others pause from their activities. Pap stands before his hoe in his potato patch, believing the inevitable. Each aware of the trouble between Harness, Arnie, and Wilbur, causes them to imagine the worse. It is common for men to hunt for game anytime, but the succession and time of these shots signal something different.

Everyone will miss Roxie's gait gracing the countryside. Some crude people say they are more upset by her death than by the death of her master. She was a pretty horse, a dark brown color with a blaze of white down her forehead, muscular, and well disciplined. The countless trips to town and trips to the homes of acquaintances, both to Laneville and Jordon's Run, had perfected her physique. She was a well-tuned athlete from her massive head to her well-placed hooves. Never again would she pride the roads or livery with her presence, nor be rubbed down and praised by the Ostler working there. This day she would rest in the creek bed, and remain there until predators are gorged. The rigging would hang in a barn somewhere or, worse yet, be worn by an inferior horse. If there is any consolation in her death, we could say that she lives on in the lives of these - those who have been privileged to benefit from her death.

Entering the head of the Gap is Wilbur's brother, Provey Hawkins, and his one horse sled traveling to Ped's to get a load of corn, and climbing the Gap below are Milt Cornshakles's horses laboring to pull a farm wagon up the steep road. The wagon is driven by young Thaddeus as his dad walks along behind. As Arnie and Wilbur exit the Gap, they warn Provey Hawkins to keep his mouth shut, as he startles them in their hurried flight to escape.

Thaddeus eyes a figure in the road and brings the unsuspecting horses to an abrupt halt. Habit would have pushed them forward here, but the body prevents that. Thaddeus quickly draws the brake and yells for his dad.

Milt makes his way around the rear of the wagon, walking down the narrow path between the road and the wagon. As he walks alongside the wagon, he clings to the harness to keep from falling over the bank. The khaki jacket makes it apparent as to who is in the road. Not especially moved with emotion, Milt sends Thaddeus to the store to have someone travel to a phone to call the doctor. Milt stays with the body until Harry shows up.

Harry, hearing the shots and seeing the boys making their

quick exit, causes him to reenter the Gap to investigate. Milt asks Harry to wait by the body until he takes the team back the way they had come, so as not to disturb the body until the investigation is over.

The Gap fills with people following the killing - Dr. J. B. Groves, Coroner; Grant Roby, Justice; on lookers: Al Clower; Russ Smith, and others. A preliminary hearing or inquisition takes place immediately. Kimble, with an uncanny backwoods manner, asks each in attendance what they know of the killing. Men with stammering lips try to evade responsibility with alibis. Milt Cornshakle, by this time, has brought his wagon back into the Gap and endures the questioning before going home. Harry Hanks waits his turn, as well, to be questioned by Kimble.

Dr. Groves examines the body carefully, turning it over, then back again. Actually, some of the locals do much of the handling. He observes the entry by washing the wound area above the left eye with some creek water. The exit is a mangled mess of clotted blood and flesh. The doctor saturates the area with a wet cloth and parts the hair to further analyze the wound and determine the angle of the shot. Locals can do nothing but stand around and view the lifeless body. All are silent while Groves throws out a volley of technical terms describing the wound, which fall deaf on mountain ears, only distinguishable by the recorder. The facts are recorded and the outcome is now in the hands of townspeople.

Pap stands talking to Sister Dolly. Her face is tight with anguish, knowing it falls on the preacher to take the terrible news to Bib's wife.

Pap questions, "Mustin yer heart break a little whenever ya hav' t' break th' heart of 'nother? It must be th' hardest thing ya hav' t' do."

I knew from observing long ago that the minister was familiar with misfortune. Somehow she would have the right words to say to Harness's wife, I assured myself.

— XX —

THE TRUTH TALKED ABOUT

Looking down at a knothole in the oak boards that line my porch floor, I watch as the sun filters its way to the predetermined location, indicating one o'clock. I determined earlier that as the sun makes its way through a crack in the wooden shingles to that knot, it is reasonably close to that time of day. Close by, a spider makes her way to who knows where.

There is not much on the road today. The mail carrier will likely be the next traveler. Blaze, my dog, senses the carrier long before my ears pick up the sound of hooves. Getting the paper delivered to my home is a luxury I choose to afford. It keeps me informed of the news and gossip. I anxiously await this week's printing since it will include the editor's take on the killing.

Suddenly, Blaze's ears move as he raises his head to get a better perception of something in the distance. Lying there with energy like a coiled spring ready to vault at anything out of the way, he looks at me for approval to investigate. I give him a little nod to stay put, but as the sound becomes louder, he raises to his feet. That allows me to grab his shaggy coat so he won't get the thunder kicked out of him by the mailman's horse. The horse pulls up to within arm's length of my

THE TRUTH TALKED ABOUT

porch and I reach from the rocker to retrieve the paper and a couple of duns.

He clears his overfilled jaw of tobacco by spitting toward the woodpile, and drawls, "Howdy, how's ever'thin' goin'?"

He is one of those who carry the news in more than one way. A raw-boned man, with knobby knees, elbows and knuckles. Of all God's creation, he is one whose beauty was sparsely rationed. As Boy declares, "No doubt, th' ugliest man in th' county!" But that doesn't affect the carrier's self-esteem. He kicks his right foot from the wooden stirrup and throws his bony leg over the pommel and blurts, "Ever'bidy over't town 'lows th' sheriff has Elias Rohrbach locked up fir th' killin'. Nobidy knows who done it, an' proley neer will!"

"We'll see, the law has it now, somebody's sure to rat on the killers," I reply.

"Time 'll tell, no tellin' what'll 'come of 't," he mutters. Taking a bite out of a cud of tobacco with the few remaining snags of teeth, the carrier sorts through some mail in the leather bag slung across the saddle.

With beady eyes, he looks back toward me with his heavy mustache and overgrown eyebrows, aware of the beautiful weather, states "Purty day, hain't it?" Without waiting for a reply, he looks to my garden. "Garden lookin' mighty good, too." The sun noticeably beaming through the fluffy, floating clouds - shining so brightly it seems one could light a pipe by them.

"Not bad, not bad at all," I reply anxiously wanting to begin reading the paper and hoping he soon gets his animal's mind and mouth off my roses and on to his deliveries.

He takes an old rag out of his flannel pocket to rub over his brow, going under his tattered hat to his balding head. "Better git on," he garbles as he kicks the sides of his horse, whose flanks shine wet with sweat from the trip thus far.

As he pulls away, I cannot help comparing his horse to

those who have performed similar functions in the past. My mind goes to the Pony Express and those who sped from their stops to race on to their next destination. It is said that a Pony Express horse was considered broken "when a rider could lead them out of the stable without getting his head kicked off!" Unlike the Pony Express, our man has time to socialize and his horse has developed the same unhurried attitude as well.

Opening the paper, my eyes fall to the long-awaited front-page news. The Grant County Gazette, May 13, 1921, reads as follows.

"Murdered"

"Harness Bibs* Shot From Ambush in Hopeville Gap."

"We do not suppose there is any right thinking mind in the county but that deplores the tragedy of last Saturday, and is willing to do all they can to bring the murderer to justice.

Human beings have been killed by their fellow man before in this county, but they were usually attended by circumstances that in a way relieved the slayer. In the present case it is different. Harness Bibs* had many enemies, tis true. Whether it was his fault or not is useless to discuss. The glaring fact confronts us that a man lay in wait and deliberately shot Bibs*. The mindless, cowardly and dastardly act a man can commit.

Bibs* had been in Petersburg most of the day Saturday and about two o'clock started for his home up the North Fork. At Hopeville, he turned up the Gap and after going about one-half mile, his murderer, who was waiting among the rocks, fired, shooting him in the head, causing instant death. The horse [Bibs] was riding continued for about one hundred yards and it, too, was shot.

It was about four o'clock when Bibs's* body was found lying along the side of the road. The alarm was quickly given and an

THE TRUTH TALKED ABOUT 135

effort was made to get bloodhounds but none could be obtained. Squire Roby empaneled a Coroner's jury who discovered the deceased came to his death at the hands of parties unknown.

Sheriff Kimble came over Sunday night and with Pros. Atty. I. D. Smith took charge of the case, both of whom have been very active in an effort to unearth the perpetrators of the crime.

On Monday evening, Sheriff Kimble arrested Elias Rohrbach* upon suspicion and he is held awaiting a preliminary examination."

Looking up from the paper, I can see Pap in the distance making his way down the ridge to read the latest, or better stated, have it read to him. Bless his heart! If it were not for my honesty, I could tell him anything. He's in a dead run, in a matter of speaking, not too fast. The fast has left for the safe. He has learned that he'd rather go slow than tumble down the ridge. As everyone, Pap anxiously awaits the news, feeling perhaps the writer has some information we are not privy to, having had opportunities to talk to the law officers. Pap listens intently as I read the article to him, frowning once in a while. Only once does he say, "hold 't, go back over th' part 'bout, the mind cowardly and dastardly act." So I read it again, still not sure he understands.

I had also gotten the Keyser paper, "The Mountain Echo," dated May 14, 1921, to get their take on the story. Opinions form as I read the stories, but not a word, only moans and facial contortions from Pap, expressing anger and disbelief.

"Farmer Ambushed"

"And Horse and Rider Shot by Unknown Assailants in Grant County Sunday Morning" (Sunday is a known mistake - the killing happened Saturday).

"Harness Bibs*, age 40, a farmer of near Hopeville, Grant County, was shot from his horse and instantly killed by unidentified parties at North Fork Gap, several miles West of Petersburg, last Saturday morning.

The shooting is thought to have been the outcome of ill feelings against Bibs* in that neighborhood. Bibs*, it was said, had been accused of informing on moonshiners to revenue officers and had been told by residents of that section to leave. It is also alleged that Bibs* had informed on a draft evader and had gained animosity in that.

Several shots were fired by more than one gunman as the horse Bibs* was riding through the gap was shot and killed the same time as the rider."

The writer of the local paper seems to feel as most that this might have been justifiable homicide if only the victim would have had a chance.

Pap spoke up, "Yea, an' th' story might be wrote different if ole Harness had a seen 'em first."

To add to Pap's thinking, I add, "He might have at least escaped and met them on equal terms. Well, if they hadn't allowed jealousy to become so deeply rooted. If Bibs hadn't turned them in, he would no doubt be here today and his family would not have to suffer through this."

Elias Rohrbach is a suspect because he was known to have courted Harness's wife. He became suspect when his horse was seen tied outside the residence when Harness was known to be away. Many saw him make the trek across the five ridges that separated their houses. The relationship may have been blossoming to the point that he wanted Harness out of the way. Everyone says he has an alibi that positions him with others that day. But they may be lying to cover for him. Arnie and Wilbur certainly are suspects since it is believed that Harness had them arrested for being slackers.

As soon as the needed evidence gets in, they will have their day in court. Most hate to get involved. To suggest Elias as the guilty party would be to separate a man from his family and to implicate the boys would put them away again and for a much longer time. Some figure that living with guilt will be punishment enough. Others reason that Harness had it coming to him. Then, too, some do not want to say anything that might incriminate them. If nothing more, the subject of their involvement with moonshine might come up.

Some are humbled by the incident and refuse to hide behind pride. They rather are ashamed that the community must be tarnished and upset by this uncivilized act. I often talk with Pap, who is especially broken by the incident and what it has done to disrupt the community. He assures me that all will be well with the passing of time. He says time is not such a cheap commodity and it's a shame to waste it on foolishness, but when men are full of wrath, all must suffer. Like floods, the scars will soon disappear from the land and thoughts of most folk. Only those who have been directly affected will care.

Pap and I find ourselves against the Four Knobs overlooking Harness's gravesite. Harness didn't have the stature as others, so few attended. Pap lays aside some of his usual jesting and seems to be anxious to get settled to the service. Sister Dolly opens with the thought that you can be sure your sins will find you out, and that God's love contains forgiveness for whosoever will. A tear makes its way down a crease on her cheek to be dried with an ever-present hanky, as she opens her heart in love. It was a tear of concern that comes from empathy.

She stresses, "Them who done this evil 'll have t' give a 'count, as them who do any kind a evil." She spends much time emphasizing the need to bind together.

Everyone forms a circle to sing a closing hymn and

again realize their dependence upon God and each other. The congregation leaves, as do I, feeling somewhat uplifted, knowing that there is a place where the weary soul can come to find rest in times of trouble. There are tempers and many questions, yet a confident hope that this will be an end to this violence.

Standing off to themselves at Bibs's gravesite are Jess Bass, Pete and Jeb. Martin made his efforts to pay respects as well. In the mind of each was the incident at the schoolhouse when Brose lifted Jess from his horse. Plaguing Martin's mind is the harassment Jess displayed earlier at Hopeville.

Before leaving the mountain, Pap hopes to travel on to the Cornshakle farm to see its monstrous bovine. Pap had heard about it and just had to see it for himself. He makes his way to talk to Woodrow. I anxiously follow, wanting to see the beast as well.

There is a fair amount of turmoil and distrust after the killing. The old folks don't think kindly of people convicting the boys until the verdict is in.

Before leaving the gravesite, we find a seat on some surrounding rocks. Pap leans forward and closes one eye as he begins. "Purty weather we're havin'." He knew Woodrow attended the funeral out of respect and not that he wished to talk of Harness or his death since his son was a prime suspect.

Woodrow, always glad to see Pap, answers, "Yea, th' weathers been good, rains come in time, 'pears like we'll have a good season."

Pap continues, "Woodrow, I hear tell ya have a awful bull over 't yer place."

Woodrow replies with a slight grin, "Well, yea, Pap, I reckon ya could say that. Won't ya come on over an' take a look at 'im?"

Without missing a step, Martin joins us as we take the road further west. It has been more than a few miles to get here for the funeral, now we are walking further into the mountains. Worse yet, Mom will be expecting our return before midnight! Before Pap and Woodrow get done talking, I'm sure darkness will overtake our trip home, causing us to be traveling through the eerie Gap under the canopy of a blackened sky.

Jess and the boys pull up to us on their animals not far from the cemetery. Jess hadn't had a fight for a while and was looking for a diversion. He also, being eager to determine who is the better man, he or Martin, states, "'ave ya seen that heifer Jezebel since I'd last seen 'er?"

Martin turns on his heels to engage the mountain man. Once again Jess hasn't the time to react before realizing himself being drug to the ground. The large boned giant quickly rises to his feet. Before a full recovery is made, the quicker Martin places a well-intended fist to Jess's nose. Blood spurts from both nostrils. Jeb and Pete come to his side. Jess pushes them away shouting still, "There 'll be 'nother day!" Anxiously, we move on to the Cornshakle place.

Upon reaching the Cornshakle farm, Woodrow takes us by the hog pen to show off his prize sows, some with pigs. In another pen basking in the mud lays a boar, the size of a cow. For an instant, Pap thinks this is the animal everyone is talking about. "Woodrow, I 'clare if that's not th' biggest hog I ere seen!"

Woodrow throws a couple of ears of corn over the rails to get him up. The beast rises to its feet to satisfy an insatiable hunger – its appetite an allegory of want. Woodrow has something else to show his visitors and leads us down the path to the barn. We wait by the fence that surrounds the barn. Pap places his hands on the top rail and leans forward to peer between the rails. Woodrow begins calling to an animal we could see just glimpses of through the barn logs. He rattles the trough and out through the mud tramps the largest bull ever to set foot on the mountain. Flat footed, he easily towers over the fence. Pap, with eyes as big as saucers, quickly exclaims, "My, my, my, what 'll he weigh, Woodrow? Looks like you've done an' corralled a buffalo!"

"I have no idie, but some of 'em guess a ton," Woodrow answers, as he rubs the bull's massive head, then the huge hump over its neck and runs his fingers through the curly hair that lines the back. "He's a pet, but does his part 'round here."

Our stomachs are finally set down to enjoy the bounties of the mountain. As always, there is hog meat and vegetables from the garden. Woodrow asks Pap to say grace, to which he appeals to God to help this family in time of need, and thank Him "fir th' pervisions." The prayer sounds more like a prayer for strength to endure, rather than one of blessing and to enjoy the food provided for us.

We eat more than enough and move to the porch, where stories and conversation continues. Mom Cornshakle and the girls put things away. We sit gazing at the countryside.

To the west is the Black Place, the Sods lay behind us, and the Open Ridge School stands in the skyline to the east. Against North Mountain stand two rock pinnacles: Chimney Rocks and Seneca Rocks. These structures we can see from Woodrow's porch. They rise perpendicularly from the slope of the mountain, to the height of several hundred feet above the surrounding forest. They tower as obelisks or spires of gigantic masonry, whose summits seem to touch the clouds.

At the base of Seneca Rocks, the Mouth of Seneca empties into the North Fork River. Setting beside the North Fork Turnpike and the pack-horse road coming across the Alleghanies from Beverly is a small village. There is about one-half dozen families who live there, with the conveniences of a store, post office, a blacksmith's shop, a schoolhouse, and a meetinghouse and what used to be an apple-jack distillery.

As we set on the porch, Woodrow sees he has my attention and anxiously pulls a story from his vast repertoire. "Some time back," he begins, "I'd a pretty fair horse an' was a comin' out a town when a young feller pulled up 'longside me, an' wanted t' race. I took a quick look at th' slip of a feller an' his horse. My horse had better blood in its veins than most ole mountain hacks, but he was a settin' astraddle a young'un. He wanted t' put up a ten dollar bill fir th' race, an' I said alrighty, ya got yerself a bet, ... figurin' I could use th' money an' would be 'llright. I grabbed m' rifle tighter, an' kicked th' sides of m' mare. Th' young horse took off, like scered by a haint. First thing ya know, th' young feller's horse run int' a saplin' branch that spooked 'im. Fin'ly got straightened out an' we was a ridin' neck an' neck 'till we come ont' flock a chickens an' some women a comin' from milkin', in th' road. Chickens an' milk splattered in ever' direction. Next thing I knowed, his horse took t' a ditch an' sent him sailin' head over heels.

"Well, all that scered my horse, causin' her t' run fir dear life. She was heavin' fir air an' out a control. I pulled on th' reins 'til m' shoulders ached, but didn't do no good, 'cause th' bit was in her teeth. Finally I got 'er turned t' home, but there at th' gate was m' big Berkshire sow a sucklin' 'er pigs - thirteen of 'em an' not a runt in th' bunch. M' mare's forefeet hit right square int' th' litter, killin' some an' crippling what lived. Once t' th' barn door, I turned 'er in, where she dropped t' 'er hams, tuckered out. As she was a goin' down th' gun went off an' killed m' big red rooster. But m' fall was broke when I hit m' hound dog layin' there sleepin'. Worst thing t' find out, I broke three of m' dog's ribs!"

Being the first to question, I ask, "Did you ever get your ten dollars?"

Woodrow chuckles as he responds, "Al, I seen 'im a comin' up th' lane a limpin', but didn't have th' heart t' ask 'im fir th' ten dollars."

Pap and Woodrow talk of simpler times, and acquaintances, both living and past. Eventually, Pap turns the subject to home. "Woodrow, we'd better be headin' off th' ridge 'fore nightfall."

Woodrow returns with mountain hospitality, "Al, ain't no use goin' this late, you fellers jist as well stay th' night."

Pap returns, "Well, I would, but we got th' animals t' look after." All the while, I am hoping he will oblige the offer. He continues, "Mebie next time." Pap turns toward Woodrow, then to the meadow. I think I hear sadness in his voice, knowing both are getting older, and realizing the stress Woodrow is under with his son. Pap finishes, "Next time I come, we'll plan t' stay th' day, and mebie do some huntin'."

Woodrow follows us to the edge of the porch, where he bids, "Don't make it s' long next time, till ya come. Ya be cereful off th' ridge."

Martin heads across the rise to his home and we decide to go down Wolford hollow to leave the mountain, allowing us to avoid the Gap, but adding a mile or two to our walk.

While walking, I ask Pap, "Do you reckon that story about the horse race is true?" Pap answers, "Ya should a ask 'im, seen what he'd a said. Poor ole Woodrow has had 'nough trouble lately t' drain th' sap of life right out a him, but he kin still banter a feller."

While walking off the mountain, a Barred Owl sounds from a tree top. The stars and moon do their best to brighten the sky and shine some light on our path as we pass Hopeville. Providing some company are the yellow lights shining from farmhouse windows. One more ridge to climb and we will see the lights of home.

— XXI —

HE'S NOT A RELIGIOUS MAN

Harness's death is the focal point of every conversation - either he or the conviction of the killers. The Hopeville Meeting House is especially popular. It gives folks a special reason to attend, arrive a little earlier and stay later. Today, Pap courageously honors the congregation as he plays "O Happy Day," then follows singing the verse, "Happy day, happy day, When Jesus worshed m' sins away! He taught me how t' watch an' pray, An' live rejoicin' ever'day. Happy day, happy day, When Jesus worshed m' sins away!"

The locals, families from up the Gap, and some from the Four Knobs, came down Wolford Hollow to attend the service. After service, men and women stand out front and speculate as to who did the killing and what will happen to Harness's family. The most memorable comment I've heard while under the oak was from Arlie, in his usual backwoods draw, "Ere, 'ell back ere on th' moun'ain, there's talk of Arnie an' Wilbur a runnin' scered."

If only we could rid our lives of those who make and sell moonshine. That is asking too much out of most men. As blame is placed, Mom demands, "It's them no good boys on th' mountain an' th' makin' of moonshine that's brung sech trouble!"

Pap cannot let the remark lie as he responds kindly, "Mom, hold it there, th' boy's ain't all bad, they have some good. I figure they's some good in 'bout anybidy. Th' boy's 'ould do anything fir me, er most fir that matter, but they 'tend t' settle this score."

Mom, like many granny women, has the vice of dipping snuff. Often, one can see snuff-stained teeth and a broom straw protruding from their mouth. The excuse is medicinal, such as, cuts, wasp stings, helps with digestion. I heard Mom some time ago ask our own Sister Dolly in a most deliberate manner, "Will my usin' snuff keep me out a heaven?" To which our pastor responded most compassionately, "Why no, honey, all they want up there is yer soul."

Pap tells a story of an elderly woman who condemned a minister for drinking coffee. The woman adamantly declared, "It's a sin t' drink that wicked, strong stuff!" Sometime later, the minister had the occasion to visit the woman and saw her snuff use, to which he declared, "That snuff dippin' 's a sin!" The poor woman was somewhat taken, but humbly replied, "Surely t' goodness, somethin' that tastes s' good, can't be all that bad!"

Religion, moonshine and other vices are always opponents in the mountain arguments. They are as poles as far apart as North and South. To defend one's actions or the actions of another, the usual defense is to proclaim, "They're not religious nohow!" They make the comment, almost bragging. Pap says it's usually the non-religious that bring wrath on this community. I suppose it's their way of proclaiming strength. Inwardly, they must know that it takes a lot more strength to restrain from alcohol, adultery, and other vices. Pap reminds me, "Th' true Christian never hurts nobidy – not without them a needin' it!" He continues, "Real strength comes from th' inside. Settin' a good moral example is more important in buildin' a decent place t' live, than slanderin' th' godly! Don't ya worry, when they lose their health, money an' friends, they'll see their need of God!"

As I lie on my bed, Pap's words keep ringing in my head about the religious man. I have heard men brag about not being religious, almost giving them a license to do whatever. They do as they wish and live the life they want with little restraint or concern for their fellow man. Reinforcing the ideas in my head is the reality that most of our congregations are made up of the female gender. More than one congregation is supported almost entirely by women. Men somehow leave minding the kids and spiritual leadership up to their spouses.

Feeling a bit of inspiration, I know I had better put my thoughts on paper before morning - that will be too late. Reaching to the side of the bed, I fumble to find the wick stem of the oil lamp and turn the light to full brilliance.

"HE'S NOT A RELIGIOUS MAN"

The story is told, tis true,
About a man who made some dew:
   He was excused by the local clan,
   For he was not a religious man.

He lived his life for himself,
Cussed, cheated, disregarded his health;
   It was overlooked that he didn't stand,
   For he was not a religious man.

His wife and kids all went astray,
Couldn't understand why they went that way;
   But was approved by those he ran,
   For he was not a religious man.

Then one day he pillowed his head,
Too proud to regret the life he'd led;
   Tearfully, God said he'd built on the sand,
   For he was not a religious man.

HE'S NOT A RELIGIOUS MAN

As quickly as the room had been brightened, it darkens as I turn back the wick, bringing an end to another day. While awaiting sleep, I relive the recent happenings in and around our community. I think of Maynard and where he must be tonight. I wonder if Big Jake and Ocie have gotten over their ill feelings. I remember the evening at the church social when Ocie moved his hand ever so secretly under his bibs. I think of the tearing in the hearts of Martin and Sara Jane. If only culture would allow their union.

Coming to memory are the boys on the mountain who are scared because of all the incriminating talk, and Elias is yet nervous. He had been hanging around Harness's house when Harness was away. He had been hauled in for questioning, but there was not enough hard evidence to place him at the crime scene and he was soon let go. It was determined that he was home at the time of the incident. There is a chance that his name will resurface, however, because of the allegations.

The next court term doesn't come up until April and by that time, Sheriff Kimble hopes to have enough evidence to have the boys tried. Evidence is mounting as he makes his rounds and listens to the gossip of the locals and townspeople alike. He has questioned those who served Harness in town that May 7th and those who heard the threats made by the boys. By court term, he should be ready to try those who are of suspicion. Until then they will be free to roam the mountain.

— XXII —

APPALACHIA'S HEART

No doubt, one of the greatest pictures that can be painted as I look out my cabin window is one of my rich loam garden in June. Added to this portrait is a charcoal gray sky sending a gentle rain down to water the plants and refill my pond.

This is a steady one - appears it has set in for the day. The low Nimbus clouds have blanketed the sky with no indications that they are about to move. It is a fine, slow rain, with no wind to shake the moisture from the already burdened greenery, laden with this year's crop. Farmers say that after this refreshing, you can "hear th' corn grow" and maybe you can, because it grows so rapidly. Surely, ole Ped must be happy to see his corn at Hopeville jump from the ground.

On days like today, there is nothing better to do than to catch up on some reading and do a few things inside. There is always a danger of getting too casual and sleeping the day away. Blaze has already taken advantage of that and the heat from the Home Comfort. I love the thunder as it roars overhead. Pap laughingly jests, "God has gone an' upset th' tator wagon." As the rain pounds on my metal roof, it soon lulls me to sleep, but that's okay. This is my reward for doing plenty the many days before and there will be more weeds to hoe as a result of this.

Summer always brings with it unlimited chores. The hay crop is top priority since the animals depend upon it for next winter and I on them for my existence. The summer Timothy is waist high with full tops, indicating their degree of ripeness and readiness to be cut. It must be cut at its highest, but not in the seed. Seeds rob nutrition from the blades, and since cows cannot digest seeds, it is of little value.

I am fortunate to have a sickle bar mower to cut hay and two fine Belgians to provide the power. Without a doubt, the most important rule regarding mowers is that a person should never operate one if he is inexperienced with horses. The chatter of the cutter bar and the noise of the cogs as they ratchet causes excitement with horses.

Some say that you're a lazy, inconsiderate horse owner if you ride the machinery. To do so places extra stress on the horses; of course, that's different when it comes to a mower. I sometimes justify a ride, realizing the role of my horses and their tremendous strength. They handle the John Deere mower like a child with a toy, as they pull it around the field. The Timothy rolls off the cutter bar like trees falling under a great "Northerner." Farmers around here rake the hay with a buggy rake, then make shocks and drag them to the stack by wrapping a rope around the bottom to pull them. The most difficult work is creating a stack so the rain will run off. Those techniques are learned early.

Some have oats that must be threshed, but must wait for the thresher to move through the area. These are pulled by a giant steam engine. The only other steam engine in these parts is the one at the sawmill. Most of the crew comes with the thresher and are paid by the bushel. These steam engines are as slow as molasses in winter, but are not denied when pulling a load. They sure aren't as personal, but can do the work of many of our horses and do not get tired.

Pap paid a visit last evening, which went well into the

night. Before leaving, he got around to asking me to help "git" his hay in as soon as it dries off. Since he doesn't have any decent equipment, my mower and team come in handy. He only has an old spavin, wind-broken mare, a milk cow, and a few sheep, so it doesn't take much winter feed. The most difficult thing about working his place is maneuvering the steep hills. It's common to experience the sliding of iron wheels down the hill with each pass. But I feel pretty safe with all that horseflesh out in front. My two Belgians weigh about a ton each. It is somewhat like hanging on to a giant kite as the wind slings it through the air. Actually, I enjoy working behind my team, and to think, I actually get paid for doing it - indirectly. When I feel the mower slide, all I have to do is hold on to the upper side for dear life.

The hay has dried sufficient to allow me to get in Pap's field in early morning. With everything working fine and the mowing completed, the fallen hay looks great basking in the sun. I head the team to the house for supper. After tying the team by the barn, I stop by the porch to wash up. Grabbing the dipping gourd from the post, I enjoy a big swig of mountain water. It comes to the house through an aqueduct made of locust logs. These were drilled and laid end to end in a ditch from a spring against New Creek to the back porch where water shoots out about twelve feet. Winter's freeze makes this the most ornate sculptor display of all creation.

Mom has supper ready and again fixes enough to feed a small army. Her company never gets up from the table without a second helping. Always the statement, "Ya sure wadn't very hungry t'night, was ya?" She has the usual summer staples this evening: "tators," beans, bread, side meat, garden vegetables, and more than a few kinds of jelly. All are picked nearby and "put up" in the cellar. After the main course, we help ourselves to dessert, where awaits Blackberry Cobbler.

"I'll have some pie with a helping of sweet cream over it," I suggest.

Conversation continues as Pap, with gray hair and a philosopher's face, looks toward Hopeville, then to the Four Knobs and the Sods. He always seems to know what is critical and what is peripheral. The shock that has hit the community has been devastating. People wandered in and out of the Gap every day to view the site where Harness was shot. Trophy hunters have already collected a piece of horse skull, a horseshoe, and a 32 caliber shell.

Pap says, "I wonder what 'll 'come of his wife?" We knew the gossip and that she had not been faithful to him, but are sympathetic; after all, there are two sides to every story. Most knew Elias Rohrbach had been sparking her.

I reminded Pap, "You know he was arrested a while back."

Pap, in his motionless way, responds, "Elias could be th' blame fir th' killin'. Mebe he put th' boys up t' it. An' I'll tell ya 'nother thing, dadburn if I don't believe ole Hense is a holdin' in somethin' more than air!"

"It does make sense," I answer, then continue, "Pap, you might just be on to something, but don't forget that the trouble started when Harness turned the boys in for evading the Army. They no doubt took matters into their own hands by killing him. Then, too, we cannot overlook the business they were wrapped up in. Everyone knows about the jealousy over their moonshine sales. At any rate, that has fueled many conflicts."

We talk of the good church services lately and the comforting sermons. Pap reminded me of the sermon in the Grant County Gazette, dated May 6, 1921, that I read to him the day Harness was killed. It discussed God's will in our lives. He understood the gist of the article and brought up a good point, but I am not sure these have much impact on our rural audience. They often appear quite lofty, being the scholarship of city-educated preachers. Many of our folk have but a fifth grade education and often don't place much weight on print, which lacks a personal touch. The text was taken from Psalm 143:10 and entitled:

"The Will of God"

"The perfect organization of all the material universe ought to be sufficient evidence to any reasoning person that the God who called into being the perfectly working machine from that which had no being before has certainly done no purposeless thing, neither in the creating nor the arranging by laws of his own making, all that is.

Design, purpose and will of the greatest Architect and Designer are in abundant evidence in every star that shines and every wave that beats. Greater still are the evidences of a master Planner and Builder in the plants whose seeds produce after their kind and the animals that are so perfectly adapted to their native haunts. If these seem wonderful, and they are, how much more wonderful is He from whose loin we sprang. Adam, who was created in the image of God in the Garden of Eden, which the records infer, was so perfectly prepared to meet his need.

We are little and helpless before Jehovah, and yet, does not the fact that we have been so "fearfully and wonderfully made" indicate to the thoughtful person that we are made for a purpose, and not for no purpose? Intimate love has met every need of ours, both spiritual and physical, in the material world. Could it be possible that God cares for us enough day by day to supply all our need, even by giving His only begotten Son to make possible the salvation of such as should receive Him, and has no will for us who represent the climax of all the material creation? And if He does have a will for us, is it possible that He is willing for us to grope about, and content to see us stumble and fall in our groping to find what His will is? If He has a will, it must be better than ours, for He holds the future in the hollow of His hand. More certainly than we hold the fragmentary knowledge of the past in our puny brain matter. If He knows what thing I ought to do better than I know, I should doubt His love if I thought it were not possible for me to find out.

A knowledge of His general will was given on tables of stone for Moses, and all who would, to read, long, long ago, but we are not any more alike than two flowers are alike, so there must be small details of His will that differ as we differ. For instance, He certainly does not want everybody to teach, not to preach, nor to farm, etc. I think it was the highest personal compliment God ever paid an individual soul to have a plan for his life that differs just a little from any other plan in the world.

Certainly, no life can be said to be at its best that dares to live without making any effort to know whether God's will differs from his own. Perhaps our very curiosity makes us wonder what His will for this step and that may be, but it would be as casting pearls before swine for Him to make it plain if we had no intention whatever of obeying. Our willingness to obey before we know is no more to be criticized than the willingness of a child to learn the simple texts first given it before it is able to see what it is to learn in the future. If we only acted as the frail children we are before God, how much easier we could learn to rightly interpret His approval and His restraint as we lay our plans bare before His infinite wisdom, and His matchless love. The Holy Spirit wants to use our consciences as the vehicle for carrying the knowledge of His will, as it were, by a still small voice. If we do not harden them by disobeying the will as we already know it."

"Pap, it's tough to imagine some events as being His will, but the minister who penned that sermon may have had the mind of God and was used to prepare our hearts," I declare, as I give Pap my unsolicited opinion. For whatever the reason, these mountain people have come to accept His sovereignty.

Pap adds, as he arches his eyebrows and turns from the sink, "That's a good piece, but our preacher ain't doin' bad herself. She preaches, 'God is hindered when our will gits in th' way an' causes us t' sin. His love don't stop, but His forgiveness can't git beyond our stubbornness!' Ever'bidy knows she's a good preacher. If only these precious souls could see th' need t' 'tend our services."

I remind Pap of the Grant County Gazette, May 5, 1920 article that carried Harness's death announcement, also carried a sermon on adultery. Sermons come from impressions as ministers meditate, or see a need in the community. Pap and I had talked about the alleged courtship of Elias with Harness's wife. Incidences such as this no doubt sparked this sermon. The minister used Exodus 20:14; Matthew 5:28; I Corinthians 6:18, to address the subject.

"Thou Shalt Not Commit Adultery"

"We are dealing here with a very delicate, yet a very pertinent subject, one requiring the wisdom and tongue of an angel. However, despite our human limitations, we dare not pass by or skip the sixth commandment. It is sinned against too frequently, and such sins are too often winked at, to make its discussion unimportant and unnecessary.

Holy Writ tells us, God instituted the holy estate of matrimony to perpetuate this sacred mystery of human life. He gave the first woman to the first man and joined the two in an indissoluble union. This occurred before sin seized man's soul. Marriage is in no way responsible for the Fall, as many suppose. It is holy, not only just because it was ordained of God the Father, but also because Jesus gave it His presence at the marriage of Cana and the miracle He performed there. The Holy Spirit, likewise, pronounces a benediction upon the marriage state by likening the relation of earthly spouses to the union of Christ and the Church.

The Roman Catholic Church errs when it teaches that the marriage estate is less holy than celibacy or the unmarried estate. It also goes to the other extreme when it counts it a settlement. God simply shows that marriage is honorable and holy, and essential to the home, family, society, state, and church.

The sixth commandment is given to protect the honor of the home, to keep pure the very virtues of life by emphasizing chastity upon all.

Young men and women, this commandment forbids you to do or say anything in secret which you would be ashamed to do in the presence of honorable virtuous men and women. Guard your virtue as you would a priceless treasure, even your life. Be chaste, pure and devout in all your life so that you will never know the shame, regrets, and heartaches of the forward and indecent. If you do this, your bodies will not be polluted with loathsome diseases, nor weakened by self abuse, and you will be able to endure His holy estate of matrimony with a conscience void of offense before God and man.

In conclusion, a word to those who have entered the marriage estate. The divine purpose in instituting marriage was to enable God's children to lead chaste and decent lives in word and deed. It was intended to be a means of blessing, never an instrument of torture. Accordingly, marriage should be a union of mutual love and honor, in which the man is the head and the woman the heart, in which husband and wife enjoy consolations of each other's presence and fellowship, and mutual encouragement and assistance during life's joys and sorrows, prosperity and adversity."

While waiting for the blackberries and heavy cream to digest, we rehash the subject of adultery and the attention given to it and marriage in scripture. Another subject of equal importance and space in scripture is that of fornication, I remind Pap.

Pap answers, "It 'lmost seems it's a cruel joke fir a bidy's hormones t' kick in s' early. Why, a kid's hardly out a diapers 'til he's ready t' mate!"

"It does certainly seem unreasonable that God should permit youthful urges so young. Why didn't He wait until one was old enough to support a family?" I add.

Pap remains quiet as he reflects on the question, without a comment. I turn to the windows and see the sun beginning to fade, and the lengthening of the shadows in the timber, and back to Pap, "I had better be getting off the hill before darkness sets in."

Pap had set out a bucket of oats for the team, so they had some time to rest and eat before heading out. "Do you need anything else before I leave?" I yell as I pick up the lines.

"No, but I'll 'spect ya back in a day er two when th' hay's dry," Pap answers.

Soon, the clanging of the machinery drowns out the other evening sounds. I take it easy going home so as not to tear something up. In these mountains, it's necessary to treasure everything since it comes so hard. I had worked in a distant city and conserved enough to buy some things to get started - turns out that I have more than a lot of folk who have labored in these mountains all their lives. I just thank God I am able to help out. But then, they are always anxious to return a favor.

— XXIII —

CATCHIN' TROUT

Pap has been busy with his old mare plowing corn. His cornfield and potato patch lie against the sun-side ridge of Jordon's Run. There, Curt Rohrbach was shot by Yankee soldiers while trying to round up all the Southern sympathizers. Feeling a bullet pierce his ear, he "played 'possum." Rushing to his side, soldiers saw that blood had covered the side of his head. They gouged him with their rifle barrels only to see no movement. Figuring he was dead, they continued pursuing others.

Just across the ridge from Pap's cornfield is Gap Run where Harness was shot. There, one can stand at the High Falls and see his field as it follows the contour of the hollow. Surrounding the field are Paw Paw, Gum, Red Oak, and Locust trees. At the bottom is a faithful spring where livestock and wildlife drink. Every now and then, we place a log along the bottom to dam up the watering hole. The field is about two acres and produces pretty good crops, but only second to Ped's down on the river.

Seeing Pap's field of corn reminds me of Boy Awer's hired hand. Boy says, "Th' man 'ould work good, 'long side a me. Why, in no time we'd lay a pile a corn by. But th' low down skunk 'ould come back at night an' steal 't. I know 't fir a fact!"

I hurried to get my own work done so I would be ready to finish Pap's hay. We started raking around noonday so as to get it ready to shock by mid-afternoon. We drag them to where Pap has made stacks for the last fifty years. It's a matter of habit, I guess. He says, "Some habits kin be good, 'cause they're time savin', an' they keep a feller from strayin' too far int' unknown territory." I see him lumbering back to the house as I top out the last stack. I finish laying the fence of Chestnut Rails around the stack to keep the sheep out. Looking towards the house, smoke curls as it comes from the chimney. That's a sure sign that supper is being prepared and another night I don't have to cook.

Before going to supper, I pick up the jug of spring water we had stowed under the stack and carry it back to the spring to be refilled for another day. I'm captivated by the aroma escaping the kitchen as I stop on the porch long enough to wash my hands. I unlatch and push the worn door open to enter. Hitting me as I enter is not only the smell of food, but the smells associated with a home where old people live: the smell of cooked cabbage, hog meat, Merthiolate, and stale air as a result of some windows that are seldom opened. I grab the bench once more and sit down to a fine meal of side meat, spuds, cooked cabbage, and a salad of dandelions and watercress. We talk about an assortment of things, ranging from Pap and Mom's health issues to our plans to do some native trout fishing tomorrow.

The Rainbow, Brook and Brown Trout are the most beautiful fish in these waters. Their color may not surpass the bluegill, and size may not exceed the bass, but when one considers all the features, trout outclass the rest. Their sleek bodies enable them to maneuver riffles, jump falls and inch up fast flowing streams. When left alone, they will grow to twenty-five inches, but their predators (man and beast) prevent that. Man, bear, coon, and fox have a keen appetite for

CATCHIN' TROUT

these delicacies, thus destroying any possibility of growing to massive size.

Only the brook is indigenous to this area. They can be distinguished from both the rainbow and the brown trout because they have a greater number of lateral-line scales. Their background color is brownish to greenish and their back is laced with light, twisting, wormlike lines. The sides have some light and some red spots, both with blue halos. The first rays of its pectoral, pelvic and anal fins are milky-white, which is not true of the brown or rainbow.

The rainbow has radiating rows of black spots on the tail, back and sides, and no teeth on their tongue. They have a longitudinal reddish stripe along their side. They differ from the other two in that they spawn in the spring.

The brown has a square tail which has few or no spots. Their adipose fin has some spots. Their sides are light brown to yellowish with black spots and usually some red or orange spots. These spots often have whitish to bluish halos.

All trout prefer the cool mountain streams, although temperatures must remain slightly lower for brook trout survival; however, brook trout are found within small creeks and ponds in greater abundance than the brown trout. They feed on a variety of foods: insects, larvae, plankton, crustaceans, frogs, small fishes, fish eggs, crawfish, and worms.

Pap and I have learned some secrets of trout fishing. The best time to catch them is from the first peep of day until nine o'clock in the morning, or from five o'clock until eight in the evening. The best season is from the first of May until the last of July. During this early season, they are running up the streams and the favored bait is the common red worm. In the later months, the streams are smaller causing them to settle in deep, cooler, still water. At this time, all skilled fishermen prefer the crawfish tail. Others relish using the small grub-worm as bait. Some say that the small, rough-looking white worm, found in rotten wood, surpasses all other bait.

So there is a certain amount of opinion, season or technique connected to which bait is best. Also, one needs to master skills regarding tying and baiting the hook and using line, which will blend with the various water colors.

Pap declares that in middle of August the trout begin to decline in quality, becoming poor; the meat is dry and some even attract worms. In September, the brown and brook commence spawning. They paddle up the small streams where they may be seen in great numbers depositing their eggs in sand or aggregate beds. October comes and the brooders return to the deep water at the mouths of the warm branches or springs, where they remain until spawning time again. In February, the young trout, scarcely an inch long, can be seen in schools of a hundred, in the safety and freshness of the cool mountain streams that churn over and around rocks. They remain in these smaller streams until they are sufficiently strong enough to keep out of the way of the larger fish. Once able to take care of themselves, they swim down to the deeper water where there is plenty of food, and no chance of becoming trapped in a dried up creek.

Taking the team home off Wildcat, I watch the swaying team as they trudge along, and am blessed to see a falling star. I've seen several in these darkened skies, but that doesn't take from the magnificence. To know that they are innumerable and so many millions of miles away, yet provide a brilliance to guide the wayward traveler and enlighten our nights, gives them purpose. But perhaps the greatest mystery is to contemplate the night when the Magi were led by a star to Bethlehem to see the Christ Child. I focus on the outline of the constellations, trying to locate Job's Pleiades and Orion, which Pap has shown me plenty of times. To most, they make no more sense than gravels would if they were tossed against the sky. "Ya hafta use yer 'magination," Pap declares!

Pap and Maynard arrive early this morning. Fishing causes me to sleep with a hair trigger and I'm out of the sack by daybreak. I've been prancing the floor, anxious to go and hoping to hook a lunker.

"I have some night crawlers in a bucket," I state, as we step to the porch.

Pap interjects, "I'm set on havin' some red worms m'self, but 'll use th' night crawlers if we run short."

Out by the barn there are plenty of damp places to dig for worms, the night crawlers we'll save for eels. I raise the rocks and dig while Pap and Maynard pick worms. Soon we have enough to last the day. Blaze tags along, as we make our way up the Fork. We need to go a couple miles to Manuel Run, where it is almost certain the natives will be hitting. It is necessary to creep up on them like you sneak up on a deer. Our clothes and a day growth of beard act as camouflage. Nearly each time a squiggly worm hits the water, a wild eyed native has our line, taking it, in hopes of getting away. Most are not big enough to give one bragging rights, but every once in a while ,we snag a twelve or fourteen inch one - those with shoulders and jaws that make good stories to tell around the store.

The native trout know how to put up a fight and fend for their lives, unlike the stocked trout. Pap hollers with laughter every time he latches onto a decent one. Some can bend a pole double, but all require a mastery to balance a small line with the fierceness of the fight.

I kneel by a spring that bubbles from the bank and begin to clean our catch. The tastier ones are more pinkish because they have been in the water longer. Those I throw in a pan with a helping of cow butter for taste and savor the smell as they fry over our small fire. Pap catches a few more as I ready the fish to eat on homemade bread.

Having fought Braken Ferns and brier patches, yet satisfied to have caught several, we head for the Fork, where in the backed-up foaming water, there is sure to be Bass and Goggle Eyes waiting. The Fork also has trout, deep down, in its continual alteration of flashing rapids and transparent emerald pools. These glide amidst mirrored pictures of the graceful overshadowing trees and singular rock pinnacles, which adorn the banks. We have our favorite fishing holes, but there is one cardinal rule of every devout fisherman and that is to keep that information secret!

We stop by the blackberry patch on our trip home and begin filling a bucket we brought along for that purpose. These and more will be used for pies and such. Pap wades into the patch, seemingly unconcerned about the rattlers that may be lurking there. Everywhere our eyes fall, vines are laden with lush berries. In no time, the bucket is full and we continue homeward.

Conversation is filled with other enjoyable summertime ventures. "Sangin'" is one of them. Ginseng is used by the Orientals for medicinal purposes. Many Mountaineers go "sangin" every time they get a chance or combine the search with fishing, hunting, or working in the woods. Since early times in our history, men would eagerly dig the root to trade for salt and other articles at the markets.

Close to the mountain people is another plant, the "ramp." Ramps are dug early in the spring and can be eaten raw, but we'd rather fry them in hog lard with a helping of eggs and potatoes. Their taste is somewhat like an onion, but reacting to the acids in one's stomach makes friends few and far between. The smell can be remedied, however, when everyone eats them!

Before reaching Hopeville, the threatening rain shower breaks through the clouds. Thinking we may find adequate shelter under a ledge proves to be wrong. We continue on until we reach the store, looking like drowned muskrats. Thankfully, we find a towel and wait out the storm.

— XXIV —

ARE THESE PEOPLE REALLY THAT LAZY?

Today I sit at my desk, surrounded by the four walls of my little cabin, nestled between mountains, contemplating some observations I have made over the years. Fortunately, for me, I've been able to live, walk, talk, weep, laugh, and sit at the table of many here, and considered to be their true friend. One can use the finest rhetoric to describe situations and people, but not really know them until having gone through some of life's experiences with them. As I think of individuals that have impacted my life, I cannot help but think of the way they have been characterized by the outside.

As with all cultures, there are unique characteristics among all groups. Appalachians have been characterized as illiterate, gun-totin', moonshine guzzling hillbillies. They have been viewed as a subculture and taken advantage of, or were simply given a government check and ignored. Unfortunately, many gladly accept these subsidies. They have been treated unfairly, victimized, been characterized as "dumb hillbillies," while at the same time, there are unique traits in people everywhere, who in no way meet a standard. But there are some reasons that have caused him to be handicapped. The mountaineer has suffered from his lack of business education, opportunities, and exploitation by outside entrepreneurs. However, within the mountain communities, one can see that family obligations and a good work ethic are important to most.

The question posed has been asked frequently when a passerby has viewed some of our laid-back lifestyles and some, no doubt, deserve that description. Appalachians are stereotyped as folk reclining on the front porch with a demijohn filled with moonshine, barefooted, and wearing shredded, dirty clothes. The house is usually depicted with chickens peering out the kitchen window, with someone sitting on the outhouse facility. Why don't they have a job? someone asks. These probably do not want one - that is a steady one or cannot find one without traveling some distance. While one does not see too many mountaineers vagrant like the Gypsy, they may work just enough to earn the necessities of life. They have a different list of priorities and the accumulation of things is not one of them.

There are those, however, who work from sunup to sundown, which the critics ignore. Then there are those that have been dealt a hand that is difficult to overcome and struggle every day of their existence. The mountaineer has a difficult image to overcome and there are some who have done so. Perhaps another way to view the Appalachian is to understand his values and his priorities.

The mountain folk, for the most part, do not have very much interest in things outside these mountains because they seem a million miles away. Most of these things have little impact on them and they cannot change the situation anyway. The things that really matter are those that directly affect their lifestyle and the way people relate to them. All too often they view themselves as looked down upon, or that they are second-class citizens. They, at times, may act proud, which is but a facade to overcome the intimidation felt when townspeople are around.

Even within the mountains, there can be discrimination. There are those from the city and the country people. Many view the townspeople as looking down on the country folk. It is said that they strut around like they are a cut above those from the country. The exception to this is Sara Jane, who has won our hearts. She comes to our socials and accepts us for who we are in our hearts and not our outward fashions. Truth is, she values the transparent and honest ideals found in Martin and most of the folks here.

There are negative overtones when one works in the woods or with the soil as opposed to those who run businesses. In the country, there are one or two who have large river bottom farms that have respect, but there are many who earn a mere existence. They do this on a few acres, or working for a timber entrepreneur who usually lives in town.

Our rural kids attend school only to the eighth grade, and usually not that long. The older boys normally must begin working to help the family, and the older girls either get "in th' family way" or do not see the need to continue their education. They see their future as becoming housewives and marrying one of the local boys. The children from town have the privilege to attend school until the twelfth grade and do so because they have been shown the advantages of being well educated. It would be cost prohibitive to provide boarding for our children so they could access the same privilege.

The cycle continues because of this formal education experience. Normally, those who continue school become more successful businessmen. It is true that rural folk may own some timber, but the businessmen from town who market it get rich. The training our young men receive from their employment does not prepare them for high dollar jobs. Even if they should inherit the home place, it is divided between several children, causing it to become less supportive.

The country folk are marked by the way they walk, by

the way they talk, and by their social circles. Education and cultural opportunities have cultivated a certain style for the townspeople, whereas the rural folk's vernacular prevents communication in certain circles and inhibits business opportunities. All of this attitude and demeanor often makes our children shy and lacking confidence.

There is a noticeable difference in the dress fashions of the country folks as compared to the townspeople. There is the city-bred merchant dressed in his fustian frock and the backwoodsman with his linsey or leather hunting shirt, or the farmer with his bibs and coat, or the wagoner with his flannel vest. Today, because of the financial standing, our children frequently are seen with feed sack material sown to make a dress or shirt.

This trend may even follow them to the grave. The townsfolk make the front page of the local paper. Harness's death announcement made the fourth page! Granted, he didn't own a large farm, or sign large checks, but his death affected many. "Why didn't his death make headlines?" they ask.

Pap scolds me for thinking these things. Although he never voices his feelings regarding this, I see it in his actions. For the most part, I try to be on the upbeat, but I cannot hide the fact when our people are treated inferiorly. He constantly says, "Over there th' grounds level. Ever'bidy's th' same over there!" That keeps these folks going in the struggles of life. If only men could recognize each other for their true worth, rather than what they possess!

Mom, who is nearing her journey's end, is such a huge asset toward helping me understand the inequalities. She, with that look of contentment, focuses on the things we have: food, water, and the ability to breathe - the necessities of life. They remind me that the most important thing is to be able to pillow your head, knowing you have made a positive moral difference and have not harmed anyone undeservingly.

— XXV —

THE COUNTRY FOLK

Late summer brings with it scores of jobs needing done to help face the winter. Wood cutting ranks among the largest of them. I need to get my woodshed full and help others who do not have the strength. As I was thinking of Pap, I hear footsteps on the porch. The timing is right, because I need to get my crosscut saw sharpened.

"Pap, do you want anything to eat?" Acting as if he doesn't hear me, which may be the case, he walks over to the stove and feebly pours himself a cup of coffee. On the table sets sweet cream to flatter the taste. He makes his way across the kitchen to the wooden table and pulls out the bench, worn free of splinters, and sits down. His thickened fingers unable to fit in the cup's handle, he pinches it as one would the tail of a squirming fish, then brings the coffee to his lips. Next time, I will set out another. On the table there's a bowl of onions, some homemade bread, and cow butter. The onions are Pap's delicacy.

"Here's something that'll stick with ya," I state as I set the potatoes and warmed-up ham down in front of him.

"We'd better say grace," but Pap already has his head bowed for it. With that, he begins as usual. "We thank thee,

Lord, fir yer pervisions, thank ya agin fir all yer benefits, our health, our friends an' fam'ly, an' we pray fir them less fortunate. Most of all, thank ya fir yer Son that giv' his life fir our sins. Now we ask ya t' bless this here food t' our bidies an' our bidies t' yer service. In yer Son's name we pray. Amen."

"I'd rather eat a onion dipped in coarse salt, an' fried tators, than ary a thing on God's green earth," he declares as he lifts the iron skillet to rake out some potatoes. Having done that, he dips a large onion in salt and takes a bite out of it as one would an apple.

Pap lifts the once-defined hat from his head and with a flannel sleeve wipes his forehead. His gray hair is in disarray from the sweaty walk off the ridge. After clanging the spoon against the side of the cup, he stirs the heavy cream and begins sipping. "I hear tell th' law has its eyes on Harness's killers, 'bout ready t' round 'em up."

"Well, it seems to me somebody needs to be brought to justice, but that takes time," I add.

Still sitting on the bench, he looks out the sink window to the mountain, "Th' sheriff might have more trouble than he bargain fir, when it comes t' takin' 'em t' jail. It'd be mighty temptin' fir 'em t' skip th' country. If they'd done their killin' an' kept their mouths shut, nothin' would be knowed as t' who done 't. But ya kin 'lways be sure yer sins 'll find ya out!" Pap adds as he lifts his cup to his mouth.

Having finished breakfast and gotten things put away, we move to the porch. I pull my heavy coat around my ears to beat the morning chill. Pap picks up the crosscut leaning against the door jam and asks, "I guess you're a needin' yer saw filed?"

"Pap, I don't know how you can time your visits so well," as I attempt to hand him a second cup of coffee.

He nods for me to set it on the nearby stump. His experienced hands guide the file across the teeth, bringing them in tune as a violinist brings life to notes. It's a very meticulous job and must be done in a precise way.

Sawing wood is one time you need to conserve every bit of energy possible. Sawing with one who doesn't know how will work you to exhaustion before the job is done. The theory is to let the saw do the work as you pull the blade. Pap says, "Ya never pursh, jist pull." He's done it for years, so I guess his advice is trustworthy.

Pap again can't resist telling me of the fellow who, when asked how he felt, would always say, "I feel like a crosscut saw!" Each time Pap tells this same story, he rears back and laughs, and reminds me of what the guy meant. "It takes two men t' handle 'im!" We've got men like that in these mountains. The townspeople might have it over them in polish, but when it comes to being a man, well, there's no contest. Pap has told dozens of stories of those who "cleaned house" when a fight arose with some cocky town boys.

Pap has the saw ready and lifts the coffee to his mouth. Looking down over the glistening teeth, it is apparent they are in tune and well set for the day's work. Pap again reminds me, "Ya know that th' set is right if a needle will slide from one end t' th' other, sort a like a plow in a furrie." With that, we empty our cups.

I pack a can of apple butter, bread, a couple of tomatoes, and some water to enjoy later. Pap has a sandwich tucked in his pocket (his trademark). We look about the place, trying to see the horses - with no luck - then beat against the feed trough. Over toward the stand of oaks, we hear a giant pounding of the earth as the horses come to attention.

Only needing one horse today, I grab Barney's mane and lead him to the stall. The fact that he has been around unforeseen circumstances longer makes me more comfortable. He stands sixteen hands tall which makes it a chore to get the heavy harness over him. But he stands there attentively as many times before. With that chore completed, Pap picks up the reins as I shoulder the saw and pick up the poke of food.

Having fastened the axe and wedges to the harness, we're on our way.

"The tree that had fallen with last winter's ice storm on North Mountain will make a good start," I tell Pap. The walk is nice to the riverbank. Here it becomes rocky, swift and chilly. Barney doesn't mind anything, it seems. His huge frame takes to obstacles like nothing is unconquerable. The fallen tree just needs the limbs and butt trimmed. It was a widow-maker for sure, but since it was already down, no one need fear that. Some of the limbs are so large that they need the saw; others we trim with the double-bitted axe. Having done that, Pap swings Barney into position. With the grabs secured, I'm careful in connecting the singletree to them. More than one logger has fewer fingers while making the connection. Barney lunges toward the harness with a massive heave, causing timbers to crack. Pap roars with laughter as the dormant oak tears loose from the entanglement that has held it for so long.

It's a relief to reach the river where the buoyancy of the log makes it pull easier. By the time we near the opposite shore, the log is washed free of the dirt once wedged in its bark. Pap pauses to give Barney and himself a breather after the steep climb from the riverbank. Although the air is a little chilly, sweat has formed under the huge leather collar. Standing there, Pap drops the lines and walks to the water's edge, then back to the horse where he leans against Barney's sweaty flank.

"Ya know," he says, "This ole river has no politics. It goes wherever it wants; don't worry 'bout a thing. But over time, it wears at th' things that'd like t' control it. Kind a 'minds me of some people. Mebie if some of our moun'ain folk 'ould git more 'volved in th' system, they could have a better life. It's too late fir me, but young men like Martin an' yerself could do better, like businessmen an' important folk. Fir too often our people would rather not have th' extra aggravation that sometimes comes 'long with a shot in business. They'd rather do what is pleasin' for th' time bein' an' not think 'bout th' future. Jist like this here river, it don't worry 'bout nothin'. Too many 'round here don't worry 'bout nothin' an' ya know, nothin' ain't worth nothin'. Our men would rather spend time huntin', 'stead of lookin' t' th' future. If only they could break from that an' be some 'fluence 'round here. Mebie our preacher could preach 'long them lines."

Now rested, Barney prances to get moving again. Pap picks up the lines, gives a slight twitch and Barney charges. The water's edge has lodged the log against rocks and quagmire, causing it to resist the pull. Knowing a few tricks of the trade, Pap swings Barney around so as to pull from an angle. Unrelenting hindquarter muscles bulge and Barney's huge chest pushes deep into the collar, shoving earth behind him. The trace lines stretch as tight as fiddle strings and something must concede. The log breaks loose with a forgiving surrender and we're on our way.

We pull up to the house so as to prevent carrying wood so far. Sawing begins as we cut the oak into stove length sizes. Pap has done this before which makes it easier. Although old, he can pull his own weight. My goal is to get it cut up in blocks so I can do the splitting later. The log will make several ricks when finally stacked.

My growling stomach causes me to think of dinnertime and the soup beans I had put on earlier. I had built a lasting fire in the Home Comfort this morning that should complete them to perfection. Sure enough, we open the cabin door and smell the aroma of the beans and corn bread. Several helpings of this with cow butter spread on corn bread are reward enough for our hard work. We eat our fill and set to rest a bit.

Martin rides up on his horse. Today he has Sara Jane sitting behind him. Most of the ladies would think it immodest to ride astraddle a horse, but she sees that as a personal thing.

Anyway, she wishes to ride some of the trails with Martin, whom she has grown to love. They do not get to see each other often and like to make the most of it when they do.

Martin pulls his horse to the porch and smiles and greetings are conveyed as we move outside.

Pap comments, "Jist th' person we've been lookin' fir, but I see ya have somethin' else t' take up yer time." Sara's face wreaths with a smile, giggles as she hides the indignity of her situation behind Martin's strong back. Yet there is no compromising of her femininity. Martin assures us that as soon as he delivers Sara, he will return to help. She left her buggy down behind Jake's store, and Martin was taking her there so she could return home.

If there is ever a gentleman and right-hand man in these hills, it is he. Noting the timepiece in Pap's overalls, Martin asks the time. Pap lifts the chain on the pocket watch with care and holds it out to where his eyes can adjust, "Gittin' 'long t' 'bout half past one." Just then, he gets somewhat philosophical about his watch, "Some think it's fir tellin' what time a bidy should eat. I got th' answer t' that! A man don't need t' look at a watch t' see if he's hungry!"

Martin turns to Sara to obtain her expression, smiles gently and turns back to us, "We'd better get goin'." He turns his horse toward the road and quickly puts him into a reckless gait. It is not long until he returns to help us finish the day. The ladies have planned a quilting bee tomorrow afternoon, so we must do our best to put in a full day here with the wood.

The quilt making is to be combined with the men making apple butter. A good day waits with rich fellowship and fine eating. The ladies cut the apples and will prepare them for cooking. We had gathered them from the trees in the orchard, just down from the cave.

Inside the church, the quilt frame was set up and ladies gathered around busying themselves. Some of the older ladies take charge in designing the quilt. The greatest competition and confusion, as it appears to us, is who can get a word in. They gossip about everyone and everything under the sun. It's a woman thing, I have heard. It's been reported that some of the women who traveled with their husbands West became so lonesome for the fellowship of their own gender that they literally lost their minds. It becomes apparent when they have some titillating gossip going when the speaker's volume decreases to a whisper. At other times, the chatter can be heard for a country mile!

Outside is a different story. Pap runs things since he has more experience than anyone. He takes time to show me the techniques of mountain living, and some lessons taught to him by his predecessors. The old men sit around on stumps, whittling and talking usually in smaller groups, when not stirring. We started the apples at daylight, so along about midmorning, our stomachs begin to growl. The ladies unpack the sandwiches they prepared. They are able to take a break to eat, but some of us have to keep stirring so the three kettles won't burn. The apples take about eight hours from start to finish, provided they cook up well. We eat in shifts, with each taking turns with the stir. By three o'clock, the butter is ready to come off and go into the crocks. After cooling, a cloth placed on the top protects it in the weeks to come. Each takes his share. The quilt is put up for another day and we are on our paths home.

Mountain chores have been discussed throughout the day, everything from butchering to gardening. The fragrance of apple butter spawns talk about syrup making. It is an enjoyable time in the mountains for those who have a sugar maple grove. Some mountain farms have up to fifty trees to tap. The Four Knob farms have especially great stands of maples. After the first thaw of February, the sap begins to run. Men drill small holes in the trees and insert a spout made of a small piece of wood. A nail is driven above the spout to hang a bucket on. The buckets are emptied every day into a barrel, which is transported to the boiling pan. A fire is built under the pan to boil the syrup to the consistency desired. It is put into jars to keep over the coming months.

— XXVI —

THE ACCUSED

By February 8, 1922, Sheriff John A. Kimble has compiled enough evidence to file a warrant, approximately two hundred seventy-seven days after the killing. It states – "did feloniously, willfully, maliciously, deliberately and unlawfully kill, slay and murder one Harness Bibs." Kimble and a couple of his deputies filed past my place early this morning with two extra saddle horses, one for Arnie and the other for Wilbur.

Without much resistance, the law does its job of capturing the boys. This would be the last time their arms would move freely and walk without hearing the clank of chains - at least they thought so.

Looking up from my chores in the heat of the day, I see the procession making its way back to town. News had already reached our ears as to the lack of defense. The boys, no doubt, figured they had fought long enough. Sooner or later, they would have to meet their fate. The law had done its job. Pap and I wave and watch until they fade over the hill.

Arnie and Wilbur are taken to Keyser to appear before R. A. Welch, a Keyser lawyer. They are placed in separate compartments to prevent collaborating. Arnie makes a statement to Welch, between nine and eleven o'clock. For the sake of room, Arnie is taken to Parsons by way of the Western Maryland Railroad, the evening of the ninth. Two days later, he makes a confession, either conniving to squirm out of the conviction, or figuring Wilbur may place all the blame on him. He also supposed that his brother Gus had confessed everything since he had little to lose or perhaps confessed as part of a plea bargain since he was in jail for another crime.

Arnie outlined the event stating their intent, but stated that his gun choked and Wilbur had done the killing. Wilbur confessed the previous evening about 9 o'clock. It is not known who shot the fatal bullet, but each declared the other did it. Later, on February 16, B. Grant Roby commits Wilbur also to the Parsons jail, to be held until a court date in April, since it is a larger holding facility.

Court day finally arrives and Pap shows up at my place about daylight. For the past one-half hour, we have been "chewin' th' fat." In short time, Boy's team pulls up to my gate. We board with Pap taking the middle. Boy and I sit on the outsides of the little seat. Boy lifts the reins and spews out some unintelligible commands that I suppose his horses understand. The best translation that I can come up with is "Git in there, Dick, pull up there, Tom!"

We figured we would go today since it most likely will not last long, plus we wish to get in on the first trial and have the news first hand. Pap sits motionless in the cold as we travel, although sandwiched between Boy's fleshy body and my extra coats. Boy's mustache fills with drippings from the cool air against his warm breath. I am interested in the character of the trees and the architecture of different farmers and the way they have blended their buildings with the contour of their surroundings. I enjoy the fragrances of the barns and springtime. The feeding animals are also of interest as they look toward us in wonder - their heated bodies cause steam to rise.

Finally, we pull into town and make our way into the court house, where lawyers and townspeople look as if to say, "Where on earth did these people come from?" That is not to say we look weird, rather they stare like a calf looking at a new gate.

We walk up the wooden steps to the court house, hoping to get a seat by the stove, to no avail. As I take inventory of the surroundings, I observe the judge looking as if he is living a hangover. His robe once fit, but that was many pounds past. What we can see over the oak chamber are shaggy brows and an attitude of wanting to get this over. Manacles have been fastened to Arnie and Wilbur's wrists and apparent that the unyielding iron has cut deeply into their flesh.

The gavel sounds and the April court session begins revealing these findings.

** First to the stand is Miles Hausshalter, a witness on behalf of the State, who being first duly sworn in, testifies as follows:

Direct examination by Prosecutor Attorney Isaac D. Smith:

Q. State your name, residence.
A. Miles Hausshalter, Pendleton County, Mouth of Seneca, but I get my mail over here.

Q. About how far do you live from Petersburg?
A. Nineteen miles, I suppose, the way Mr. Hawkins said that Mr. Groves measured with an automobile to his place.

Q. What is your business?
A. Farmer.

Q. Did you know Harness Bibs?
A. I had part acquaintance with him, nothing in particular.

Q. What day of the week did you see him in Petersburg?
A. I couldn't say, but to the best of my recollection, it was Saturday, but I wouldn't be positive that it was.

Q. Did you see Harness Bibs after you left town on horseback?
A. Yes, sir, he overtook me in the road.

Q. Tell the jury whether or not you continued up the road in company with Harness Bibs.
A. Yes, sir. Up to the creek, where he turned up the hollow. Just between Charley Hanks's and Ped Rohrbach's there at the creek; ford in the creek.

Q. What did he have with him?
A. Had a little oats, I believe, in a sack; pretty sure he had.

Q. How long did it take you to go from Petersburg to where he turned up the hollow?
A. I couldn't tell you that, the horse traveled along at good speed, but I couldn't tell what time we was on the road.

Q. Couldn't you give the jury about what time in the afternoon it was when you reached Old Hopeville?
A. No, the nearest I could give it, we met the mail carrier just right close to where Henry Awers turned to go up to his place. I suppose it was a few minutes of 2:00.

** Next to approach the stand is Milt Cornshakle, from back on Jordon's Run, an elderly man, who lumbers up to the witness stand. Milt begins to tell his version of the quandary that has perplexed the community these many months. He speaks with his usual broken English, but ever exact in his reconstruction of the incident.

Prosecutor Attorney Isaac D. Smith: Were you at town May 7?

Milt: I suppose I was.

Prosecutor: Did you see Harness Bibs that day?

Milt: Yes, sir, he overtaken me up against Abe Redman's place. He was riding a mouse-colored horse, some people call them different, I don't know.

Prosecutor: Where did you next see Harness Bibs?

Milt: Hopeville Gap.

Prosecutor: What was he doing?

Milt: Wasn't doing anything but layin' in the road.

Prosecutor: About what time was it when you found his body?

Milt: Between 3:00 and 4:00 o'clock, as near as I could tell. We had no time piece.

Prosecutor: Give us your recollection of how you found the body.

Milt: The boy was driving the wagon, when it come to a sudden halt. I had to walk around the team to see what was the matter. About ten to fifteen steps ahead laid a body. I sent the boy back to Ped Rohrbach's to tell him there was a man in the road. I stayed with the team while they sent Jabe Hawkins to the nearest phone to see what to do.

Prosecutor: So you were the first to come upon the body. You were with the body by yourself for some time?

Milt: That's right, until Ped Rohrbach and others come. Harry Hanks stayed with the body while I brought the team out of the Gap. Ped Rohrbach and me went back up and stayed until they held the inquest and I went home.

Prosecutor: Tell the jury how you found the body.

Milt: Head was layin' in wagon track on left side of the road; feet lying against the bank. Head was layin' down the Gap, with blood and brains scattered about.

Prosecutor: What else did you see?

Milt: Saw a sack layin' in the road with some stuff in it.

Prosecutor: Did you see any blood before you got to the body?

Milt: Saw blood 35 or 40 steps away. A little rain shower come up before we started in the Gap. That made the blood travel further.

Prosecutor: What is the condition of the road at this place in the Gap?

Milt:About eight to nine feet wide, and very rugged on each side.

** Next, Ped Rohrbach, a witness of lawful age, who being first duly sworn, takes the witness stand. His broad calloused hands nervously placed on the Bible for the swearing, wishing they were instead embracing plow handles.

He lives near Old Hopeville, right where Old Hopeville Gap Road turns off North Fork Pike, above our present school. He had been plowing in the field below the schoolhouse. He didn't identify the body to be Bibs when he first went up the Gap, only later at the inquest. Bibs was face down with his coat thrown over his head, but Milt knew who it was because he recognized the color of the coat, having seen him earlier that day in town. He referred to an old schoolhouse, which was up the Fork from his house, to point out where he had been plowing.

Prosecutor: Mr. Rohrbach, I want you to describe to the jury the manner in which those shots as you heard them were sounded?

Ped: I hardly know how to get at that, sir.

Prosecutor: I mean for you to state how they sounded with respect from the time you heard the first one until you heard the next one.

Ped indicates by snapping his fingers four times, a short interval between first and second snap, then another interval, followed by snapping fingers twice in succession.

Prosecutor: What did you do after you heard the shots?

Ped: Went to plowing then.

Prosecutor: Didn't interest you any at all, did it?

Ped: No, didn't seem to.

Prosecutor: What experience have you had with guns?

Ped: Well, sir, I have shot Winchesters and I have shot shotguns and I have shot Home Rifles and as far as having any experience with high-powered guns I have not.

** Dr. J. B. Grove approaches the stand, a witness of lawful age.

Dr. J. B. Grove, physician and surgeon, went to the Gap to hold an inquest and conduct an autopsy, about 7:00 P.M. He found the tail of the khaki colored coat thrown up over the head. The body was apparently undisturbed from the time it had hit the ground. Milt didn't move the body to trot his team by so he could take them home, but backed them to a place to turn around, and exited the way he came. Harry Hanks stood guard over the body while the others were gone, not fearing for his own life or that he could have been shot by the killers.

After being first duly sworn, testifies as follows:

Prosecutor: Was there an inquest held over the body?

Grove: There was.

Prosecutor: Was Harness Bibs wearing a coat, and what was the position of it?

Grove: Yes, a Khaki-colored coat, with the tail thrown up over head and face.

Prosecutor: What was the nature of the wound?

Grove: A bullet entered just over the left eye, passing into the head through the left hemisphere of the brain and making its exit, taking away a piece of the skull and brains. The left hemisphere of the brain was entirely destroyed, a portion of the brain coming out of this opening behind and surrounding the head in the road for about two or two and a half feet were sprays of arterial blood.

Prosecutor: Wish you would take the hat I now hand you, examine it and say whether or not this is the hat found below the body of Harness Bibs.

Grove: Yes, that is the hat.

Prosecutor: Did the bullet pass through the hat, doctor?

Grove: Yes, sir.

Prosecutor: Can you state, doctor, what direction the bullet came from that passed through the head?

Grove: It was from a higher position than Bibs.

** Next comes W. D. LaFevre, a witness of lawful age, who being first duly sworn, testifies.

W. D. LaFevre is the County Engineer who visited the Gap on Monday with two assistants, Paul Shobe and Percy Welton, his wife, Miss Virginia Ervin, and a number of others were up there at the time. Isaac Smith, States's Attorney, showed him where the body was found, and locals demonstrated where the killers had waited. He constructed maps of locations and calculated that the body was found 2200 feet from the mouth of the Gap. Blood was 175 feet from Bibs's body. The horse was 573 feet from it. The road is at a 20% grade, with heavy woods to the left and perpendicular cliffs to right of the body, 50 or 75 feet in height. There are pockets in the cliffs further up the gap road, which open four or five feet in width and probably the same in length.

** Next to approach is H. C. Bennett, age 40, jeweler and photographer. He had gone into the Gap with Isaac Smith to photograph the position of the individuals. He states that Milt Cornshakle and Charley Hausshalter were there. Locals posed in the ledges as well as where the horse and rider were. These pictures were instrumental in helping the jury understand the case.

** Next comes Big Jake Hausshalter, a witness of lawful age, who being first duly sworn, testifies as follows:

Prosecutor: State your residence and occupation.

Hausshalter: Live out about three or four miles beyond the Corner, back in the mountain. I do a little farming.

Prosecutor: Were you up in the Gap after Bibs was killed?

Hausshalter: Sunday morning, couldn't tell what time in the morning it was, along in the forepart.

Prosecutor: What, if anything, did you find there?

Hausshalter: I found a 32 Remington shell.

(This shell became inadmissible because it could not be determined when it was shot, and nothing was said of the other shells - if they were even found.)

** Charley Hausshalter takes the stand, whom proudly had his picture taken where the killers were believed to have sat. This location was based upon the tracks in the ledges around a Spruce Tree.

* Milt Cornshakle comes back to the stand to testify regarding his posing for Mr. LaFevere. (He had reenacted the scene of a man in Harness's position on a horse, and had lain prone on the ground to assimilate the scene).

** Next to the witness stand is M. C. Stonestreet, who lives on the mountain. When asked about his occupation, he said that he owns a farm and works in the woods. He had been near Flintstone, Maryland, on Thanksgiving Day, 1920. He saw Arnie and Wilbur on the train and had conversed with them on the return trip home. He spoke of Arnie as a free talker who asked if Harness Bibs was around up in that country? M. C. returned, "As far as I know, Harness Bibs wadn't, he's afraid t' stay in that country!" M.C. went on, "As well as I 'member, Arnie said, 'By God, he better not stay 'round up there er I'll kill 'im!'" M.C. concluded, "Hold on, that's talk nobody ought t' make. Suppose he'd be killed an' this talk got out, you'd be blamed with it. Arnie answered, 'It's pretty big talk t' have, but, he better not cross our path er we'll kill 'im!' Arnie had looked for Harness Bibs earlier the morning he was arrested for being a slacker, and said that if he had seen him, he would have shot him."

** Hense Cornshakle takes his turn at the witness stand, Milt's brother, who had told Arnie and Wilbur that Harness had gone to town. At question was the remark that it had taken him four to five hours to go the six or seven miles to travel to the top of the mountain. He defended. "Well, it's all up mountain, takes a person a good while along the road."

** Provey Hawkins, brother of Wilbur, approaches the stand. He lives near the head of the Gap. He says that he heard the shots and went into the Gap to investigate. He came upon Roxie and saw her bleeding from the nose. He also met the boys. Arnie warned him, "Not t' tell anybidy er he would get it as well."

** Approaching the witness stand next is Gabe B. Cornshakle, Milt's brother, who lives at Hopeville. On May 7, he went up on the Alleghany to the Mosey place with his cattle. He stopped by Woodrow Cornshakle's place about 11:00 A.M. and ate dinner with them. He stated that he had seen Arnie and the two old people there, referring to Woodrow and his wife.

** Next on the witness stand is Gus Cornshakle, Arnie's brother, son of Woodrow. (He had been staying in McDowell County working on the road. He had been sentenced March 22 and serving time for moonshining. He had also been accused of raping a girl). When asked if he was Arnie's brother, he answered crudely, "Supposed t' be." Mr. Kimble, the sheriff, offered him a hundred dollars to find the killer, because he was accused of the murder as well. He was reported to have said to someone that the 303 was the gun to kill Bibs with.

    The day was well spent, and darkness falling fast as we head out of town. Boy, Pap and I discuss the day's proceedings. Of particular interest to Pap are the intervals between the shots. Boy comments, "By gummies, if only th' sound could a some way be done agin fir all of us t' hear, then we could tell which gun done it!"

    The court report indicated the frequencies of the shots. The court also questioned the volume of the sound so it could determine which gun was responsible for the shots. There is no accurate means to measure the sound, only opinion, but it would be an interesting test.

    We continue to discuss the many possibilities as we travel in the road wagon. If we can determine anything from the succession of the shots, there are many possibilities.

One, the first bullet could have missed, and the second could have hit Harness. Roxie could have taken one of the two remaining. Secondly, Harness could have been hit by the first, Roxie any of the other three. Thirdly, the first could have hit Roxie, Harness may have crouched down behind her, and while doing so could have been hit in the head by the next shot. Roxie could then have bolted the five hundred seventy three feet up the road, with the remaining shots missing while she ran. The last observations I wish to make are as follows: the distance was approximately one hundred sixty three feet. Most would have aimed for the chest, being a larger target. Very likely, anxiety would have hampered a well-placed shot. Also, Harness could have seen them, and reacted in a downward motion, causing a bullet to the head. At any rate, fate carried the fatal bullet, and a man lay motionless in the rocky road.

Some say Harness had forty bottles of strychnine in his possession when he was shot. It has been reported that he declared to poison every creek from the Mosey Place to the Jordon's Run Post Office. There's no wonder people were indifferent to him. This raw boned man had gone from a caring family man to a man separated from everyone. He moved into this area to homestead and build a life for his family. He tried to make a living working on the Ervin farm, but the money to be made from "bootlegging" was too attractive. The moonshine market was too enticing to resist, the money too good. This market led to jealousy. This led to his death in the Gap.

Instead, lying on the Four Knobs, under a locust is a prematurely broken down grave marker, situated for cows and wild beast to trample. Weeds and wild grass are overtaking the site and pushing through the fresh dirt. Cow piles already fall indiscriminately as animals pass in their feeding. Off to the side are a few other graves, now mere fading memories.

After traveling well into the night, we descend the last

grade before leveling off to where the road follows the river. Boy, out of his big heart, decides to drive on to Wildcat to give Pap a ride to his door.

Pap inches up the steps as Boy backs the team to turn the wagon around. Once off the ridge, Boy stops at my yard gate, allowing my dismount, then continues on to his house. During the next few days, we await the sentencing.

After the April court, the sentencing was declared. Wilbur had changed his plea from "not guilty" to "guilty," reducing his penalty to five years. The judge's gavel sounded out 18 years for Arnie. The prison doors swung shut and stayed that way for many years. Here, permanently recorded, are the emotions of the boys - that of pain, fear, and death. The inhumane guards, the misunderstood boys from the mountains, the strange surroundings did little to make life easy. The thick steel doors with a rectangular opening at eye level are cold and unbreakable. The bars expose men as cattle on watch. On occasion, there is a need to fight back schoolboy tears. Any sudden move by Arnie causes an ache in the poorly healed shoulder that had been wounded during the earlier capture. All mail from home is read, reread, every syllable, every word, every line, between the lines, the questions pondered. Each grip the worn Bibles their Mothers had sent. If ever they return to the mountain, things would certainly be different! The old people will be gone, and Bibs. Each hoping this bitter incident will not be repeated, but a warning down through the generations to the young and old alike.

— XXVII —

THE GAP'S HAINTED

Pap and I stand looking into the Gap from the ridge above. Suddenly, yet calmly, Pap turns and looks at me, stating with conviction, "Th' Gap's hainted!"

From above, the Gap looks as if someone had taken a huge hand and scratched across the rock-infested mountain years ago. It gives the resemblance that the longest fingernail had dug deep to shape the creek bed, giving it a most irregular symmetry. Some have said that its rugged characteristics make it look like Hell with the fire put out. There is no particular design, but was simply designed by the unmovable structures that dictated the water's path. Every few yards, an outcropping of ledges forced the architect to go a convincing way. There are thousands of crevices and boulders to hide anything or anyone. It is no surprise the boys chose this place to commit their crime.

Although not healthy, fear plays a role in the mountains. Economic fear and venturing into a new business comprises many of these fears, the latter stemming from the uncertainty of jobs. Fears related to health matters stem from the disadvantages of services. It is not uncommon for some to claim sickness most of their lives, even if they don't seem too bad. There is also a certain religious fear. Many have served God for fear of damnation, not for reasons of love. Some ministers have built churches on a theology of fear, causing parishioners to never truly experience the positive things of serving God. Out of protection, children are taught to fear almost everything and everyone. Fear is used as a tool to discipline children. Many parents send children to fright, telling them "Th' boogie man 'll git ya." Children are often seen peering out from behind a curtain. This often prohibits them from having otherwise enlightening experiences and childhoods.

The pioneers not only lived in a world filled with the perils of wild animals and the difficulties of making a living, but imagined dangers of witchcraft and superstition as well. Witches were believed to have the power to generate havoc among the households by causing sickness and disease and even casting spells on livestock and other animals. Some supposedly have jinxed an enemy's chickens to prevent them from laying eggs. Many an old woman has cited incantations over warts and other abnormalities. Fear of the mysterious has governed many lives.

In some ways, most Appalachians rarely admit fear! Come what may - mountain lions, floods, or men - they see no fear. They rise to the challenge. In dealing with the tangible, to accuse one of fear is to challenge him to a fight. They may experience fear, but never admit it. When it comes to the unknown - the spirit world - there is fear!

Throughout the mountains, there are many stories of a ghostly nature. Most of these were concocted to exaggerate the opponent in a storytelling session, or to simply provide entertainment on winter nights. But then, there may have been omens to coerce someone back in line.

Flurries of tales are spun around the Potbelly Stove at Jake's Store. Men take their turn repeating tales of "strange occurrences." A night of sitting on the bench can provide hours of entertainment or fright. It is a matter of decorum not to have any unnecessary interruptions while one has the floor. The only exception to this is to lean forward to relieve oneself of tobacco juice in the partially opened stove door.

Pop Berg tells the hair-raising account of one living up Ike's Run, who had no head. When anyone approached the cabin up in the hollow, an image appeared at the creaking door. He says, "Us boys liked t' see who was th' bravest, we'd run up t' th' cabin, pursh th' door open, an' run like crazy, just t' see th' tattered suit in th' door. We'd run all th' way off th' moun'ain, bruisin' ourselves from head t' toe!" The excitement, the planned interludes, the fluctuation in his voice constructs a mood that is spellbinding.

The story is told about Arlie, who in his younger days had been sparking a young lady a couple of ridges away. On the way to her house, he had to pass by a graveyard. All the boys knew he was terrified of haints and strange happenings. Regardless of the horror of passing by the graveyard, he knew an evening with his girlfriend would be worth any possible fright that could occur. Saturday night, he put on his best clothes and began the journey. It was only natural to take along some token of his love, so he had picked a few flowers along the fencerow. The trip home was not a particular bother since the evening had gone well, and he had music in his heart. Up ahead, the boys were waiting in the graveyard, behind the trees and tombstones, disguised with white sheets covering them.

Upon seeing these, fear pumped Arlie's legs full of adrenalin, propelling him to run for his life. He didn't stop until he reached the porch steps of home. The normal trail wasn't bad for the countryside, but this time he took every possible shortcut, causing him to scale barbed and split rail fences, and other hazards, at break-neck speed. When he arrived home, the barbwire and briers had ripped away at his cloths. Breathless and terror still raging in his veins, he looked down at his bloody body to see just a mere belt remaining, and a few tattered pieces of belt loops.

No one dared asked him anything about his trip home. Eventually, he did talk about the experience, always being careful not to express too much fear. All he ever says is, "Err, I'll tell ya one thing, one time I run up aginst a whole mess a haints! Liked t' scere me t' death, reckon it would of, if I wadn't th' man I am."

Pap leans back against a big gum tree overlooking the Gap. In his voice is conviction that the "haint" exists. He relates his past experiences of working farms up the Fork. As is typical, he was paid in goods of linsey, pork, beef, honey, or corn. At other times, a calf, pig, sheep, and skins have been used for money. His travels created the need to pass through the Gap about 4:00 in the morning. This provided ample time to be at the farm at daybreak. The normal sounds heard while passing through the gorge were the cracking of the slate under his feet, an occasional night owl and once in a great while the peal of a panther, but sometimes he declares he heard others. "Some of th' noises," he declares, "were frightful an' harsh as th' bellowin' of a mad ox!" He went on, "Many times I looked over t' th' crevice where Bibs's killers set that day, an' saw a lantern there. It had nary a reason t' hurt me, but liked t' scere me t' death! Ask Lissie, he'll tell ya 'bout th' lantern!" Pap continues, "I 'member goin' out t' th' point of th' rocks t' cut a honey tree. When th' tree come crashin' down, it seem like all th' rocks in th' Gap caved in. Th' earth made such a mad sound that it seemed like th' whole Gap was a fillin' up with rocks. It liked t' scere me t' death! It 'peared we must a bothered somethin' we shouldn't."

I made a trip to talk to Arlie about the scary incidents on the mountain. He told me about the haints at the graveyard, then about the haints in the Gap. "Err, I'll tell ya one thing, ya better not go down in th' Gap by yerself. They say there's a haint in there that 'll scere th' livin' daylights out of ya.

Some have seen that lantern all up an' down th' Gap!"

Perhaps the greatest problem that looms over the Gap is the scar that was cast upon some lives. Many years have passed since I first made my venture into the Gap to study the past. The time has slipped by so quickly since Pap, now a grizzled old man, and I took our walks in the Gap to inquire about the killing. The old Gap is more worn and so are the lives it has affected, and most notably, Arnie and Wilbur. Wilbur has returned home to find much of the mountain the same. The changes are those within. It has been said that he can't find a place to live where he can find peace. They say he has to have the light on throughout the night. Wherever he sleeps, he awakes to the torment that "horses are after him."

Arlie tells the story about him and Wilbur coon hunting recently. They stop to rest, build a fire and listen to the dogs bark as they run their prey. Arlie occupies himself by tossing sticks into the fire and watches sparks fly into the darkness. Wilbur drifts off to sleep and is awakened by a tormenting frenzy. "Arlie, do ya hear all them horses comin' after us?" Arlie reacts in his slow speech, "Err, why no, Wilbur, there's no horses 'round here." A while later, the dogs return with their tongues hanging out, awaiting a pat of reward, and a signal to move on. They immediately put the fire out and head off the mountain. Arlie says the re-occurrence of the haint torments Wilbur of the Gap incident.

Pap, without a doubt, reveals the most humorous story when he tells of a memorial service back near Whitmer. Pap says, "There was this 'ere man who had a humped back, couldn't straighten up. Well, he died, an' they had t' strap 'im down in th' casket with some rope, t' hold him straight out. 'bout half way through th' service, th' rope broke an' he all of a sudden sprung up. Ever'bidy run fir th' outside an' like t' run over one 'nother! Th' preacher declared, 'Dadburn, a church with only one door!'"

Pap declares, "Sister Dolly ain't a scered t' take a stand on th' matter! She knows th' stories an' th' 'posed Gap Haint." Speaking from Saul's encounter with the Witch of Endor, she points a fragile, yet dynamic finger, denouncing any toleration of familiar spirits. "Ya folk who set 'round tellin' them made up stories of lanterns, ghosts, an' such ought t' be 'shamed of yerself."

She makes her point by emphasizing the importance of thinking on heavenly things, and not leaving yourself open to Satan's activity. To take it a step further, things in nature portray good and the evil. Men tend to fear the darkness and be bold in the sunlight. I suppose that is the reason some will not venture into the Gap after dark, unless they have company. Sunlight brings out the brave. There is something scary about the night sounds and the unseen. Only those who do not fear the devil or do not have a deep-seated confidence in God have a reason to be afraid of the night.

— XXVIII —

THE REFINED AND THE NOT SO

Appalachians brought their religion with them as they moved into the mountains. Even when desires came to divorce from religiosity, they wished to hold on to the basic values. They found it impossible to entirely escape their roots. There has been a church within reach of every home as soon as the population merited it. The density of churches is expressed greatly in West Virginia. It presently has more churches per capita than any other state. One must ask, why the problems? Why the abundance of inter-relational, economic, and health issues? It is difficult to articulate all of the reasons the large number of churches do not reflect less problems. It is difficult to come up with statistics, but one answer may address attendance. While there are more churches per capita, attendance may not be any greater per capita. Many attend church only in time of need, such as a funeral, or to attend Christmas or Easter celebrations. Adults sometimes maintain they should not force their children to attend church, but allow them to decide for themselves; subsequently, children often quit when they find something more exciting, albeit temporal. Ironically, adults force their children to do many other things less important.

An added conflict is the strict observance of tradition. There is a deep allegiance to the faith of one's ancestors and strong arguments that all other faiths are heresy. As to how faithful one is to his beliefs is often disregarded and not important in this argument. This adamant proclamation goes toward destroying another's faith, differing often in mere semantics. The fact is, the otherwise positive moral influence is destroyed by negative remarks or rumors.

Gossiping about someone in the church, or out of the church, for that matter, is a deterrent to some that might otherwise attend. Critics often feel that church people should be perfect. They somehow feel they do not want to be a part of a group where there are hypocrites, yet failing to realize hypocrites are found everywhere and every institution. This mountaineer sees church hypocrites as having a potential to be helped. To be pious in this argument and not attend is neither doing themselves a service nor their children.

Many mountain ministers are often less educated and present a less effective gospel. They preach a gospel of emotionalism and little emphasis on fact. They have been called "farmer-preachers." These have been converted in revivals and "called." A local church acknowledges their leadership, which has often been ordination enough. Some have not been able to read, but can proclaim at least part of the gospel and offer hope to the sick and dying. These, in many cases, are suspicious of education, lest it interfere with the simple preaching from the heart. It has been said, "Colleges and seminaries have ruined many a good preacher." They either feel "God-given" insight is sufficient, or justify this approach to defend their lack of dedication to be educated. In some cases, however, formal education has been compensated with learning scripture, history, and theology with personal devotion.

Many of those without a formal education tend to direct worship that is informal and unrehearsed. Sermons are long and loud, with a major emphasis on the need for immediate conversion. Some preach entirely emptying their lungs of air without stopping to breathe, then with a sudden deep inhalation, inhale. The message of hell, promises of heaven, invitations to receive Christ before it is too late, attacks on worldliness and personal immorality characterize most sermons. The latter places strict restrictions on how women should adorn themselves. Some of the regulations demand a woman to be fully covered, no pants, hair that is never to be cut, and no jewelry. Other acts preached against dancing, tobacco, liquor, cards, gambling, illicit sex, and worldly amusement.

As Pap and I discuss the matter further, I conclude, "Pap, we can't defend the social gospel preached by some outside Hopeville!"

Pap declares, "Education is th' sharpenin' of th' axe, not th' axe itself! Ya need it all!"

I respond quickly, "But some rely totally on experience, and often experience that runs in search of a theology! It seems to me we need to incorporate both in our practice - a sound theology and a good dose of experience."

Mountaineers often fail to see the compatibility of education and religious experience. Usually when there is not this balance, there is little character change and guidance to aid one in being successful in other areas of life. Some dance, shout, and amen a preacher, but these alone do little to sustain one spiritually throughout the week. But when there is too much reliance upon education, the spiritual needs go unmet, leaving an inner void. A good balance of fact, faith and feeling can prepare people to be successful in all aspects of living.

Apart from the message of salvation presented in the churches, there are many benefits, some of which will be revealed in eternity. Knowing the mountains, it is easy to envision the otherwise large number of welfare recipients, additional health problems, demand on counselors, the suicides, the added drunkenness, and other vices. The fact that a church and its influence reside in an area brings blessings and often prevents the proliferation of these problems. The mountain churches have always encouraged the broken hearted, aided in the battle against illiteracy and have provided social opportunities and preparation for eternity.

Across Appalachia, churches have sprinkled the landscape. Few have experienced harassment from the law. They cross nearly every spectrum of religion. All of the churches offer something to the Appalachian. One may view this as a smorgasbord opportunity. Humans have a variety of needs and appetites; thus, all the churches should serve Appalachian needs. Another view sees this as an ordained way to spread the gospel, as the different branches of the military contribute to combat the enemy. One often sees churches side-by-side, sometimes representing a past split. This illustrates that the number of church increases using the old adage of "multiply by dividing." But think of the influence larger churches could have with less overhead per parishioner.

The geographical isolation, theological conservatism, and rugged individualism created a spirit of independence in churches. They appreciated this freedom to worship, to construct churches and adored the autonomy. And apart from ministries who assemble "cult followings" or those from cults, Appalachian churches have always sought to prepare souls for Heaven and circumvent Hell.

The Presbyterians and Methodists blanket the mountains. Their services are generally more orderly, ministers more educated, church life more uniform and perhaps less independent than that of other mountain groups. This is an example of the diversity in desires, knowing that most mountaineers appear to be less regimented.

Another group under the banner of John Calvin, the Baptists, sprinkled the landscape. Although there are variations in their churches, "Eternal Security" and the need to fulfill the "Great Commission," stands out in their theology.

Eternal Security is one of those circular arguments represented by renowned minds on each side. Those holding to Eternal Security believe salvation cannot be lost. If one has been "saved," he will not do any wrong resulting in backsliding. If he should do wrong, Christ's work on the cross is sufficient to cover any sin, but if he should fall into sin, for which he is unrepentant, he was never "saved" in the first place. The latter can be confusing, particularly if he were a minister who turned to the world. Also, there is always the question as to how many charlatans are filling pews or pulpits, knowing others have professed and turned.

Those not believing in Eternal Security believe they can lose their salvation when distracted and having turned from a life of righteousness back to the world. Some believe this can happen too easily and fail in expressing confidence in the atonement, but most reserve the right to God to determine when one falls from grace. In neither case can one judge another with certainty or does the belief cause one group to live differently than the other.

Coming out of the Anabaptist movement, the Brethren and Mennonites maintain close-knit communities. Again, variations prevail in their churches, but the pacifist cause stands out. An early Mennonite minister was jailed for advising his flock to not serve the war effort in any way. The statement, in essence, demands adherents to contribute nothing to a fund used to run the war machine. Another practice that is closely followed is "Feet Washing" observances.

Lastly, "Pentecostals" make up many congregations. They are the same as other Protestants, in that they believe in traditional dogma: trinity, creation, virgin birth, atonement, and resurrection. They, however, follow Joel 2:28, 29 and Acts 2:1-4, that is, the "Baptism of the Holy Spirit," with the initial physical evidence of speaking in unknown tongues or "glossolallia." There is spontaneity in their worship of shouts, emotional enthusiasm and praying aloud.

A few of these are the "snake handlers," who literally follow Paul's writing in Acts 28:3, and Jesus's commandment in Mark 16: 17 & 18. Espoused by Tennessean, George W. Hensley, these followers may also practice "fire holding" and "poison-drinking" observances. These practice the "snake handling" ritual to prove that God can protect them while doing so, thus making the principle a common practice. Most opponents believe the intent of these statements by Paul and Jesus advises Christians of the protection if one should be bitten accidentally and believe one should not tempt God.

Pentecostals have been labeled superstitious, ignorant, and plagued with emotionalism and uneducated. But every group has had its share of criticisms to which time will tell the truth. My hope is that each can contribute toward personal morality, sound theology and politics, and concern for personal conversion and evangelism.

One must conclude that if there were more of a concerted effort, then the goals of each church may be reached. If only they could focus on the similarities, rather than their differences, at least when encountering problems outside the church, our world might be different.

Church buildings and pulpits have seldom been shared. More charismatic personalities may become a difficult model for the local pastor to compete with, or worse yet, a group may be proselyted. A local Mennonite group loaned their building to another group to hold services and subsequently realized they had lost the majority of their members. So the building was moved to better suit the Mennonite needs.

Pap laments the time to come when the lack in church attendance or cults may one day replace the Judeo-Christian Theology and their shouts may sound across the hills and hollows, where only hallelujahs have been heard. He senses a change is imminent, causing him to proclaim, "Jist th' other day, somebidy told of some group a comin', preachin' somethin' from some book other than th' Bible."

Frequently, when mountain people realize a need, whether social, financial, or spiritual, they become religious and genuinely change. On the other hand, some resort to drinking to solve their problems. Some drift from one solution to another. When things are not going well, they drink and at other times, they go to church. Then there are those that, no matter what, take things into their own hands, and think it cowardly to do otherwise. They view it as unmanly to attend services and may even want to entertain themselves by disrupting it.

Recently, such an incident took place in a neighboring community. A young man was on his way to church when he met up with another, with whom he had a quarrel. He was assaulted, but refused to fight in front of the church, and chose to run. The story picks up with the recent news article printed in the Grant County Gazette, May 5, 1920, left by our same snuff spitting, boney postman. He, as others, is aggravated at the inability to get along.

"Brutal Assault at Circleville"

"Arthur Fields*, son of Rev Benham Fields* of Circleville, was the victim of a brutal assault on last Sunday evening when he was assaulted with a knife or razor by Lige Teter*, who lives in the Teter Gap, near Circleville.

The assault occurred in front of the church in Circleville while services were being held.

Mr. Fields* was on his way to the religious services when he was assailed by Teter*, who was drinking, and had evidently come to the religious meeting for the purpose of provoking a disturbance and disturbing the services.

When but few words had passed between the parties, Fields* insisted that was not the place for a controversy and urged that they adjust any differences at another time. Teter* made a savage slash with a sharp instrument at his head, cutting a gash to the bone down over the forehead and another across the throat, which, if a shade deeper, would have been fatal. A stiff collar checked this blow. Another cut, probably aimed at the heart, struck a tin tobacco box in the coat pocket and dulled the blade. Another slash at the wrist cut the arm about half off, and from this wound the assaulted man lost the most blood.

The first blow felled Fields* and it was while Teter* had him down that the other injuries were inflicted. Fields* called for help, but several friends of Teter* prevented the boys who were present from going to Fields's* assistance.

After receiving these injuries, Fields* succeeded in getting to his feet and ran for his life with Teter* following some distance, slashing him in the back, cutting his coat to shreds. He succeeded in reaching the home of Henry Harper, where Dr. I. H. Jordan lives, and fell exhausted from the loss of blood and remained unconscious for many hours. Dr. Jordan was out of town and friends used every remedy they could to check the flow of blood, while Deputy Sheriff Allen Fields*, a brother of the victim, hurried to Riverton in his car for Dr. Teter, who arrived an hour and a half later, barely in time to save the life of the man.

Mr. Fields* was carried to the home of Allen Fields*, where he is receiving the best of treatment and under the most favorable conditions may recover.

After the brutal assault, Teter* fled and was not located until Monday night when Deputy Sheriff Fields*, with several assistants, surrounded the home of Jacob Arbogast on top of North Fork mountain, and captured the prisoner in the upper story of the home about 3 o'clock A.M. He was taken before Squire A. J. Helmick, at Circleville, where he waived a preliminary hearing, and being unable to give the bail required, was brought to the jail at Franklin to await the action of the grand jury at the July term of Circuit Court."

— XXIX —

THE LONG HOLLOW BURYING

Long Hollow is but a few miles from Hopeville, the way the crow flies, on the way to Seneca. It is hardly a community since the houses are so scattered, and there are two less now since Lek Cornshakle burned them to keep unwanted squatters out. The name comes from the long hollow sandwiched between a small mountain called Round Bottom Ridge and the higher Alleghanies. The road to Long Hollow ascends Red Bud Ridge, a section of which is called "Crows Ridge," known for the massive number of crows seen there. A pair of Bald Eagles makes their home just behind Red Bud, in the Rich Woods, against North Mountain. They chose a convenient place to swoop down the narrow canyon to fish.

It is also a favorite roost for buzzards. Before nightfall, they soar above the trees in a circling pattern, at great altitudes until finally selecting branches on which to settle for the night. Their silhouette can be seen against the starlit skies as they keep watch over the valley below. In early morning, they are privileged to be able to launch their rested wings from such height as they sail to distant farms, hoping to find carrion.

The Fork road makes three switchbacks before topping

Red Bud Ridge, then drops sharply on the other side to circle down by the school, then snakes its way on up through Long Hollow. There are two important buildings in the area. The school, where approximately twenty-four students attend, sits just down off the ridge at the lower end of the hollow. Sitting at the western end of the hollow is the Mullenax store.

Just as centuries before, the sky darkens on this cool December night, over the murmuring, transparent creek that flows by the school. A mist hangs over the valley due to the frigid weather conditions. Although running very swiftly, Moyer Run manages to have a lot of ice along its edges. The Alleghany winds are fierce because of the natural sweeping to the region, bringing rain, sleet, and swirling snow to the hollow, causing huge snow drifts here and there.

Gathered in the schoolhouse are friends of Ocie, who care about his making it through the night. He struggles to survive a gunshot wound he had received earlier in the day. Godfrey Stats, who lives across the river, and a couple of his boys await the outcome. They live on the other side of the Potomac and must ford it by boat or horse to travel outside their farm. Others also are trying to console their friend by staying by his side throughout the evening.

Earlier in the day, there had been a funeral at the head of the hollow for Stella Hawkins. Many of Stella's lifelong friends paid their last respect, as Sister Dolly commemorated her life. Her worldly life was over. The Alleghany winds blasted across the meadow, causing folk to brace themselves in order to stand. Each bared the cold wind as they sang hymns and listened to precious words.

She spoke from Psalms 23, a well-known chapter that folk here readily identify with. Then continued on with Hebrews stating, "An' it's 'pointed unt' men once t' die, but after that th' judgment." She didn't mix words telling those around the coffin to straighten their paths of living, as if reading their mail. Sister Dolly reminded those gathered that often it is difficult understanding God's ways. She insisted that God views life with the backdrop of eternity while we see things in the light of an hourglass. Important to God are things as they relate to eternity; earth is but for rehearsal. She went on to say that we hurt when anyone leaves our midst, especially the young, but God sees the big picture. He wishes to have them with Him, knowing we shall do the same, and who knows what trouble a seemingly early death may prevent.

The ladies present were dressed in their finest solemn outfits. There was hardly a dry eye as Stella was lowered in the shell grave, surrounded by locust. More tears flowed as each remembered her rich contribution to her friends, her contagious smile and caring ways. Each contemplated how they had often taken each other for granted. Now they were saying their goodbye's, never to see their loved one again. At least they could visit the site and lay a flower to represent their love.

Reaching as deeply as possible, I can only sympathize with those along the Oregon Trail and the tearing in the heart as they laid their children and spouses in unmarked graves, to move on, never returning. Pieces of their heart remained behind, along the trail. How many sleepless nights would come and go? How many tears would wet the goose down pillows? To ease the pain, they thought of their future homeland where there will be no more parting.

The men hung around to shovel dirt on the pine box that held one of the mountains most thoughtful citizens. Pap takes a rest from his shoveling and mumbles through his hurt, "It's not th' coffin, but a pine box, not th' box, but th' corpse, not th' corpse, but a bidy, not jist a bidy, but Stella, an' not her, but her house, she, she's gone, gone to her eternal reward, over there, bless God, over there!"

I could not help sense Pap's emotions - his sorrow for her death, but the conviction of again seeing her. "Well, Pap, I see you have it all figured out," I respond.

"Yea, but do th' rest of 'em," he demands with tear-filled eyes.

Preparing to leave the gravesite, Big Jake does not wait long before passing a snarled look to Ocie, stemming from the bearded bronze turkey accusation. His forehead wrinkles and brows draw over stern eyes conveying malice. When some mountain people get something on their mind, it is often there to stay! This funeral makes no exception.

Ocie moves his hand through his open blouse and inside his bibs to rest his hand on some comfort in the event things get uneasy. He wasn't at Hopeville now, but Long Hollow, home where he can do as he pleases.

Everyone heads home. Some towards the mountain and others down the Fork. Many hitch a ride on Boy's wagon to their destinations, where they take winding trails to mountain homes. Pap throws his trusty cane on the back, and with some effort climbs aboard, allowing his legs to dangle off the rear. With a jerk, the team leans into the harness, creating a need for everyone to hold onto the wagon as it begins to move. Pap is one of the few that will have a ride practically to his doorstep.

Upon reaching the school, they stop at the nearby shed to unload. Women folk head home while the men linger by the shed to discuss the passing of their acquaintance, the weather, farming, and hunting - usually in that order. Up in the cool of the rafters, a pint of the perfectly clear liquid is retrieved and passed around. Each, in their own way, expresses their missing Stella and the gracious home cooked meals. Each takes a sip of the powerful stuff, afterward making facial expressions as if there is distaste, but undoubtedly the palate indicates differently.

Ocie had stopped off at his house, but soon joins the group. Jake again accuses Ocie of stealing his turkey and demands retribution or reap the consequences! Ocie calls him a liar and ever so discreetly slides his hand inside his bib overalls to finger the handle of his revolver.

Big Jake stands head and shoulders over Ocie. Ocie is no match for Jake without an equalizer. Jake becomes angrier by the minute and is determined to settle it once and for all and to defend his reputation. But there is concern as to what is under Ocie's bibs. Earlier in the day, he was certain he heard the sound of a cocking hammer, but he has comfort as well, having retrieved a pistol of his own. Knowing he may be outgunned, Ocie heads toward the school, an attempt to prevent getting killed. Men at the shed ponder the situation.

Godfrey stands hoping, "Maybe ole Jake 'ill have time t' cool off."

Slow-talking Arlie muses, "Err, why don't somebidy do somethin'?"

Jess Bass, with folded arms, figures, "A man's might is th' law 'round here, let 'em work it out 'emselves!" He then takes a drawl on his corncob pipe and watches the smoke swirl to the sky.

Traveling ever so slowly through Jeb and Pete's half-witted minds is, "We's a gittin' out a th' way when lead starts flyin'!"

Shots ring out as Jake chases Ocie around the schoolhouse, firing the pistol. Realizing the ineffectiveness of the handgun, he sends the boy after his Johnson twelve gauge shotgun. He brings it to his shoulder. It sounds off, but misses its target.

The guineas are again scattered from their browsing, as well as Jeb and Pete. Ocie turns and ineffectively returns fire. Jake fires again. Lead perforates the schoolhouse and finally a load penetrates Ocie's blouse, bib straps, undergarments, and on to his vital organs. In seconds, he falls to the ground as organs begin leaking precious blood.

Strength leaves his once powerful legs. The shots now reverberate against vital organs, as an arrow quivers in the

THE LONG HOLLOW BURYING

body of its prey. In seconds, the battle is over. Jake, satisfied with his revenge, walks the deep path, through the roses that form an archway over the yard gate and up the steps to his home.

Help rushes to Ocie's side. Someone reaches to the ground to pick up his hat and place it over his whitened face. Soon the decision is made to carry him into the school. The sun falls below the ridge in the clearing where the road fades out of sight. Quietly, the mountains settle for another night of rest. But in the school, the evening is spent in suffering as Ocie hangs in the shadows, between life and death. Friends try in vain to comfort Ocie as he lay on the floor next to the stove. Some tend the fire and some pray for God's tender mercies.

After little deliberation, Godfrey faces a darkened sky straddling his horse, turning her toward Red Bud to ride for the doctor. The many miles down the Fork takes him past Pap's place, where he can see an image peering from the window, knowing Pap is wondering, "Who in their right mind 's on th' road at this hour?"

Time will not allow Godfrey to stop to warm, although his pants are buried with wind swept snow and sleet. Between the stiff leather saddle and legs is a growing layer of ice where the heat of his body condenses against the cool of the night. In his hair and mustache resides a frozen mass of ice.

Down off the ridge, Boy's lights are out and the only sounds are the barking dogs that were awaken from their nest. It would be hours before any would hear a word.

After many miles of riding the difficult, steep, rough, crooked roads, Godfrey returns to the school. He strips the rigging from his horse and turns her loose to feed. She shakes furiously to rid herself of the ice frozen in her mane, gives a whinny and rushes to find something on which to graze.

Tired and wet from rain mixed with snow and showing the effects of a long hard ride, Godfrey rushes to the stove, late and without the promise of help. In a state of hopelessness, onlookers are filled with anxiety. A horrendous fever causes Ocie great grief. In the wee hours of the morning, a final groan comes from the scraggly gray-bearded life of Ocie, as breath leaves him.

The body is covered, knowing there is nothing anyone can do. Unwillingly, Lottie leaves the side of her husband, as she is lead to her home.

The lamp is blown out and the door pulled shut. The fire in the stove is left burning, knowing it would die before morning. Godfrey and the boys walk down the lane under a faint moon to the river. They shove the boat off the bank into the rushing water and quickly jump aboard. Once on the other side, they make the climb to their home in Rich Woods. Everyone goes to respective homes, saddened by the loss. In the morning, the mountains would awake to the news of yet another soul passing.

— XXX —

LONG HOLLOW INQUISITION

Since early morning, I have seen Pap's coal oil lamp as it shines through his windows. I finish the chores while waiting to go to the inquisition. Looking in the direction of the Sods, I see Boy hitching the team to the frozen harness. He will be along soon to provide a ride to Long Hollow. Pap's place is on our way so we will pick him up at his doorstep. It seems such a short time ago since we went to the trial of the boys from the mountain and now another. Friends will be there and we need to make our presence known.

Descending Red Bud, we see many people already at the school, where Ocie yet lies. It will be a long day, and especially long for those on the witness stand.

The Long Hollow School House has many memories of school and church activities, but December 31, 1926, it serves as a courtroom. It's been many a moon since it has served in this fashion. Many travel to Long Hollow to give voice and listen to the proceedings.

B. Grant Roby, a Justice and acting Coroner, upon the view of the body of Ocie Fields, there lying dead and in the presence of the jurors, after having been duly summoned and proclamation given as required by law, and being duly sworn to inquire when, how, and by what means the said Ocie Fields came to his death, began the inquisition.

First, Ben Fields, a witness of lawful age, being duly sworn, stands before the congregation of witnesses. He had been here before as a student and to attend church services, now an entirely different matter.

By I. D. Smith, Prosecuting Attorney of Grant County.

Smith: You may state your name.
Fields: Ben Fields
Smith: Your age?
Fields: Thirty-three.
Smith: Where do you live?
Fields: Grant County.
Smith: Near the Long Hollow School House?
Fields: Yes, sir.
Smith: Are you married?
Fields: No, sir.
Smith: You have been married, have you not?
Fields: Yes, sir.
Smith: And you are a widower?
Fields: Yes, sir.
Smith: How many children have you?
Fields: Seven.
Smith: Are you acquainted with Ocie Fields?
Fields: Yes, sir.
Smith: How long have you known him?
Fields: Ever since I was a little boy.
Smith: Do you identify the dead body now lying before this jury as the body of Ocie Fields?
Fields: Yes, sir.
Smith: Do you know Jake Hausshalter?
Fields: Yes, sir.
Smith: How long have you known him?

Fields: Ever since I was a boy.
Smith: Where does he live with reference to the Long Hollow School House?
Fields: Near the schoolhouse.
Smith: Where were you yesterday afternoon?
Fields: At a buryin'.
Smith: Whose?
Fields: Stella Hawkins's.
Smith: Who did you go with and what time was it?
Fields: I went with Godfrey Stats an' Ocie Fields, but I don't know what time it was.
Smith: About one or two o'clock?
Fields: I don't know. It might 'ave been.
Smith: Did you see Ocie talk to Jake Hausshalter?
Fields: Yes, sir.
Smith: What did they talk about?
Fields: About the buryin', I guess.
Smith: Did you have anything to drink up there?
Fields: No, sir.
Smith: What time was it when you left the burying?
Fields: About three or three-thirty, or somewheres along there.
Smith: How did you and Ocie come down the road from the place of the burying to the Long Hollow School House?
Fields: I walked most of the way and then Boy Awers come along.
Smith: Who did you see at the schoolhouse?
Fields: I saw several standin' around talkin'.
Smith: You had headed home and asked to come back. What did you first see?
Fields: Jake comin' out with his revolver and firin' five or six shots.
Smith: Where was Ocie?
Fields: In the county road.
Smith: What did Ocie do?

Fields: Fired two shots back.
Smith: What did Jake do?
Fields: He got his shotgun.
Smith: What kind was it?
Fields: A Johnson
Smith: You may state, if anything, what Hausshalter said when he fired the shot that killed Fields?
Fields: Not a word.
Smith: What did you do?
Fields: I went down to Ocie and raised his head.
Smith: What did he say first?
Fields: "Praise th' Lord."
Smith: What did you do next?
Fields: I pulled his cap over his head and went home.
Smith: Who carried him in the schoolhouse?
Fields: Carrie Fields and my son.
Smith: They carried him in the schoolhouse and started a little fire?
Fields: Yes, sir.
Smith: And this happened on Thursday, yesterday?
Fields: Yes, sir.
Smith: Now, how did this conversation start up about this turkey business?
Fields: Ocie told Jake that he heard he had tried to send the state police on him.
Smith: What did Jake say?
Fields: He said he did not, that he would not talk to him about it now because he was drinkin'.
Smith: When Ocie had started down towards the school house and you had started towards your home, what was it Jake said to Ocie?
Fields: He said "Now plod along."
Smith: What did Ocie do?
Fields: He plodded on.
Smith: Not another word said?

Fields: Ocie started on, and I thought I heard him say somethin', but I don't know what it was, and Jake commenced shootin'.

** Next to take the stand is Ocie's wife, Lottie, who was thirty-five years old, fourteen years younger than Ocie. She is asked if her husband had been drinking. She responds, "I don't know. He had gone to the burying and said he would be back for supper." When asked if he and Jake had been having trouble, she said, "Nothin' serious. Nothin', only somethin' over a turkey gobbler."

Smith: When you reached the schoolhouse, your husband was here on the floor near the stove? (Pointing to the body).
Lottie: Yes, I went around to where he was, and he said, "Mamma, you come," and I said yes. He said, "I will never get well." He said, "Brother Jake", once, is all that I heard him say. Then he asked about the children.
Smith: He told you that he would never get well.
Lottie: He said, "I will never get well."
Smith: What did he tell you about who shot him?
Lottie: He said, "Brother Jake" once, is all that I heard him say.
Smith: He was perfectly conscious, wasn't he?
Lottie: Yes, but he didn't care about talkin'.
Smith: What else did he say right after that?
Lottie: He asked me if I had brought the children, and then he went on groanin', and then he said, "Brother Jake."
Smith: Did you stay until he died? Lottie: Yes, sir.

** Next, to testify is Lester Stats, fifteen years old, who attends the Long Hollow School. He is asked who his teacher was, to which he states, "Mr. Bernard Pittensbarger." He testifies, "I was tryin' t' git Ocie's feet warm. He complained of 'em bein' cold an' I was tryin' t' git 'em warmed."

** Next to witness, Russel Stats, eighteen years old. Testifies that Ocie "Groaned an' said he was goin' t' die, an' he wanted a drink of water still."

** Next to the stand is Godfrey Stats, who testifies that Lottie stated that night, "I told ya 'bout foolin' with Jake." He states that he was, "At th' school fir jist a little bit an' I went fir th' doctor." He had gone the fifteen miles to town on horseback in the middle of an Allegheny winter, and at night. One can't help admire this horseback trip, placing it alongside renowned deeds of philanthropy. Looking back and into the future, this deed will always be viewed as a noble act.

** Next to swear to tell the truth is Dr. J.B. Grove, who performed the autopsy, December 31, 1926 at Long Hollow.

Smith : You may state at whose request you performed this autopsy.

Grove: I.D.Smith's, Prosecuting Attorney of Grant County.

Smith : You may state whether or not you were able to identify the body of Ocie Fields.

Grove : The body was identified by Boy Awers and Will Turner.

Smith : You may state the result of your autopsy and then state by what means the said Ocie Fields came to his death.

Grove : The body showed no bruises or broken bones. The back was perforated by numerous shot holes with a few shots under the skin. On opening the chest, the cavity was found filled with blood, both right and left lung was perforated with shot, causing hemorrhage in the chest cavity.

From the base of each lung, we removed two shots - two from each lung. Abdomen found to contain considerable quantity of free blood, due to the perforation of the stomach and upper part of descending colon. The remaining organs of the abdomen were free from any injury. On opening the skull, there was found to be no pathology in the brain. Heart normal. Conclusion: This man came to his death by a gunshot wound delivered from a shot gun in the back, the shot perforating both lungs, stomach and upper portion of descending colon, causing death from hemorrhage.

Smith: There were a number of shots that entered the body, were there not?

Grove : I did not count them, but I would judge forty, at least.

The inquisition concludes in the schoolhouse with witnesses called, dictation taken, and a re-enactment of the tragedy. The case was clear as to who did the shooting and the anatomy of the event. The primary question was motive. Was there a justifiable motive to defend Jake? The few hours of questioning concluded. Afterwards, some socializing and then all steer toward home.

Pap nervously reaches for a sure seat.

"Ya better grap a hold," Boy yells! He then commands the horses to move ahead as he gives the lines a flick. Realizing he has unseated his passengers, he chuckles. The wagon jerks as it moves out of the frozen snow caked around the wheels. Creaking sounds emerge from the wooden structure at every twist imposed by the rocky road. Guineas and chickens cackle as they take to the air to escape oncoming hooves. The large iron shoes have no mercy as they pound the earth. A hard pull awaits the team, as they take Red Bud.

— XXXI —

THE TALK AND HEARING

Again, I wait for our local newspaper to get the reporters take on the killing. Blaze's growl lets me know there must be something on the road. He had been curled up on an old rug on the porch, but now has risen to his feet, listening attentively. I pull the curtains aside to peer out the window where I can see the mailman coming at a trot, obviously because of the cold. I wrap a warm coat around me and meet him at the yard gate. He digs in the satchel to retrieve the newspaper.

"Howdy," he drawls. "Been cold as th' dickens, haint it?" He pulls his scarf closer to his neck for warmth and takes his forefinger and thumb to sling the drippings from his nose - first one side, then the other.

"Yea, but it's that time of the year," I exclaim, wanting to get back to the stove.

He clears his throat and spits a stream of tobacco through his frozen mustache to continue, "Bad killin' up th' road, wadn't it?"

"Yea, certainly was an awful thing right here at Christmas time."

"Ole Jake 'll git put up th' river," he states.

"They sometimes forget there is a law around to handle those matters," I added.

"Better git on, it's cold 'nough to freeze a crowbar," he declares, attempting to smile in spite of the bitterness. He pats his horse's withers to give her the signal to move on.

I settle by the stove to read the paper, knowing later I must climb the ridge to read it to Pap. Our Grant County Gazette, January 6, 1927, recounts the killing.

"A BAD AFFAIR"

"The North Fork section of our county was the scene of another homicide Friday afternoon, when Jake Hausshalter* shot and killed Ocie Fields*.

Both men reside near Long Hollow and married sisters. They attended a funeral the day of the shooting, and it is reported had a few words sometime during the day. On his way home, Fields* passed near the home of Hausshalter*, who came from his house and pointing a pistol at Fields*, told him to hurry along. Fields* continued on his way and when near the schoolhouse at or near Long Hollow, Hausshalter* began firing his revolver at him, but missed him with about five shots. Hausshalter* then called his son Eber*, a young man about twenty years of age, to get his shotgun. The young man went to the house and returned with the gun, which he handed to his father.

It is not certain how many shots were fired from the gun, but we understand more than one. Anyhow, Fields* was trying to keep out of range by running around the school house, but finally Hausshalter* got close enough to let him have the full charge of the gun about the middle of the back. Fields* fell and only lived a few hours. Pros. Atty. Smith, with Squire Roby and Dr. Grove, held an inquest, the result being to charge Hausshalter* with the killing.

The state police, with Leslie Flanagan, arrested Hausshalter* who offered no resistance, at his home, and he is now in jail awaiting the action of the grand jury. Both men have families. Fields* being about 50 years of age and Hausshalter* is probably about the same age."

Not many days pass until acquaintances file by my place on their way to the hearing over at town. Pap didn't feel up to going, so Boy and I didn't make plans, either. After all, we would miss his company during the trip, and I need to be with him today. We'll just have to wait for the results when friends return.

The preliminary hearing takes place at the courthouse on January 6, 1927, before B. Grant Roby, Justice of the Peace of Grant County. Dr. J. B. Grove came first to the witness stand. He was asked to state what he did in making his examination and performing the autopsy.

He began: "This body was identified by Boy Awers and Will Turner - was a man apparently fifty years of age, height 5 ft. 8 in., estimated to weigh one hundred sixty or one hundred sixty five pounds. Rigor mortis was well established in the body. We then removed the clothing from the body, around the chest from the outside in, over-all blouse, sweater, shirt and undershirt, also overalls and a pair of trousers. In the pockets of this clothing, we found one coin of five cents, which was turned over to Justice Roby. No bruises or broken bones. On the anterior surface of the body, there was no blood, but on the back extending across to the upper part of the loin to tip of shoulder blade was perforated by shot holes, probably from thirty to fifty, some of them under the skin and some of them deeper. The chest was opened and found filled with free blood; the base of both lungs perforated by shots. Two shots were removed from the lower lobes of both lungs, which were turned over to the Justice. The heart was found to be normal and abdomen contained considerable quantity of free blood, caused by perforating the stomach and upper portion of descending colon. The remaining organs of the abdomen were apparently normal. The skull was opened and the brain examined and found to be normal."

Next, Ben Fields testifies that on Thursday he had been to a burying. He states that he knew Jake and Ocie, and that Ocie lives across the river from the Long Hollow School house, and that he would have to go past the school to return home.

Smith: Were there any other persons with you when you went to the burying?
Fields: Godfrey Stats.
Smith: Where did you go after it was over?
Fields: I went home. I walked. I overtaken a wagon.
Smith: Whose wagon?
Fields: Boy Awers'.
Smith: What persons were with Boy Awers on that wagon?
Fields: Ocie, Laura Hawkins and Claudie Rohrbach, then I got on.
Smith: And you, Jake Hausshalter and Cal Hawkins came back from the funeral together?
Fields: Yes, sir, as far as Amos Dolly's.
Smith: How long had you been up to the schoolhouse - the wood shed before this trouble started?
Fields: We went up to the turn of the road from the schoolhouse and waited half an hour.
Smith: Was Jake at the schoolhouse?
Fields: Yes, sir, and he told Ocie to keep poderin' on.
Smith: Don't you know that Ocie was carrying a 32 Smith and Weston?
Fields: No, sir, I don't know that.
Smith: You had been drinking with him?
Fields: No, sir.
Smith: You had had a drink?
Fields: Yes, sir, in the wood shed at the schoolhouse.

Smith: Who did you take it with?
Fields: Jake Hausshalter.
Smith: You may state what time the shotgun was brought to Jake Hausshalter by his boy. I believe you stated that he was over near his corncrib building.
Fields: Yes, sir.

The trial concludes that all had been drinking. A pint jar had been passed at the turn in the road, as well as down at the wood shed. This intemperance, as was so often the case, had no doubt brought about the resulted killing. The information above was brought out in the court case; however, there are some other issues in the local gossip.

Perhaps these were true, or may have grown out of one's bias to the story. It is said that Jake accused Ocie of being too friendly with his wife. Another possibility is that Ocie had reported Jake to the revenue agents for making moonshine. If true, this may have been Jake's way of getting back at Ocie because he believed Ocie had stolen a turkey gobbler. However, it's hardly thinkable that Ocie would offer information that may incriminate him in some way. Another incident that prompted the conflict was that Ocie believed Jake had chopped into the floor beams of his house. The court found Jake guilty and sentenced him to serve time in the penitentiary. The full sentence was never served because he was killed while there.

Early spring brings me once again to one of my favorite stomping grounds. I again muse over the event while leaning against this giant White Oak Tree, an event caused largely by moonshine. Since early this morning, I've been squirrel hunting, first on Red Bud, now here in this hollow. There are but ground squirrels stirring which gives plenty of time to contemplate. Looking above me, there is a chicken hawk perched, no doubt after the same prey as myself. He was annoying at first, with the jumping from branch to branch

- knocking twigs and acorns down, causing me to confuse him with the antics of a squirrel.

God must have thought it terrible for people to have just come from a burying and to act so foolishly. Stella had lived her life, but Ocie died prematurely. Selfishness and moonshine are the culprits, which have caused so much strife in these mountains, and not that of being poor.

I look up, trying to imagine how God must have felt as He viewed the scene that day. I wonder about Ocie's widow. Jake's wife left to raise the family in these hard times. First, Harness's wife must strive alone, now Ocie's. Memories forever shadow the schoolhouse, a permanent memory, left behind by the shots embedded in the molded siding. I think of the canning jar that was passed that day. Whose hands have the guns fallen into? I can almost hear the stretching of the harness and the clanging of the single trees, as horses labored under wagons loaded to the hub, and sleds that day.

There are a couple of Shagbark Hickories, oaks, apples, and plenty of saplings. The fall colors situated against the mottled blue sky display the most gorgeous artwork known to man. Each stroke of God's imagination uncovers unmatched beauty. I love to travel these hills and cannot wait to round the next bend, for it is always prettier than the last. Pap says the old Long Hollow School used to stand just below where I sit, before it was replaced with the new one down at the run.

Rocks are scattered around with much character. All have unique shapes and many are covered with moss of the most beautiful green color. The rough road is deeply sunken to about four feet in places where it has been worn and washed. Often it becomes so muddy that deep wheel grooves are made and harden to form furrows for the horses to slip and slide on. If only men could relive the day of the killing. God wishes to operate in the affairs of men, but they must allow Him. This old hollow will change with the passing of time and many newcomers will one day travel up and down, not knowing of Ocie's death. The scars are usually just left on the hearts of a few. The hollow will never be perceived as playing a part in a shooting. A place was provided and it was a time when men simply were not appreciative of their surroundings. If only they would have taken time to cherish the things that I hold dear today: creation, health, and community.

Another trip and another day takes Pap and me high on North Mountain to where we can look down and see what God has wrought, and all that man has impacted. "There is beauty when man adds his touch to cultivation, or buildings, but the things that bother me are the extremes we talk of," I remark.

For some mysterious reason, Pap seems so distant. It is as if his mind is taken up with another conversation. Feeling like I am being ignored, I ask, "Pap, Pap, are you listening to me?"

With some delay, he answers, "Why, yea, boy, I'm a listenin'."

While catching our breath, we peer across the way to Dolly Sods, then against the Four Knobs and to the West, where in the distance is Spruce Knob. The green pines stand as proud sentinels displaying God's handiwork. The massive ledges on North Mountain and New Creek display the marks of the terrible deluges. No word needs to be said to describe the Gap incident or that of Long Hollow. Together, our eyes fastened upon dear Old Hopeville, where so many had gathered for school and church, and where countless needs were met. If only there was a way to number all the blessings received there.

Just to have Mom around again to give words of comfort. She has been gone now for a few years. Just one more opportunity to hear Sister Dolly, or one of the old concerned ministers pour their heart out. I feel that much of the innocence of the past is gone. If only we could capture a simpler time - a time when men were neighbors - a time when moonshine hadn't disrupted so many lives.

Pap listened as I spoke freely, then offered his advice, "Ya know that kin never be, ya can't turn back th' clock of time. Sister Dolly is gone, many of th' others are gone, but you kin be brave, a leader fer a new time. Things aren't simple, but you're called t' take up th' torch."

I knew that as long as Pap was around, he would have all the support a man would ever want or need. Feeling better about the future, I grab my Iver Johnson squirrel gun, and move off toward Kimble's Ridge, with Blaze by my side and Pap following at a distance. I am confident, somehow, that the legacy left behind by great men and women that have toiled here will provide a great mold for future generations.

Pap concludes our conversation with, "It's been a good day."

"Indeed it has," I respond as I take aim at another Fox Squirrel.

— XXXII —

THINGS SEEM TO MAKE SENSE

While traveling the trails - some sunlit, some darkened - I sometimes catch a glimpse of Pap walking ahead of me. A few months back, I cradled Pap in my arms as he closed his eyes for the last time mumbling, "If I don't see ya in th' air, I'll see ya over there."

He had lived by those words. That was his hope and inspiration. He laid several days curled on his cot, with skin sagging over protruding bones. My heart sank as he could no longer eat. His last bite to eat was a little coffee soup. His skeleton could be well felt as he attempted to turn toward the windows that line the Fork, to get another view of Hopeville that he loved so well. I wiped his forehead and thin hair with a hanky as I brought a glass of water to his mouth. The lamp scarcely illuminated the room and his Bible as it lay open to Psalm 91. He mumbled, "Read it again."

"He that dwelleth in the secret place of the most High shall abide under the shadow of the Almighty. I will say of the Lord, He is my fortress: my God; in him will I trust. Surely he shall...," a couple more struggles of breath and he was gone. Tears streamed down my cheeks and landed on the pages, leaving a stain. I hugged him, knowing it would be the last here. Heaven became silent at that awful moment. A pen would be powerless to express my hurt.

I relive the event and reach to the stand beside the bed. I pick up his Bible to find words of comfort. To my amazement, tucked away in the front pages, I find a treasured letter from those who years before had moved away. There, too, is a tattered picture of a young boy on horseback. Inscribed on the back is a note in faint form, the handwriting of a woman, "your grandson;" me, why? Why didn't he ever tell me? There had to be a reason. He gave me all the privileges of a blood heir, yet could not permit me to know of our kinship. With all the old people gone, it will be difficult to obtain the facts, but in time, I may.

I have come to realize that it is time for me to pick up the mantle, to provide inspiration for those who follow. There is always someone who is reaching out for advice. There are those following in my tracks. Pap had always been there for me, but now exists only in my thoughts.

I suppose there are some ideal "Paps," but I never had the pleasure of having one. I could only borrow one for short intervals. Many times on the trail in these mountains, I wish I could have had a clearer interaction with Pap, and a better understanding of things. He was personal, but distant, inside, but seldom beside. I could never quite grasp the intimacy which I desired. There are other men like Pap who have wisdom, foresight, and discretion, which has helped, but their lives are taken up with children of their own. I am fortunate to have had the privilege to meet some of these, although for a short time. I'll always keep Pap in my vision to aid and guide my steps. My time has come to work on the traits I find so admirable. I wish to finalize this race as Pap did. I will leave the remainder of my feelings to be judged, rather than attempt to describe them here.

As is so typical in the mountains, many had a say as to the funeral arrangements, so as not to have hard feelings. All were affected by his passing and attended the funeral. The procession was a difficult one, in some ways not unlike that long funeral procession when Charles Goodnight fulfilled Oliver Loving's request to return his body the six hundred miles back to Texas for burial.

The minister spoke from Paul's writings, and applied them so deservingly to Pap. "I have fought a good fight, I have finished the course, I have kept the faith, henceforth there is laid up for me a crown of righteousness."

My friend Martin, that big Appalachian, has struggled to see Sara Jane for quite some time now. His ache has more than once been felt by Pap and me. The difficulty made so because of distance and acceptance. You see - he is an Appalachian. He may be colored as an everyday hillbilly, but his character speaks of a more refined lifestyle. Pap, on the other hand was, in most ways, a hillbilly, knowing he was deep rooted in the myths and beliefs of the mountains. He could do little about it. Martin looks beyond the chains of being characterized with poverty and plagues of the mountain ways. He wants more than the barefoot, lazy, and dirty image that characterizes some. These have stereotyped all mountain people the same. Martin doesn't like the stigma associated with hillbillies and works hard to shirk the brand. Martin reasons, "If only he could get Sara's dad to see that side of him, to trust him, to give him a chance. He knows I work; I'm strong, responsible, and honest. With all those credentials, how can he resist having me as a son-in-law?"

Their seeing each other has always been in secret, and Sara is getting anxious, as is Martin. Martin realizes he will never convince Dr. Eye of his qualities and reasons with Sara to have a quiet wedding. There is no hoop-lah, no crowd. It is a small quiet ceremony before the local minister at Hopeville. Though in her beauty, Sara has no family there, but Martin is what matters most. Martin has found his life's companion, and together they seek their dreams. Martin has never been one to talk much, and saves one of his most prolific gems for today when he whispers to Sara Jane, "God sure must a been smilin' th' day He made you." He speaks of their love, friendship and the joy of her by his side.

If only the old folk could be here to enjoy this occasion. I could only envision Pap in the corner, mingling among the guests. If only we could have a minister of Sister Dolly's caliber here to witness the ceremony. We miss these, but life goes on. They would have us to aspire forward and to form a society that is kinder and considerate to all honest men. They had standards and were not tolerant of those who did not place godly principles first, but attempted to nurture a society where all could get along. Perhaps one day, Martin will meet the "standards" of Dr. Eye, but then perhaps not. Martin and Sara Jane would play a great role in that drive. They build near Hopeville and continue on in the principles of the mountains. Pap would have appreciated his respect for these, but Martin is more progressive. Pap did not revere the hard and uncertain times in the mountains but wished to face the future with pleasant anticipation.

Much of the outlook of the mountain culture is regressive, the stories of the past, the songs relive the historic, the news unfolds, and so it goes. Martin wants more than the basic needs of life and desires constant improvement. From time to time, Martin climbs North Mountain to view the outside where so many have gone, always thinking. Hardly a day goes by that he does not share his vision with Sara Jane. He repeats over and over, "I'll labor until the opportunity comes, when we can do as others."

There are innumerable things he appreciates here, but a wedge is driven between his love and them. The passing of friends causes a dying sentiment for the mountains, creating a greater reason to dream of flat fertile fields, virgin forest, and a level political playing field where all can have the best there is to offer.

— XXXIII —

THE WATER FLOWS ON

The water that drains the Alleghanies has cut ravines and created an environment, which ultimately formed men's lives. The rocks and ledges for centuries have provided beauty for men to behold, yet hiding places for their evil works. Men worked hard to hew out a living. The ground has been unforgiving, and at times failed to yield. Others from the outside often took advantage. They oppressed, they exploited, leaving natives with leftovers. Amid all of this, future generations can look back with a proud heritage for the principles and beliefs. The greatest lessons to learn are that we benefit from their experiences. We must learn from our history, so as not to suffer the things of those before us.

In the mountains, there were things that seemed unrelenting, so troublesome, but the coming of morning over North Mountain brings freshness that enabled inhabitants to forget yesterday's problems. The coming of spring makes one forget the harsh winters; the birth of a child, makes one forget the travail of birth pains. Somehow, through the night, minds and bodies are able to recoup. The driving force preserving these mountain people and stimulating their journey is their persistent desire to reach Heaven. I believe Pap would have summarized the most important principle as Solomon did centuries ago, "Let us hear the conclusion of the whole matter. Fear God, and keep His commandments: for this is the whole duty of man." Then, too, I pray to live within the boundaries of God's plan, that when I arrive on eternity's shore, I may do so with the redeemed, and not suffer an ill fate.

The Appalachian mountain chain has indeed been awakened from her long sleep. The once virgin forests, now gone, cause bursting streams to speed faster than ever to their destination. Flora and fauna must now jostle for position on trampled terrain in order to exist. But thanks to their residual design and resistant behavior, plants yet squeeze from between rock crevices, and deer move about undetected. Hewn log dwellings have been replaced with those constructed from sawed lumber. The once lone pioneer family is no longer alone, but is among the hurried who attempt to acquire more than they need.

Change was inevitable. The mountains awoke to new sounds, never to return to the former slumber. The Bald Eagle I had seen earlier, thanks to preservation, is still in her holding pattern, searching for prey. Nearby, her mate keeps watch over the nest, but now more carefully.

You, the Geologist, can rejoice in the abrasions, upheavals, contortions and the agonies of Creation. Up the North Fork, you will find things that measure up to your satisfaction.

To the Artist: a venture through this wild country will fill your palate with studies worth a trip around the world.

To the Architect: a study of the North Fork will give you a fresh imagination and acquaint you with the works of the greatest master in your craft.

To the Seeker: time spent in the Alleghanies will enhance your spirit, and in so doing, may you find God's perfect peace.

This book has emerged, not from the pen of a mere observer, or from someone from another place, but from a native Appalachian, and from experience. Experience which has taught respect and birthed deep feelings for Appalachia and her people, and I trust, some insights into them. I have worked, talked, visited, eaten, rejoiced, and wept with those of all ages. Some mountain people, no doubt, will read anger into these pages; some will mistakenly believe that I am characterizing all Appalachians in these pages, but I hope that is not the case. My heart is troubled when the mountaineer is treated as inferior, or when anyone suffers unduly at the hand of another. My heart and my continuous intentions are to be of inspiration to the Appalachian.

This is a tribute to my brother, Marlin, who died of Lou Gehrig's disease during the writing of this book.

THE CARPENTER

Around Hopeville, there a story is told,
Where's little hot, but plenty of cold;
Fingers bruised from the hammer's steel,
Each lick strikes home as if sent to kill.

Eyes set deep in a weathered tan,
Ever so determined the race he ran;
Often set back, but onward he trod,
Realizing life soon, returns to the sod.

Then one day an enemy came by,
Evil enough to force the tough to cry;
He fought like a whale, as few ever can,
But never mistake, he was a whale of a man;

Then a blacksnake whip on the chargers flung,
God signaled an angel to gather him home;
Out of Hopeville they made their journey,
Across the skies to the blue yonder eternity.

I figure God needed someone to plan so keen,
To layout the mansions of John fourteen;
The others must be gladdened to see such help,
Struggling now over for there's God to envelope.

Up there buildin' are carpenters untold,
Where wood's replaced with silver 'n gold;
Hopeville's entry has caused quite a stir,
And good to work with the Master Carpenter.

HILLBILLIES AIN'T POETS

Hillbillies ain't of th' rhyming kind,
Neither are they really all that refined:
While others pen fancy of all their times,
Hillbillies just ain't of th' poeting kind.

Cowboys write of their little doggies,
Dogs an' horses stuck out in th' soggies:
A coyote's howl an' th' lone prairie,
Grass high as your head in big sky country.

The NW woodsmen tell of th' big blue ox,
Cold winters, woolen hats an' baggy socks:
Paul Bunyan's exploits make ax swinging fame,
Treacherous work certain t' make one lame.

Pirates sing of riches an' sparkling gold,
Freedom t' do, sworn not t' be bought or sold:
Life on th' edge of all that matters,
Drink after drink down th' ole chatter.

Cotton pickers tell a sad story in song,
In hot, sweaty fields a country mile long:
Speaking in whispers a code of their own,
Forever planning of finally going home.

Easterners write within White House walls,
Fancy words penned t' labor others with laws:
As long as th' hillbilly is in th' hills t' stay,
It's okay he's no poet, he's there out of th' way.

Endnotes

[1]Post Office Info.   National Archives
                       P.O. Box 100793
                       Atlanta, Ga. 30384

Paper to Paper Copies (Mail Order)
    Postal Site Locations 12E3
    Town of Hopeville Grant County, WV
    Row 20 Compartment 18 Shelf 3 Box 741

Microfilm/Microfiche to Paper thru 11 x 17
Records of Postmaster Appointments M841
Roll 183--Grant Co., WV
Vol. 29--Pg. 352,353
Vol. 51--Pg. 53,54
Vol. 72--Pg. 85,86
Vol. 99--Pg. 377,378